MW00941368

MORE THAN MUSIC

Also by Elizabeth Briggs

More Than Exes
More Than Comics

MORE THAN MUSIC

A **CHASING THE DREAM** NOVEL

ELIZABETH BRIGGS

Copyright © 2014 by Elizabeth Briggs
MORE THAN MUSIC, A CHASING THE DREAM Novel

All rights reserved. This book or any portion thereof may not be reproduced or used in any manner whatsoever without the express written permission of the publisher except for the use of brief quotations in a book review.

This is a work of fiction. Names, characters, businesses, places, events and incidents are either the products of the author's imagination or used in a fictitious manner. Any resemblance to actual persons, living or dead, or actual events is purely coincidental.

Cover Designed by Najla Qamber Designs
Model Photo by Lindee Robinson Photography
Models: Madison Wayne and Chad Feyrer

ISBN (paperback) 1499607997
ISBN-13 978-1499607994
ISBN (ebook) 978-0-9915696-0-1

www.elizabethbriggs.net

To Gary
For ten years, and many more to come

CHAPTER ONE

Tonight was going to be epic, I could feel it. I edged closer to the stage, pushing past emo kids with sweeping black hair and girls in fishnets and combat boots. Julie and Carla followed, our hands linked so we wouldn't lose each other while I searched for the perfect spot. Not right in front so we looked like obsessed groupies hanging all over the band, but close enough to get a good view of the stage and feel the music vibrating under our skin. After some maneuvering, the three of us wedged into a space in the crowd and clinked our beers together.

"Here's to the end of finals," Julie shouted, over the noise of a hundred conversations going on at once. "And the end of our junior year!"

"I still have a final tomorrow morning," Carla shouted back. "What time are they going on again, Maddie?"

"Any minute now," I said. "Don't worry. Kyle's band only has one album. We'll be out of here in an hour." I had a final early, too, and normally I'd be studying right now and then going to bed at a reasonable hour to make sure I got an optimal amount of sleep. But it wasn't every day a friend's band got a gig like this in a club on Hollywood Boulevard. Besides, I was a music major. This totally counted as research.

I rocked back and forth on my feet, full of that intoxicating mix of excitement, anticipation, and longing I always felt right before a concert started. The club was dark except for the spotlights highlighting the equipment on stage, poised and ready for the band to come out. People with dyed hair and tattoos and piercings pressed all around us, and I felt more out of place than ever with my black-rimmed glasses, red flannel shirt, and jeans.

Julie fit into the crowd better with her knit panda beanie, despite it being approximately the temperature of the sun in here. She'd made the hat herself and on anyone else it would look stupid, but with her long black hair and red lips, she somehow managed to pull it off. Combined with the skater dress with stars and planets that she'd also made, she was really rocking her sexy nerd look tonight. Sort of like an Asian version of Zooey Deschanel.

Carla looked gorgeous as usual, like she'd walked straight off the runway and into the club, which she probably had—she modeled on the side while pursuing her theatre major. She was half-Portuguese and half-African-American, and casting agencies went crazy for her smooth dark skin, head full of wild curls, and tall, thin frame. It was a shame Julie and I were the only ones who knew she'd rather fix old cars and play video games than do a photo shoot.

The glow of Carla's phone lit up her face as she checked her texts yet again. Probably another string of annoying questions from her boyfriend.

"Is that Daryl?" I asked.

"He just wants to know where I am."

"Don't tell him," Julie said, slapping the phone away. "He'll show up uninvited."

It wouldn't be the first time he'd crashed our girls' nights looking for Carla, convinced she was with some other guy. Probably because he knew she could do way better.

"He won't. I told him we're leaving right after the show."

A cheer went through the crowd as the band walked onto the stage, and I stood on my toes to get a better look. Hector, a Latino guy with curly hair tucked under a baseball cap, sat in front of the drums. He was followed by Becca, a blue-haired pixie in a dress with safety pins all over it. She stumbled across the stage like she was drunk, but managed to pick up her bass and slip it over her neck. Next came Kyle, his black hair hanging in his eyes and the gauges in his ear flashing under the lights. He moved behind his keyboard, but my gaze left him as soon as his older brother Jared appeared.

The crowd's cheering took on more of a screaming sound, and one girl even yelled, "Jared, I love you!" I rolled my eyes. Not that I blamed the girl. With dark hair that always stuck up like he'd just gotten out of bed, a perpetual five o'clock shadow, and blue eyes that could charm any girl into giving him his phone number, Jared was impossible to resist. I wanted to, believe me, but every time he opened his mouth and sang it was all over.

Jared gave the audience a wicked grin while he grabbed his guitar, a black Fender Stratocaster almost identical to my own except for the color. Like Kyle, he had tattoos running up and down his toned arms, and I couldn't help but wonder if they continued under his shirt.

The entire club buzzed with excitement, every one of us poised on the edge, holding our breaths and waiting for the plunge. In this moment, right before the music started, it felt like anything could happen—and I was ready.

Hector yelled out, "One, two, three, four," and the band launched into their first song. Jared's hard guitar riffs filled the small club, matched with the deep pulse of the bass, the fierce beat of the drums, and the eerie moan from Kyle's keyboard. The music ripped through me, touching the wild, dark part of my soul I kept locked away. My fingers itched to form the chords myself and play along, but I kept my hands in fists at my sides.

Instead I nodded my head to the music, picking out each note Jared played and feeling it in a way only another musician could.

When Jared leaned into the mic and sang, his smooth voice washed over me like a soft caress. It was like the last, decadent bite of a chocolate-covered strawberry. The smoky burn of whiskey as it slipped down your throat. The final night of passion before your lover left forever. I sang along to the words, feeling each line strike me deep inside. I understood exactly what he was saying, like he'd written every word just for me, like somehow he understood me in a way no one else did. Of course, every other girl in the club probably felt the same way I did. And a few guys, too.

I tore my gaze from Jared to watch the rest of the band. Hector was a blur as his muscular arms flew across the drums. Becca swayed while she played bass, her movements sluggish and her eyes half-closed like she could barely keep herself awake. Lately Kyle had been complaining about how she kept coming to rehearsals wasted, but I couldn't believe she'd do that tonight, not for their biggest performance ever.

Kyle was bent over his keyboard, head bobbing along while he played, and I loved seeing him in his element. We'd met as freshmen, and since we were both music majors who played piano, we always ended up in a lot of the same classes. We didn't hang out much outside of school or anything, but whenever we had a group project or a duet to perform we always paired up. Over the years, we'd bonded over a shared love of movie scores, superheroes, and other geeky stuff, even though he was covered in tattoos and never wore anything other than black and I thought staying up past eleven was living on the edge. Somehow we'd just clicked—but never in a romantic way.

The song ended, and the audience cheered. Jared flashed the crowd a smile full of dark promises. "Thank you," he said. "We're Villain Complex."

Julie whistled loudly beside me, and Carla covered her ears from the piercing sound. I blinked at them, coming out of a fog. I'd been so lost in the music I'd completely forgotten my friends were with me.

"They're so good!" Carla yelled.

"And the guys are so hot!" Julie added.

"I told you!" I shouted back at them. And then the next song started and I was swept away, falling under Jared's spell again.

Villain Complex had won the UCLA vs USC Battle of the Bands a month ago, securing the win for UCLA and making Kyle an instant celebrity around campus. Before that they'd only done a handful of small gigs and parties, playing both covers and songs from their own self-produced album. They were so talented it was only a matter of time until they really took off, and I'd be able to say I knew them before they were famous.

When the show ended, most of the audience crushed toward the exit like a herd of sheep. I was one of the few people crazy enough to move against the crowd and head for the stage, losing Julie and Carla somewhere in the fray. I finally made it to the front, next to a bunch of groupies gazing at Jared while he bent over to unplug something. I struggled not to stare along with them, but was saved when Kyle spotted me.

"Maddie, you came!" He jumped off the stage and grabbed me in a hug.

"I wouldn't miss it for anything. You were amazing!"

"Yeah?" He brushed hair away from his face, the tattoos on his fingers spelling out LIVE LOUD. "I was so nervous. You have no idea."

"It was a great show. Seriously. I was impressed."

"Thanks. That means a lot, coming from you." His face broke out into a grin. "Hey, I didn't get a chance to tell you the news. We have a live audition for *The Sound* on Friday!"

"What? No freaking way!" *The Sound* was a reality TV show where different rock bands competed against each other while being mentored by a famous musician. The winning band got a recording contract with a major label, and the top four bands were sent on tour together across the country. Plus, the show had millions of viewers, so even the bands that didn't win picked up a ton of new fans just from being on it.

"I know. Crazy, right?" He laughed like he couldn't believe it himself. "Jared sent in a video of us performing, plus MP3s of all our songs and a bunch of other shit. I didn't think anything would happen with it, but yesterday a producer called out of the blue and invited us to come on the show to audition."

"Wow, this is huge! I'm so happy for you." I gave him

another hug and meant every word I said—but I was prickling with a touch of envy, too. I wanted Kyle and his band to win, of course. And it's not like I wanted to go on *The Sound* or anything, hell no. It's just that, for once in my life, I'd like to do something bold like that, too. No more standing in the crowd and cheering for others, no more hiding in an orchestra or behind a piano, but on stage, living the dream out loud and in front. But that wasn't me.

A girl with hair the color of fruit punch slammed against Kyle, wrapping her inked arms around him. They kissed for the longest, most awkward moment ever while I stood next to them like a creepy voyeur. Finally they remembered I was there and broke away, grinning like two beautiful misfits in love.

"Hey, Maddie!" Alexis said with a big smile. "Wasn't Kyle incredible up there?"

"He really was," I agreed.

"I'm so proud of you, babe." She kissed his cheek, and he smiled at her like he was the luckiest guy in the world. They'd been high school sweethearts but had broken up when she'd gone to Princeton. Now that she'd transferred to USC, they'd reconnected at the Battle of the Bands and had been inseparable ever since.

"Hey, I got some killer photos of the show," she said. "I can't wait to get them on the website."

"Cool. Send them to Jared so he can put them up." He jerked his head toward his brother, who was talking with one of the groupies. "Jared!"

Uh oh. So far I'd managed to avoid all interactions with Jared for my own safety. Kyle had warned me that his brother had a new girl every week, and I knew they definitely weren't geeky girls like me. If we never met, then Jared could remain the version in my head, the guy who wrote songs that made me feel less alone in the middle of the night and who grinned at the audience like he knew their darkest secrets. Once we met, he would be a real person. But I couldn't exactly run off now, not with him walking over to us, even though the voice in my head yelled, *Go, go, go!*

"What's up?" Jared asked, smiling at us. It was a different smile from the one he used on stage, a private smile for friends that made him look even more like Kyle. I saw the real him for the first time, and it was even better than I'd imagined. I was doomed.

"Kyle talks about you all the time," Jared said to me, after we were introduced. "Great to finally meet you."

He hopped off the stage and spread his arms, moving in like he wanted to hug me. This wasn't all that shocking since Kyle was a hugger, too, but I stood there, frozen and tongue-tied for an excruciatingly long pause. It should be criminal for a man to be so good-looking. How were normal girls like myself supposed to touch the sun without getting burned?

"You too," I finally said and stepped toward him.

As his strong arms circled me, a little tremor ran through my body, like a static shock jolting right through my chest. He was the perfect height for me to press my face into the curve of his neck and breathe him in, but I restrained myself. The hug was brief, but even that second of contact was enough to leave me breathless. I quickly pulled away and took a few steps back to a safe distance.

"We're having a party at our place after this," Kyle said. "You should come, Maddie."

"Thanks, but I should get home." I had that final in the morning, and Carla would kill me if I kept her out all night. Besides, Kyle and I didn't exactly run in the same crowd, and I wouldn't know anyone at this party other than him and Alexis. And Jared now, but he was dangerous to be around.

"At least stop by for a few minutes," Jared said, giving me that warm smile again. I practically melted all over the floor, like a chocolate left in the sun. So unfair.

Alexis glanced between me and Jared with an amused smile, like she could tell how he affected me. "Yes, you have to come."

Kyle nudged me with his elbow. "C'mon. You can check out our studio while you're there."

Well…I supposed it wasn't that late yet, and I *had* been dying to check out the band's studio. It would be a good friend-gesture if I made an appearance, and if the party was crowded, I'd probably be able to avoid Jared the entire time. A few minutes couldn't hurt, right?

CHAPTER TWO

By the time I showed up with Carla and Julie in tow, the house the brothers shared in the Hollywood Hills was completely packed. We squeezed our way inside a room that smelled of pizza and beer while music pounded in the background. I immediately spotted Jared leaning over a stunning blonde in the corner, twirling her hair in his fingers. No surprise there.

I'd never been to Kyle's place before, and even though he'd hinted about his family having money, it was still a shock to walk through the piece of prime LA real estate the brothers somehow managed to afford. Not that it was fancy or anything—it was actually pretty sparse, a typical bachelor pad with few personal touches. But it was two stories, with a pool and an amazing view of the city sparkling with a billion lights, and that didn't come cheap.

"We really should head home soon," Carla said as we stepped into the kitchen, where it was slightly quieter.

Julie grabbed some drinks from a cooler and passed one to each of us. "Relax. Have a beer."

"Fine. One beer only." But Carla promptly ignored it and started texting again.

"I'm fine with leaving in a few minutes," I said. I didn't know anyone here, the music was super loud, and I had no desire to watch Jared hooking up with one of his groupies. I'd say hi to Kyle, check out his studio, and then we could go. My duty as his friend would be done, and I'd still get enough sleep for my final tomorrow. Win-win.

"Speak for yourself," Julie said. "I had my last final today, and I am a free woman for the summer. Tonight I plan to find a guy who will make me forget all about molecular biology."

Julie was on the pre-med track with plans to apply to medical school next year, but it was no secret she hated it. Her true love was designing clothes, but she said that was just a hobby, not a career. Or maybe that was her parents speaking. I was never sure.

She nudged me with her elbow. "And you should talk to Jared."

"What?" I nearly dropped my drink. "No!"

"Seriously, you've been undressing him with your eyes all night. Make a move already."

"I have not been undressing him!" The words came out way too loud, and the people next to us glanced over. Even Carla looked up at me with raised eyebrows, like she didn't believe my protest. I flushed and lowered my voice. "It doesn't matter. He's a total player, and besides he'd never go for someone like me anyway."

"Why not?" Carla asked. "You're beautiful and smart, and you play guitar, too. That already puts you ahead of these other girls."

"I don't really play guitar. I mean, I do, but only for you two…"

"Hey, you don't have to marry the guy," Julie added. "Just go talk to him. Have some fun."

"Or ask Kyle to set you up," Carla said.

"No. Definitely not." There was no way I'd ask Kyle to hook me up with his older brother. Ick.

"Fine, but you have to do something about this," Julie said. "You're practically obsessed with the guy."

Carla gave me a sympathetic smile. "You do listen to his music a lot…"

I hated when they ganged up on me like this. "Hang on, just because I think he's talented—"

"And hot," Julie butted in.

"And because I like his band's music doesn't mean I'm 'obsessed' with him."

Julie rolled her eyes. "Fine, then let's find you another guy to get your mind off him. How long has it been since you got laid?"

I rubbed a hand across my face, more than ready to go home now. "I don't know."

"When did you break up with Chad? Six months ago?"

"Something like that," I muttered, hoping she'd drop it already. Chad was a communications major who said "dude" too much and spent most of his time at the beach. He'd been easy on the eyes and pretty good in bed, but he didn't get me at all. The final straw had been when he'd bailed on one of my big recitals to go drinking with some friends. Music was my life, and if he couldn't understand that, then there was no point dating him anymore.

Julie opened her mouth to push me again, but I held up a hand. "Fine, I'll talk to Kyle, okay?"

"Yes! Go forth and conquer!" She raised her beer to me while Carla patted my arm and wished me luck before going back to her phone.

I returned to the living room and found Kyle in the crowd, dancing close with Alexis. "You made it!" Kyle said when he saw me. "Want to check out the studio now?"

"Sure." I'd promised Julie I'd talk to Kyle, but I hadn't actually agreed to bring up Jared, after all. "Or I can find it myself. Just tell me where to go. I don't want to interrupt."

"Nah, I'll take you. I locked it so no one can steal our gear." He paused to smile at his girlfriend. "You coming?"

Alexis kissed Kyle on the cheek. "No, you two go ahead."

"You sure?" He pulled her in by her waist and gave her a ridiculously long kiss while I stared pointedly at the floor.

"Go," she said, laughing and shoving him away. "Get your music geek on."

Kyle started to lead me through the crowd, but a bottle smashed near us, loud even with the music blasting. In the corner, beer and green fragments of glass dripped down the wall above Jared while Becca glared at him from a few feet away. Conversation died as everyone turned to watch the scene.

"*Another* girl, Jared?" she yelled, her words slurred. "How many tonight?" She reached for another bottle to throw, but Hector appeared at her side and yanked her back.

"What the fuck, Becca?" Hector asked. Jared slowly wiped beer off his face like he couldn't believe she'd just done that.

"Don't touch me!" She flailed her arms to fight him off. Hector immediately released her, but she stumbled into someone behind her. "Stay away from me!"

"Shit, not this again," Kyle muttered. "Here—the studio's at the end of that hallway." He handed me a key and then darted over to grab Becca's arm and help steady her. "Hey, let's get you sobered up."

"I'm fine," she muttered. Her eyes closed as she swayed next to him.

Jared stepped forward, fists clenched at his side. "Becca, this has to stop."

Kyle shot his brother a sharp look. "Let me handle this."

"Then handle it! We can't have her on *The Sound* like this. Either she gets her shit together, or she's out of the band."

Becca's eyes snapped open, and she jerked away. "I'm done anyway! Done with you, done with your band, done with all this shit!"

She stormed out the front door, and Kyle raced after her. Jared started to follow, but Hector held him back and they started arguing in low voices. Kyle had been right about Becca being a mess, and I knew they'd been through a few other bassists before, too. Hopefully he could get her straightened out before their audition.

Conversation around the room picked up again, but I slipped down the hallway and found the door Kyle had mentioned. It clicked shut and locked behind me, and the noise of the party faded to a dull thrum. The studio seemed to be a soundproofed garage with cheap carpeting that peeled up in the corners. The far wall had the Villain Complex logo and a bunch of quotes painted in black, including: "You don't know the power of the Dark Side," from *Return of the Jedi*; "You either die a hero or live long enough to see yourself become the villain," from *The Dark Knight*; and "One lab accident away from being a supervillain," from *The Big Bang Theory*. Under the quotes was a couch with an acoustic guitar flung across it and a small table covered in empty soda and beer cans. The rest of the studio was filled with microphones, headphones, pedals, amps, and cords crisscrossing the floor to connect it all.

I stepped carefully through the room, like I was walking on hallowed ground, and inspected the instruments on display. Kyle had a top-of-the-line keyboard that I wanted to run my fingers across, but I held back. I didn't see the bass Becca had used earlier—maybe she'd taken it before her dramatic exit. The drums were here, though, in pieces, waiting to be set up again.

Jared's black Fender sat in the middle of the room, propped up on a stand instead of in its case. It was already plugged into a small amp, like it was just waiting for someone, anyone, to play it. I glanced around the room—stupid, since I was obviously the only one in it—and took a step closer. I just wanted to look at his guitar, to figure out why it was plugged in when no one was here. Maybe Jared had been checking it after the show and had been interrupted. Or maybe he'd planned to sneak away from the party to be alone, just him and his music behind the soundproofed walls. If so, I could relate to that. Music had always been my way to escape and deal with the world on my own terms. I just didn't think of Jared as the kind of guy who needed to escape, too.

The guitar was beautiful, with a smooth white faceplate, gleaming struts, and a shiny fingerboard. My fingers itched to touch the silvery strings, to form a chord and let it ring out through the amp, to hear what it sounded like without all the other instruments accompanying it. And if I was honest, I wanted to close my eyes and pretend I was on stage, playing for a crowd, hearing them scream for me. The longing I felt every time I went to a concert stirred up in me again. It wouldn't hurt if I played one chord, right? That was it. One chord, and I'd put it back. No one would ever know.

Before I could stop myself, I picked up the guitar and threw the strap over my head. It settled against my shoulder, and with one hand on the fret board and the other on the strings, I was home. I closed my eyes, picturing Jared when he was on stage and how his talented fingers had moved across the guitar. I imagined him singing my favorite song of theirs, "Behind the Mask," and the words and notes melted together in my head. I strummed the guitar, the sound ringing from the amp, the vibrations traveling up the ground and into my feet. God, I loved this guitar. It sounded just as good as my own, if not better.

Now that I had the guitar in my hands, the compulsion to play was irresistible. What was one more chord, right? I was alone and the room was soundproof. The door had locked behind me. Kyle was dealing with Becca, and he'd given me permission to come in here anyway.

I knew it was a bad idea. I knew I should put the guitar down and walk out of the room. But I started strumming anyway.

I was hesitant at first, but once I started, I couldn't stop. My hands found the chords automatically, and the words flowed out of me with the music. Exhilaration swept through me with each note, and I closed my eyes and let the song take me away. Soon I was belting out the words, shredding the guitar like I was on stage playing for a massive crowd. I'd never do this in front of anyone else, but here, alone with this guitar, I could pretend. I could let myself go.

And then I opened my eyes and wanted to die.

Jared stood in front of me, his eyes wide and mouth open slightly. He must have come in while I was playing. How much did he hear? Or worse, *see?*

My fingers slipped off the strings with a screech, and I nearly dropped the guitar. Thank god for the strap. "I'm so sorry. Kyle gave me the key and I was just—"

There was no way to explain what was going on, so I shut up. I'd been singing his lyrics, playing the song he'd written. Not to mention, I'd been using *his* guitar. That was like wearing someone else's underwear. You didn't just play another person's guitar without their permission.

I yanked the guitar off and tried to put it back, but knocked the stand over instead. Hands shaking, it took me two tries to right it again, all while Jared stood there, gaping at me. Why didn't he say anything? Was he so angry he couldn't speak? I set the guitar down carefully, then backed away like it was on fire— and ran straight into the drum set. Cymbals crashed as I fell against it, knocking the equipment all over the floor. Great, now he must think I'm a stalker *and* a complete klutz. I jumped up too fast, and my legs were so unsteady I started to topple over toward the table. Jared caught me before we had another disaster, his hands gripping my arms to balance me.

"You okay?" he asked, his blue eyes holding mine and making my heart pound even faster. If I stared into those eyes too long, I'd fall into them completely.

I jerked away from his touch and stumbled back. "I'm sorry, I—"

"You were playing one of our songs."

"Was I?" I asked with a forced laugh, trying to edge toward the door to make a quick escape. "I mean, uh, yeah. I was. Obviously. But it's not a big deal. It's not like I listen to your songs a lot or anything. I just have that kind of ear where I hear something once and can play it back and uh…" *Stop talking*, I shouted at myself. *STOP*.

The thing about music was true. I could usually play anything just from listening to it a few times, but I'd also listened to Villain Complex's album about three thousand times and practiced the songs in my room with my guitar hooked up to my headphones. I wasn't obsessed or anything. I just liked their music a lot. But he didn't need to know any of that. This was humiliating enough as it was.

"Really?" he asked. "I wish I could do that."

Not the reaction I'd been expecting. I thought he'd yell at me to get out of his house or think I was another of his swooning groupies. Okay, maybe he wouldn't think that. I didn't look the part with my boring glasses and plain brown hair and flannel shirt. No, he probably assumed creepy stalker fangirl. I had to get away, out of this room, as far from Jared and his guitar and this nightmare as possible.

He started to say something else, but I blurted out, "I have to go."

I escaped through the door and back to the party, slipping into the anonymity of the crowd. Once away from Jared, I could finally breathe again, but the urge to flee was still strong. I found Alexis and gave her Kyle's key and told her to say goodbye to him for me. Now all I had to do was find my friends and get the hell out of his house.

Julie was flirting with a guy with a fauxhawk, but I grabbed her arm. "We need to leave. Now."

"What?" Julie looked back at the guy and pouted. "Right now?"

"Yes. Trust me on this." As I spoke, Jared appeared at the edge of the room, his head swinging around like he was looking for me. "Oh, god."

She craned her neck to follow my gaze. "What's going on, Maddie?"

"I'll explain when we're in the car. Now can we please go?"

She nodded, and we made our way out the front door, where we found Carla arguing with Daryl. I knew he'd track her down. Unbelievable.

"I told you, I was just about to leave!" she said to him.

"We're going now." I didn't wait to see if they followed me. I started down the hill toward where my Honda was parked, anxious to get away from the house, away from Jared, and away from the most embarrassing moment of my life.

I could never go to a Villain Complex show ever again, that was for sure.

CHAPTER THREE

Despite a restless night of sleep, I somehow managed to forget about the disaster with Jared and focus on my music history final for two hours. With that done, my junior year at UCLA was over, and I was ready for an entire summer interning with the LA Philharmonic. I'd beat out hundreds of other people to get it, and even though I'd probably spend my entire summer doing boring stuff like filing and pouring coffee, I couldn't wait.

Last night was in the past, nothing but an embarrassing memory. I'd put it behind me, and with any luck, Jared had gotten so drunk after I'd left he'd forgotten the moment had ever happened. I was over it. Really.

Except when I walked out of class, Jared was there, leaning against the wall in a black leather jacket. He stood up straight when he saw me and I skidded to a halt, breath catching in my throat. Someone crashed into me from behind, and I stumbled forward and dropped my bag. Because I couldn't have just *one* embarrassing moment in front of Jared, no, not me.

"Hey, Maddie." He picked up my bag while I moved out of the way of the students streaming into the hallway.

"Um, hey." What was he doing outside my class? He'd graduated from UCLA a year ago, so there was no reason for him to be here. I conjured up all kinds of horrible scenarios: He wanted to yell at me for touching his guitar. Or I'd broken the drums and now he wanted me to pay for them. Or he just wanted to see what kind of freak played his song from memory.

Calm down, I told myself. Maybe he wasn't here for me. Maybe he was waiting for Kyle. Yes, that made a lot more sense. Except…Kyle wasn't in my music history class.

"What are you doing here?" I asked, taking my bag from him.

"Looking for you." He rubbed the stubble along his chin, like he was thinking. "Kyle told me you play piano, but I had no idea you played guitar, too."

No one did, other than Carla and Julie. To everyone else, I was geeky Maddie who played piano—and sometimes violin or clarinet—but that was it. Only my roommates knew I practiced guitar for hours in my room, losing myself in the sound of the strings buzzing from my amp until my fingertips were sore and my hands cramped.

"And you can sing, too," he continued.

All the mortification from the previous night came back and set my cheeks aflame. I couldn't believe he'd heard me singing one of his songs.

"I'm so sorry," I said, clutching my bag to my chest. "I shouldn't have touched your guitar. I don't know what I was thinking—"

"You're really good. Do you know all our songs?"

"Yes." No, wait, why did I say that? Backtrack time. "No. Maybe. I mean, I might." I tried to shrug casually, like it was no big thing, but I wanted to melt into the linoleum floor, seep into the cracks, and disappear. I prayed for an asteroid to hit the spot I was standing in and wipe me off the face of the Earth, but no such luck.

"I need your help," he said, fixing an intense gaze on me. "We have a live audition tomorrow for *The Sound*. Problem is, our bassist quit last night, and we need a fourth member of the band."

"What?" Was he saying what I thought he was saying? No. Impossible.

"I know—worst timing ever. Can you play bass by any chance?"

"No…"

His face fell for an instant, and some reckless part of me

wanted to lie and say yes or promise him I'd learn. How hard could it be to learn the bass if I knew how to play guitar, right? Though I immediately realized how dumb that idea was because a) I could never learn bass in time for an audition tomorrow; b) I shouldn't care about making Jared happy, even if his disappointed face broke my heart; and c) none of that mattered because he couldn't possibly be asking me to join his band anyway.

"That's okay," he said. "I can play bass, and you can play guitar. It'll work." His smile lit up his face again, with a look that could charm any girl lucky enough to bask in it. Right now, that girl was me. "So what do you think?"

Jared was asking me—*me*—to play guitar in his band. In an audition on live TV. In front of four of the greatest musicians ever, plus millions of people at home. Mind. Blown. Somehow I'd been handed my secret dream on a silver platter. Next up, Jared would ask me out, too. Yeah, and then we'd ride off into the sunset on a rainbow unicorn with our million-dollar record deal.

"You want me to join your band?" I asked slowly, studying him for any sign that this was all a joke.

"Just for the audition. That should give us enough time to find another bass player to take Becca's place."

Ah, there was the catch. I would only play with them for one day, giving me a tiny taste of their lifestyle, and then they'd drop me as soon as the audition was over. No, better to never know what it would be like to play guitar on stage, to be part of a band, to make music with Jared and Kyle. Besides, I couldn't play guitar in front of the world. Guitar was my secret, my fun escape, and nothing more. My internship started on Monday, and I needed to focus on that—not on silly dreams of being a rock star.

"I'm sorry, but I can't." I spun around and rushed toward the exit before he could respond. I didn't want him to see my face and how much I desperately wanted to do it.

"Wait!" He ran after me, but I kept going, past other students who watched us with curiosity. "Maddie, wait!"

Damn his long legs. He caught up to me, practically jumping in front of me to stop me in my tracks. I kept my face glued to the floor, to the contrast of his black combat boots and my green Converse. I couldn't look up at him or I'd be tempted to say yes to anything.

He lowered his voice. "Please, you're the only person who can help us. You're an amazing guitarist, and you already know our songs. We need you."

I shook my head, looking anywhere but at him. Hearing him say he needed me with his whiskey-chocolate-sex voice made my legs a bit shaky, but what he was asking for? It was too much.

Jared got down on his knees, right in the middle of the hallway, and everyone stopped to watch us. He raised his hands like he was begging. "Please, this is our one chance, but without a fourth member, we can't do it. You're perfect and it'll only be for a day, and then I'll owe you. I'll do anything you want." He topped it off with a grin. "Help me, Maddie Taylor, you're my only hope."

Damn. How could I say no to a *Star Wars* reference from a hot guy on his knees? The word slipped out before I could stop it. "Okay."

"Yes!" He jumped to his feet and hugged me, making my head spin. "Thank you, thank you, thank you. I really owe you one."

The students around us clapped, like he'd just proposed to me or something. I gave the crowd a faint smile, feeling sick to my stomach. Jared quickly rattled off all the details about the audition tomorrow and told me to meet the band for practice in a few hours. And then he left, before I could come to my senses and change my mind.

Julie and Carla were watching *House Hunters International* when I walked into the apartment we all shared.

"You can just repaint the stupid room!" Julie yelled at the TV.

I collapsed on the sofa beside them and threw my head back with a groan. Now that Jared was no longer in front of me and the glow of his smile had worn off, the reality of what I'd agreed to do was sinking in. I couldn't go on the show with the band, but I seemed to be physically unable to say no to Jared either.

Maybe I could pretend I was sick. Or break my arm. Yes, I had to injure myself. That was the only way to get out of this mess.

"Was your final that bad?" Carla asked.

"Maybe she needs to eat." Julie handed me a box of crackers, which I waved away. Eating was the last thing on my mind right now.

"My final was fine, except Jared was waiting for me outside my class."

Julie dropped the box, spilling crackers across the hardwood floor. "He what?"

"Was he mad about last night?" Carla asked.

I'd told both girls the entire embarrassing story on the drive home from the party. They'd thought it was hilarious naturally. "No, he wasn't mad. Even worse—he asked me to join his band."

"WHAT?" Julie and Carla both blurted out together.

"I know! But it's only for their audition on *The Sound* tomorrow, and then they'll find a new bassist. It's not a permanent thing." I sucked in a breath and then spit the rest out. "And I said yes, but now I need to tell him no because I can't do it. I just can't."

My two friends looked at each other, and something passed between them. Julie turned back to me. "You *can* do this, and you will," she said in her fiercest voice.

"Julie's right," Carla said. "This is what you've been dreaming about forever. You have to do it."

"But I'm not a guitarist!" I protested. "I've never played live before or on stage or in front of…well, anyone." At least, not since my mom had flipped out on me all those years ago.

"You've played guitar for us a million times," Julie said.

"And you play piano on stage all the time," Carla added.

"Yes, I play piano on stage, and sometimes I go wild and play the violin in an orchestra. But playing guitar in a band in front of millions of people is completely different!"

"You'll be fine," Carla said. "Besides, it's only one performance. Just pretend you're playing for us."

Julie nudged me with her shoulder. "Plus this gives you a chance to get close to Jared."

"I don't want to get close to Jared!"

"Why not?" she asked. "Everyone wants to get close to Jared."

"Yes, that's *exactly* the problem."

"Do it for Kyle then," Carla said. "You've known him for years, and now he needs your help."

I hadn't thought of that. If I backed out now, they probably wouldn't have time to find another guitarist or bassist before the show. I couldn't do that to my friend. "You're right…but then, why didn't Kyle ask me to join the band himself?"

Julie shrugged. "Maybe Jared didn't tell him about your little solo performance last night."

That could be it. Kyle didn't know I played the guitar. Or maybe Jared had told him, but Kyle didn't want me in the band. I didn't exactly fit their image after all. Or even worse, maybe Kyle was upset I'd never told him I played guitar and that his brother had found out before him. Even if Kyle didn't know yet, he'd learn the truth in an hour when I went to rehearse with them. I dreaded the look on his face when he realized I'd kept this from him for three years.

"I don't know." I took off my glasses and rubbed my eyes. "I mean, look at me. I don't belong in their band. They're all so edgy and I'm so…not."

Julie faced me and put her hands on my arms, her amber eyes drilling into mine. "Stop it. Those guys would be lucky to have you in their band."

Carla wrapped her arms around both of us in a big group hug. "If you'd like, I can do your hair and makeup tomorrow before your audition, and Julie can help with your clothes. We'll make you look amazing."

I gave them the biggest smile I could muster up. "I don't know what I'd do without you two."

"So you're going to do it?" Julie asked.

I tried to think of any other protests, but when it came right down to it, I couldn't find another reason to say no. "Yeah, I'll do the audition."

Julie and Carla immediately started planning what they were going to do to me in the morning, but I wasn't feeling as optimistic. As much as I loved these girls, there was no makeup or wardrobe in the world that could make me a rock star.

CHAPTER FOUR

An hour later, I parked in front of the Cross brothers' house and grabbed my gear from my backseat. I'd brought my own electric guitar and matching amp, though I wasn't sure if I would be playing it or Jared's for practice or the audition. I'd almost brought my acoustic guitar, too, but left it behind in the end. Villain Complex wasn't an acoustic kind of band.

The studio's garage door was open, and Jared spotted me as I came up the driveway. He walked over and grabbed the handle of my guitar case.

"Here, let me help you." He took the amp, too, leaving me

with empty, sweaty hands, which I rubbed on my jeans.

His leather jacket was gone, and he wore a T-shirt that said, "It's Good to Be Bad." For the first time, I got a close look at the tattoos on his arms: bars of music surrounded by spider webs, black stars, and roses with thorny vines. Like Kyle, he also had a triangle tattooed on the inside of each wrist, one dark and one light. I'd never realized a guy's forearms could be sexy, yet somehow he managed to pull it off.

He set the guitar case on a long table and popped it open. He whistled when he saw the vintage sea foam green Fender Stratocaster inside. "Wow. Where'd you get this?"

"I bought it at a pawn shop, along with the amp." Both were chipped and dented, but I loved them. They were the only instruments I'd ever bought with my own money, right after I'd left for college. The grand piano back home, my violin and clarinet, and even the keyboard crammed next to my bed were all guilt presents from my father. My acoustic guitar had been my mom's once, back when she did things like play music. But this guitar—it was all mine.

"May I?" he asked, and I nodded.

He ran a hand over the body and neck of it with the gentle caress of someone who understood how precious it was. I watched his fingers touch each string and imagined what it'd be like if he touched me that way.

Stop it. I forced my eyes to the floor. *He's not for you.*

"Very nice," he said. "You can use your guitar for the audition or use mine if you want. Whatever works."

"I'll use mine, I guess." Even though I'd played Jared's guitar last night, it seemed too intimate now, too much of a reminder of that embarrassing moment when he'd caught me. It was bad enough being alone with him in this studio again. "Where are the other guys?"

"They should be here soon. You can start warming up if you want."

Warming up was a little too close to playing guitar, which was the entire reason I was in the studio, but that didn't mean I was ready to do it. I hadn't played in front of anyone but Julie and Carla in years. And Jared, but that had been an accident. Now he expected me to play again, and the thought made me want to run straight back to my car.

I picked up my guitar and started to tune it, mostly to give myself something to do. My hands shook while I adjusted the knobs, and I took deep breaths, trying to force myself to be calm. If I didn't get control of my fingers soon, I'd never be able to play. I couldn't decide if I was more worried about that or more hopeful.

Jared opened another case and pulled out a deep blue electric bass I hadn't seen before. Soon the studio was filled with the sound of us plucking strings as we tuned our instruments. We stood only a few feet apart but didn't speak, and an awkward cloud hung between us. Or maybe that was just me; Jared seemed oblivious to it.

"So you play bass?" A dumb question, but I had to say something to end the tension.

"Yeah, although it's been a while." His gaze swept across the studio. "I can play everything in here to some degree."

"You can?" My voice sounded a little too eager. I cleared my throat and dropped my eyes to the frets on my guitar. "Were you a music major also?"

"Nope. Philosophy. Something my brother never lets me live down."

"Philosophy?"

"Yep. And now I'm a bartender who writes angsty songs, which I'm pretty sure is what everyone does with a philosophy degree."

I couldn't help but laugh. "The job market for professional philosophers does seem to have dried up these past few years."

"Tell me about it." He adjusted his mic and raised an eyebrow at me. "And what lofty plans do you have for your music degree?"

"I'm hoping to get into USC for graduate school. They have a degree in music scores for movies, TV, and video games."

"Ah, joining the enemy," he said, referring to the rivalry between UCLA and USC.

"Maybe. There are good programs at NYU and Berklee College of Music, too, but I'd rather stay in LA."

He studied me for a moment, his bass momentarily forgotten. "So what's your favorite movie score?"

"I don't know. There are so many great ones." I adjusted my glasses as I considered. "Pretty much everything by John Williams—he did *Star Wars* and *Jurassic Park* and *Indiana Jones* and about a million more. I also love the *Lord of the Rings* scores and *The Dark Knight* and, oh, the *Tron Legacy* score by Daft Punk is amazing, too…" There I went, babbling in front of him again. His eyes were probably glazing over by now. "Sorry. I could talk about this stuff for hours."

In response, he started singing "The Imperial March" from *Star Wars.* "Dun dun dun…"

"That's the ringtone on my phone," I said with a laugh. "Wow, that probably makes me the biggest geek ever, huh?"

"Nah. I approve." He gave me a smile that sent a rush of warmth from my face down to my toes and to everything in between. "Who do you think picked all the quotes for our wall?"

"That was you?" I glanced at the wall behind us with all the quotes by or about villains. I would have guessed Kyle had chosen them, not Jared.

Kyle and Hector arrived at that moment, interrupting us. They stopped just outside the open garage door and stared at me like I was a weed in their garden. Jared must not have told them I was joining the band.

"*This* is the new guitarist?" Hector asked.

Ouch. I knew I didn't look the part, but it still hurt to hear it out loud.

"Maddie?" Kyle's mouth dropped open, and his eyes swept

over my guitar and back up to my face. "You play *guitar?*"

"Not really," I said, and then realized that probably didn't help matters, since I would be auditioning with them tomorrow. "I mean, I know how to play, but…"

Kyle turned to glare at his brother. "How did *you* know she played guitar?"

"Relax, it's not what you think," Jared said, which instantly made me flush. Great, they assumed I was one of Jared's flings. But to my surprise, Jared didn't reveal how he knew. "She told me last night at the party."

Kyle's eyes narrowed, like he found that hard to believe, but Hector cut him off. "Forget it. We all agreed—no more girls in the band. Not after what happened with Becca."

"Hector's right," Kyle said. "Sorry, Maddie. It's nothing against you."

"We don't have any other option," Jared said. "Unless you can find someone who can play guitar or bass and knows our songs before tomorrow morning."

"How do you know she can actually play?" Hector asked. "She probably just said that to get in your pants."

"Hey—" I started to protest.

"She knows our songs?" Kyle asked and then tilted his head back to the ceiling. "Actually, that doesn't surprise me. Maddie is some kind of musical genius. She can hear a piece one time and then play it back perfectly."

"That's a bit of an exaggeration," I muttered, but no one was listening to me. Maybe I should leave and let them sort this out on their own. I glanced at my guitar case and wondered how quickly I could pack up and flee to my car.

"Shit, I don't know." Hector removed his hat, spilling his dark curls, and then shoved it back on again. "We should forget this audition and wait for the next one."

"The next show won't be for another year," Jared said. "We can't wait that long. And what if they don't want us next year? No, we have to do it tomorrow."

"I need to talk to Maddie alone," Kyle said.

He led me down the driveway, far enough that the others couldn't hear us. I swallowed hard as I waited for him to speak, preparing for the worst. He stared at the guitar still around my neck and then sighed and swept back the black hair that was always falling in his eyes.

"Why didn't you tell me you played guitar?"

"Um…" I stared at the ground. I hated that I'd kept this from him for so long and that he was hurt now because of my omission. But how could I explain that guitar had been my secret all these years? Something that had just been for me. Not my parents. Not my teachers. Not even my friends. I didn't think Kyle would understand somehow. He wore his entire personality on display and didn't care what other people thought. It was one of the things I admired most about him.

"I only play when I'm alone, and not seriously or anything," I said. "I used to play more, but my mom…she didn't approve.

Told me to focus on piano, on violin and clarinet. 'Real instruments,' she called them. Probably because she used to play the guitar and that's how she met my dad..." I trailed off, but Kyle nodded. I'd told him all about my family before. "When I was a kid, she caught me playing her old guitar and nearly smashed the thing. She was drinking, of course. It scared the crap out of me, and after that, it was easier to keep that part of myself hidden. But I'm really sorry I didn't tell you."

"It's all right. I get it." He sighed again. "Are you sure you want to do this?"

"No, I'm terrified." I choked out a little laugh. "But I also want to help you."

His face softened a little. "I appreciate that. I really do. But I don't think that's the only reason you're here."

"Of course it is." I tried to keep my face blank. Was my attraction to Jared so obvious that even Kyle could see it? I didn't plan to act on it or anything.

"Is it really? Because we can't have another Becca situation."

"What happened with her anyway?"

"She and Jared hooked up about a month ago." He scowled at his brother, still in the garage. "They both admitted it was a mistake the next day, but it was never the same after that. Becca started drinking more, and she got crazy jealous any time he was with another girl. They'd fight, and then I would smooth things over and then it would happen again. We all hoped she'd get over it, but then she started showing up to rehearsals drunk—if she showed up at all—and well…you saw what happened last night. I don't think Jared actually expected her to quit the band, but none of us really want her back either."

"Nothing like that is going to happen with me. Trust me." Becca's situation hit a little too close to home, and I was definitely not following in her—or my mother's—footsteps.

"I know, but…I just don't want you to get hurt. I love my brother, but he doesn't do relationships. Promise me you won't get involved with him, okay?"

"I won't, I promise." I gave him a smile that was more confident than I was. "And I'll only be in the band for one day anyway."

"True…" He gave a reluctant nod, and we went back inside.

"Everything okay?" Jared asked.

"We're good," Kyle said. "Let's hear her play."

They all looked at me, and I froze. "What? No."

"Great, a guitar player who won't play guitar," Hector muttered.

"Don't be an ass," Jared said, hitting a button that lowered the garage door, locking me in with them. "Of course she'll play."

The time had come. They were all waiting, and if I was going to be their guitarist tomorrow, I had to show them I could actually do it. There was nowhere for me to run now. I flexed my fingers and placed them on the guitar. They hadn't told me what to play, and I felt too self-conscious to perform one of their own songs for them, but nothing else came to mind either.

I remembered Carla and Julie's suggestion earlier, to pretend I was playing for them if I got nervous. If we were sitting on our couch right now, what would they want to hear? Something mellow. Something fun. Something they liked to sing along to. My decision made, I tapped out a beat and started Incubus's "Wish You Were Here." It was a perfect choice because right now I did wish they were here with me.

The song was off at first, every chord sounding like it was being ripped from my hands instead of flowing smoothly. Turns out, playing for three hot musicians in their garage-turned-studio was nothing like playing in my apartment for my two best friends. But once I got into it and stopped thinking so much about how they were watching me, my fingers knew what to do. The music poured out of me as it always did, from my body into the guitar, out the amp, and then back to my ears again in a perfect cycle. I never felt this way when I played the violin or clarinet or even the piano. With those instruments, I was precise and controlled and didn't get lost in the music. Those were work, but this—this was like breathing.

When I got to the chorus, Jared sang the lyrics, more to himself than anyone else, and I caught the other guys nodding along, too. Eventually I'd played enough, and Hector raised a hand to stop me.

"Okay, that wasn't bad," he admitted. "But do you actually know *our* songs?"

Not bad? I'd take it. Kyle gave me a reassuring smile, too, so he must not have thought I was horrible either.

"I know them," I said.

"Told you she could play," Jared said, moving in front of the mic. "We're doing 'Behind the Mask' for the audition. Let's run through it and see how it goes."

I nodded, relieved. Jared had already heard me playing that song and must have approved, or he wouldn't have asked me to join them. All bands performed one of their original songs during the audition, even though the bands used cover songs during the actual show. "Behind the Mask" was a good choice because it demonstrated the band's sound, plus it showed off Jared's impressive vocals and had a catchy beat.

Hector started us off, but I was too slow jumping in and then had to miss a few notes to get back on track. Things started getting better, but once Jared started singing, I missed a chord again. As the song progressed, I found it hard to keep time with them. I'd never played guitar with anyone else before, and I was always just ahead or behind the guys. That made me even more stressed out, and then I missed more notes and so it continued. My only consolation was that Jared wasn't doing so hot on bass either. The song ended, and the garage dropped into silence. I knew what we were all thinking—we were terrible. Less than an hour with the band and I'd ruined them.

"Well, that was a disaster," Hector finally said. "She may know the song but that doesn't mean she can play it."

"It wasn't *that* bad," Kyle said.

"Give her a break," Jared said. "Maddie's never rehearsed with us before."

My heart beat a little faster hearing him defend me, and I had to remind myself that he needed me for the audition and that was it. Once it was over, I'd probably never hear from him again. But still, it was nice to know he didn't think I was a complete failure.

"Sorry," I apologized to all of them. "I'm just nervous. I'll get it right this time."

"Anyway, the real problem was me," Jared said, his forehead creased as he checked the tuning on his bass again. "I'm so out of practice with this thing, there's no way I'll be in shape for tomorrow."

"You'll be fine," Kyle said. "You wrote the bass line in this song. You know it better than anyone."

"Yeah, but that was a long time ago." He rubbed his face, wiping away the frustration. "Let's try it again. If we have to rehearse all night to get it right, then that's what we'll do."

We practiced the song for hours. Any time I lost my place, I focused on Hector's drumming and got back on track, and when I wanted to throw my guitar pick in the trash, Kyle's encouragement kept me going. Playing with them wasn't as scary as I'd thought it would be in the end. And standing beside Jared while he sang was even better than listening to his voice in my headphones or through my computer, even better than seeing him perform live. Because this time, I was playing *with* him.

"All right," Jared finally said. "That was good. I think if we go any longer, we'll have nothing left for tomorrow's audition."

"Thank god," Kyle said. "I was about to pass out here."

Hector stood up, twirling a drumstick in one hand. "You were right, Kyle, Maddie does pick things up quickly."

"Told you. It's freaky, right?"

I bowed my head, but couldn't hide the small grin on my face. My arms trembled with exhaustion, my fingertips throbbed, and my hands had cramped up, but I felt whole, like I'd been missing a piece of myself all my life and finally had it glued back on. And I never wanted to lose it again.

CHAPTER FIVE

The guys picked me up bright and early in their van, their gear already packed inside. I squeezed my way into the backseat next to Kyle, who wore a faded black T-shirt and a studded belt. He gave me a quick once-over as I got inside. "Perfect."

I said a silent thanks to my two best friends. Julie had picked out a black babydoll dress with a hint of lace and loaned me some ropey chain jewelry and knee-high boots. Carla had given me smoky eyes, dark red lips, and a hint of curl to my usually limp brown hair. Somehow they'd made me look fierce, but still like myself, too. Even my black-rimmed glasses looked more ironic than nerdy now.

Hector gave me a nod, too, which I supposed meant he approved. He was dressed similarly to Kyle, except with his usual baseball cap with the Villain Complex logo.

Jared turned from the driver's seat and looked me up and down. It might have been my imagination, but his eyes seemed to linger a little longer than the other two guys' had.

"You look great," he finally said, making my heart skip a beat. "We don't have much time, so let's go."

The van's door slid shut with a *thunk,* and we were off, driving along the sleepy Saturday morning streets of Los Angeles toward downtown. I picked at the hem of my dress, the whole situation surreal. I was in a car with three guys in a rock band, going to audition for a TV show I'd watched for years. It was hard to believe this wasn't all a dream.

The guys didn't talk much, and the closer we got, the more nervous I felt. This was really happening now. I couldn't back out. Well, I could, but I'd completely screw the guys over and I would never do that. Kyle was my friend, and Jared had taken a chance on me. Yes, it was only because he needed me for the audition, but I still appreciated his faith in my skills.

We soon reached LA Live, a giant plaza with restaurants, movie theaters, and clubs, plus the Staples Center, where basketball games were held, and the Nokia Theatre, where *The Sound* was filmed. The auditions were taking place across the street, at the LA Convention Center, and a huge crowd was already lined up along the sidewalk to be in the audience. We parked the van, and some guy with a headset and a clipboard checked us off and had us unload and tag our gear. He gave us a card with a 93 on it and said they'd call our number when they were ready for us.

"Are there really ninety-two bands before us?" Jared asked him.

"Nah, we hand the numbers out randomly," the guy said, before waving us into a huge room with a bunch of other people.

Judging from the wild assortment of clothes and hairstyles and the way everyone stood in groups and eyed each other with a mix of thinly veiled curiosity and contempt, these must be the other bands waiting to audition. I took in the vast crowd, and my stomach did summersaults. From the guys with long hair and motorcycle jackets, to the punk rockers with mohawks, to the country princesses who looked like Taylor Swift clones, all of them belonged here much more than I did.

"I need coffee," Kyle said. He took our orders—coffee for me and Hector, tea with honey for Jared (for his voice, he said)—and then joined the very long line at the coffee stand. All the tables and chairs were already taken, so we found a spot by the wall and leaned against it. There was nothing to do now but wait.

While Hector sat on the floor and drew in a sketchbook, Jared surveyed the room with a line of worry across his forehead. He wore a black button-down shirt with the sleeves rolled up to his elbows, showing off his inked arms. His face had the perfect amount of stubble brushing his chin and framing his mouth, and even in this crowd, I couldn't help but be drawn to him.

"You okay?" I asked, after he sighed for the fifth time.

Jared ran a hand through his hair, making it stick up more. It made him look even better somehow. "I didn't think there would be so many people here, you know?"

"Yeah." I didn't mention that there were probably dozens more on their way or auditioning on other days because I understood how he felt. This was his chance to follow his dream, to make it big with his band, and now it seemed impossible in the face of all this competition. Villain Complex was good, but we'd only spent one night practicing together, and there were so many bands here, and oh god, the more I thought about it the more I might throw up.

"How about you?" he asked.

I pressed my hands to my stomach, willing it to be calm. "Honestly? No, I'm not okay."

He laughed and sang my words to the tune of "I'm Not Okay (I Promise)" by My Chemical Romance. He continued with the next lines in the song for a minute, and some of the other people around us turned to watch him serenading me. It should have been embarrassing, but instead it made me smile and some of the tension in my shoulders relaxed. It wasn't every day a hot guy sang to me, after all.

He finished with an exaggerated bow, and I laughed. "Yes,

that song popped into my head, too," I said. "Unintentional song reference, I promise."

"It got you to laugh, so my work here is done," he said, and I melted even more.

Kyle returned and shoved coffee cups at us. "Rumor is, none of the mentors have filled up their teams yet. Sounds like we still have a shot."

He leaned against the wall next to Jared while they sipped their drinks. When they were side by side, it was obvious they were brothers, with the same deep blue eyes, perfect mouths, and striking jawlines, but Kyle was like Jared with the volume turned to full blast. Kyle showed the world he didn't conform—with his dyed-black hair, multiple piercings and ear gauges, and tattoos crawling up his neck and down his fingers—but Jared was more restrained. Only the tattoos on his arms hinted at his darker side, like his true self couldn't quite be contained and had bled ink across his skin. If he wore long sleeves, you'd never know what lurked underneath.

Perhaps that's why Jared was the one who took my breath away. I could relate to that restraint, to keeping a piece of yourself hidden at all times and feeling like everything had to be under control. There was a part of me—the part that played guitar in my room every night and felt more at home at a rock concert than in an orchestra—that I kept hidden away, too. Problem was, I wasn't sure I wanted to keep that Maddie locked up anymore.

At one point, Jared made his way around the room to talk to the other bands. He was a natural at it, with his easy charm and charisma, but all I saw were the beautiful women placing their hands on his arms and the way he stood too close to them, laughing at whatever they said. He was supposed to be checking out our competition, not collecting phone numbers. I hated that seeing him flirt with other girls bothered me so much. Kyle had warned me, after all, and it's not like anything would happen between me and Jared anyway.

"What'd you find out?" Kyle asked when Jared returned.

"Some of these people have been waiting for two hours already." He sighed and leaned back against the wall. "We're going to be here forever."

Hector grunted. "Unless the mentors pick all their team members before we even get in."

"Don't even say that," Jared said. "Just don't."

"Relax, that's not going to happen," Kyle said.

Other bands got called up and then disappeared, never to return. It was impossible to know from this room what happened to them or what our competition was like. The longer we waited, the more I was convinced that Hector was right and the mentors would fill up their teams before we got a chance to audition. No, that'd be too easy. It was more likely we'd get on stage and I'd screw up horribly, and it would be my fault the band wasn't picked for the show. How could the other guys trust me with something this big?

Our number was finally called thirty minutes later, and we all rushed to the desk at the front of the room. A woman with a high ponytail and a polo shirt with the show's logo on it grabbed four clipboards and shoved them at us.

"This is the show's contract. Each of you need to print your name and the date and sign it at the end."

I tried to read the small print, but there was just so much of it. Pages and pages of legalese I didn't understand. The guys looked just as baffled, except Jared, who was actually reading the thing like it was interesting.

"It's all pretty standard stuff," the woman said, sounding annoyed that we weren't signing it immediately. She started ticking things off on her fingers. "If you're selected during the audition, you agree to be on the show for the next five weeks. The show will pay for your hotel, plus a small living stipend. Any songs you record for the show will be sold on the website, and you'll receive ten percent of the profits. If you're one of the final four bands, you agree to go on tour in August, and if you win, you receive a recording contract from Mix It Up Records."

"Um, should I sign this if I'm only a temporary member of the band?" I asked while I flicked through it.

"No changes in band members for the duration of the show, including the audition," the woman snapped. "It's right there on page four."

"No changes?" I nearly dropped the clipboard. If I did this audition, I'd be stuck with the band for as long as they were on the show. Or even longer, if we made it to the final four and were sent on tour. That would be the entire summer—and my internship started next Monday. There was no way I could do both.

"What?" Kyle asked and then spun to face Jared. "Did you know about this?"

"No! I would never trick Maddie into joining the band. I swear, I didn't know."

Kyle tossed his clipboard on the table. "That's it then. It's over. Let's get our gear and go."

"I told you we should have waited until next year," Hector muttered.

Jared scanned the contract again. "This can't be it. There must be some other way."

Kyle sighed. "Should we call Becca? Maybe if we begged her…"

"No. Definitely not. We can't trust her to keep it together for the next five weeks."

"I know, but—"

While the guys argued, I stared at the contract in my hands. The decision I made here could impact the rest of my life, and the two choices weighed on me, heavy with their uncertain futures. I could leave the band now without any hard feelings and go back to my normal life and the internship I had worked so hard for. That was the safe path, the one I'd been traveling on for the last three years. Once I washed off the makeup and returned the clothes to Julie, I'd be regular old Maddie again, who only practiced guitar in secret and had her future figured out.

Except…I didn't want to go back to my normal life anymore.

I'd joined the band thinking it would only be for this one audition. But now that I'd played with them, I wanted more. I wanted to compete with them, to perform their songs on stage, and maybe even have a shot at winning this thing. I wanted to fight for my dream—my *real* dream—for once in my life, instead of standing in the audience and cheering for someone else.

"I want to do the show," I said, my pulse racing with equal parts fear and excitement. "If you'll have me in the band, that is."

"Are you sure?" Kyle asked. "You were so excited about your internship."

"I was, but when I practiced with you guys last night, it just felt…right. Like this is what I'm meant to be doing. I don't want to look back years from now and wonder what if, you know?"

"Yeah, I get that." He turned to the rest of the band. "Well, I'm happy to let Maddie join the band permanently. What about you guys?"

"I'm cool with it," Jared said.

"Of course you are." Hector rolled his eyes. "But yeah, let's do this."

Jared grinned and draped an arm across my shoulder, sending another spike of heat through me. "Welcome to the band, Maddie."

After signing the contract, we were taken to a small waiting room and told we'd be going on in ten minutes. Hector stretched his neck and arms while Kyle texted someone, probably Alexis. Jared ran through some vocal exercises and paced back and forth, like he was about to burst through the door and take on the crowd by himself.

I sank onto the couch, the room suddenly spinning. Now that the big moment was almost here, I didn't know if I could go through with this. My stomach threatened to bring up everything I'd had today—which, granted, had been only a small coffee. Maybe I should have eaten something this morning. Great, I was going to blow this entire audition because I hadn't thought to grab a muffin before I left.

"How are you doing?" Jared asked, sitting next to me. "Still not okay?"

"Very much not okay." I took off my glasses and cleaned them on my dress, my movements quick and shaky.

Jared placed his hand on mine, and I nearly jumped off the couch. But then his hand was gone, so fast I almost questioned whether it had actually happened, except that his touch left a lingering warmth on my skin.

"Relax," he said. "We're all nervous, but we nailed it during last night's practice. We've got this."

I nodded, but I had no doubt the rest of the band would be great. They'd all performed on stage together before, many times. I'd played with them in their garage for a few hours. Not the same at all.

Kyle dropped onto the couch, squeezing me between the two brothers. "I don't blame you for freaking out, Maddie. This whole thing is terrifying. But I've seen you perform a dozen times, you'll be great."

"That was different," I said. Today I'd be playing guitar in a rock band in front of hundreds of people and the four amazing musicians we needed to impress to get on the show. Musicians from bands I'd grown up listening to and had fangirled over for years. And if we got on the show, our audition would be aired next week for the entire country to watch. Including my mother.

"Just don't screw up and we'll be fine," Hector said.

"Gee, thanks for the pep talk," I said, and the other guys laughed. Even Hector grinned, and that sense of belonging— that feeling that this was right—struck me again. I was a part of this band now. I could do this.

Our ten minutes were up too soon, and we were directed down a brightly lit hallway and into the backstage area. *The Sound* used a special kind of rotating stage that I'd also seen at music festivals, with a platform on each side so bands could set up and break down their equipment while another band was performing. Then the stage rotated, and it began again. This saved a lot of time with so many bands playing back-to-back.

I couldn't see the band currently on stage, but their music pounded under my feet as the crowd cheered for them. We were about to be in the exact same spot, in front of that same crowd, with our music blasting through the speakers. No, I couldn't think about that or I'd run straight back to that waiting room.

We rushed onto the back side of the stage, which had already been cleared by the previous band. Our gear was waiting for us, and some roadies helped us get it unpacked quickly. After hours of waiting, everything was happening so fast. I didn't have time to think; I just shoved my earpiece in and grabbed my guitar to check the tuning while the other guys handled their own instruments. I got my distortion pedal and mic set up just as the band on stage finished their song. I heard the mentors commenting but couldn't tell if the band had done a good job or not. Either way, it meant we had to hurry.

Kyle got behind his keyboard, Hector sat at the drums, and that left me and Jared up front. My sweaty fingers dropped my guitar pick, and when I went to grab it, my knees nearly gave out from under me. When I straightened up, Jared stood right in front of me, his bass hanging from his neck.

"Ready?" he asked.

"Um, as ready as I'll ever be." Which was to say, hell no. I smoothed my hair and yanked the bottom of my dress down, wishing I had a mirror to check how I looked one last time.

"Just have fun. It'll be over before you know it." He brushed a finger against my cheek, making me shiver. "Stray eyelash," he explained. "You look amazing, by the way."

Our eyes locked, and for a second, it was only the two of us on stage, about to make music together. He offered me one of his heart-stopping smiles, and it gave me the strength I needed to go through with this.

The stage began to turn, ending the moment. Jared and I moved back to our positions in front of our mics as the roar of the crowd grew louder and spotlights flashed in our eyes. My heart pounded as an entire sea of faces stretched before me. And in front, the four musicians who would decide our fate.

This was our one shot to change our futures forever. Our one moment to lose ourselves in the music and hope we brought the audience along with us. Our one chance to turn our dreams into reality.

I was ready.

CHAPTER SIX

I sent off a silent prayer to the universe that I wouldn't screw up just as the stage finished rotating. Hector started us off with the snap of his drumsticks, and we all jumped in with the opening to "Behind the Mask," exactly like we'd practiced. My guitar rang out across the giant theater, louder than I expected but blending with the rest of the band's sound. Jared began to sing, his voice like heartbreak and salty tears, and the crowd pulsed with each word. In seconds, he'd captivated them, like I'd seen him do to the audience at the shows I'd been to.

My fingers danced across the frets, and my pick pounded

against the strings. I tried to lose myself in the music like in our rehearsal, but this time there was a crowd watching my every move. My chest tightened at the sight of the four mentors eyeing our performance, judging everything we did. Was I looking at my guitar too often? Or not enough? Should I move around the stage? Look out at the crowd? No, that would only make me more nervous. I should probably move though, instead of standing like a statue. But what if I moved too much and knocked something over? Or, worse, crashed into Jared? No, moving was out, too. Safer to stay in one place. *Just focus on the music*, I told myself. *Also, don't pass out.*

At the chorus, Jared gave me an expectant look. Right, backup vocals. I leaned into the mic in front of me and joined in, but my voice was too quiet at first. Probably because I didn't actually want anyone to hear me sing. I raised my voice and hoped Jared was hypnotizing the crowd enough that no one paid any attention to me.

Near the end of the song, the music quieted down and only Jared's vocals filled the room, haunting and pained as he sang about how no one saw the real him. His words hit me right in the gut, like they always did. When he finished the verse, I jumped back in with the killer riff he normally played, kicking the song up a notch. The other guys joined us, a bonfire of Kyle's synth and Hector's drumming and Jared's bass. The crowd went wild, and a red light lit up in front of us with a loud buzz.

I missed a note in my surprise, but the other guys never lost their place. One of the mentors had picked us! Surely the other guys were freaking out as much as I was? Hector's steady beat immediately got me back on track, but then another buzz sounded—a second mentor wanted us! Followed by the buzz of a third! I'd been scared we wouldn't even get one, and now we had *three*? I couldn't believe it.

And then it was over. With one last note, the song ended, and the crowd roared. Somehow that had been both the longest three minutes of my life and the shortest. Sweat dripped down my face—it was freaking hot under all these lights—and adrenaline raced through my veins, making my arms tremble, but I felt more alive than ever before. *This is it,* I thought. *This is what I want to do with my life.*

The audience continued to scream, and Jared raised his arms, basking in the crowd's love and in our victory. Kyle and Hector came out from behind their instruments to stand next to us, grinning like drunken fools.

Three of the mentors had red lights in front of them: Angel Reese, the former singer of the '80s glam metal band Dark Embrace, still sporting bleach blonde hair and a spiked leather jacket despite her age; Dan Dorian, the long-haired bassist and singer of Loaded River, a '90s grunge band that had played with Nirvana and Pearl Jam; and Lance Bentley, a young pop star who personified tall, dark, and handsome. He'd won the last three years of *The Sound*, but rumor had it that he'd slept his way through all the women on his team. No thank you.

The only one who didn't buzz for us was Lissa Cruz, a beautiful brunette country singer who was known for being the sweetest mentor on the show. That was okay—we needed a coach, not a cheerleader.

The host of the show, Ray Carter, joined us at the front of the stage. He was probably in his late 40s, with overly gelled black hair, skin that screamed "spray tan," and a flashy white suit.

"That was one of the best things I've heard all day," he said into his mic. "And the audience clearly loves you. Who are you and where are you from?"

"We're Villain Complex from here in Los Angeles," Jared said, and the crowd cheered even louder. I couldn't believe they were making this much noise for *us*.

"That was killer," Angel said. "I need you on my team! I—"

Dan cut her off. "Yeah, I loved the way you—"

"Hey, I was talking!" Angel snapped. "Wait your turn."

Dan rolled his eyes but gestured for her to continue. This was normal for the show; part of the draw was seeing the mentors bicker between each other. Still, it was crazy that two musicians whose songs I'd listened to for years were fighting over us. Was this really my life? How did I get here?

Angel started again. "As I was saying, I love your sound, I love your look, and I think you'd be perfect for my team. With my help, you could definitely win this thing."

"Are you done with your sales pitch yet?" Dan asked her and then continued before she could answer. "Look. You've got the raw talent. You've got the skills. You've also got some things you need to work on, but I can take you to the next level."

"No, this band is mine!" Angel said, slamming her fist on the table. "I buzzed in first!"

"That doesn't mean anything," Dan said.

"But I want them. I want them *so bad*." She practically fell out of her seat saying it, and the crowd went wild.

"Okay, you've heard from two of the mentors," Ray said. "Lance, you want to chime in?"

Lance leaned forward, his dark gaze slowly taking us all in. "Listen. I've won *The Sound* three times already. Join me and we'll win."

"That's it?" Ray asked, after a brief pause.

Lance shrugged and sat back. "That's all I need to say. They know what the right choice is."

"All right then," Ray said and turned to us. "It's up you now. Whose team do you want to be on? Take a moment to talk it over."

The crowd erupted with shouts, and we huddled together next to the drums. "What do you guys think?" Jared asked. "I think we should go with Angel."

"I don't know," Hector said. "She hasn't won before. Lance has won three times. Seems like a sure deal."

"That's why he won't win again this year. Viewers are tired of it. They want someone else to win, with a new sound."

"What about Dan?" Kyle asked. "Loaded River was my favorite band as a kid."

"I don't know. He didn't seem that excited about us," Jared said.

Kyle snorted. "He was more excited than Lance."

"Maddie, what do you think?" Jared asked.

The three of them looked at me. I'd kept quiet until now because I wasn't sure I'd get a vote. I was brand-new after all.

"Um." I turned back to check out the mentors again. Definitely not Lance, but I couldn't decide between Angel and Dan. Both of them thought we could go far in the competition, and both seemed to be good mentors from what I'd seen on previous seasons. The crowd chanted names, but it was hard to tell which name was the loudest.

"Time's up," Ray said. "Who do you pick?"

"Angel," I told the guys. "I'd go with Angel."

Hector rolled his eyes. "You only picked her because Jared did."

"*No*, I picked her because she seemed the most enthusiastic. We need someone who will fight for us 'til the end."

"My thoughts exactly," Jared said.

"Fine," Hector said, and Kyle nodded.

We turned back to the mentors and the crowd, and Jared grabbed the mic. "We pick Angel."

"And Team Angel gets another band!" Ray yelled.

One of Dark Embrace's songs started playing through the

speakers while Angel jumped up and cheered. She rushed onto the stage and hugged each of us before I knew what was happening. Her hair smelled of cigarettes and very strong perfume, and I nearly gagged.

"I'm so happy! Welcome to my team," she told us before going back to her seat. She stuck her tongue out at Dan, who just shook his head.

The stage turned so the next band could audition. Bright lights flashed in my eyes as we were taken into another room, and as soon as the door shut, we all erupted.

"We did it!" Kyle wrapped an arm around Jared and Hector's necks, bringing them in for a squeeze. "We actually did it! Alexis is going to be so jealous. She loves Angel."

"I can't believe it," Hector said, his eyes wide. "Did that really happen?"

Jared laughed and clung to the other guys. "I told you we'd make it!"

I stood apart from their guy-bonding moment. It was fine— they'd been together for years, and I was the new kid. But then Jared pulled me over with an arm around my shoulder. "Get in here. You're a part of this band, too."

His touch sent sparks through me, as it always did. I had so much I wanted to say to him—to thank him for taking a chance on me and convincing the others to let me join the band. To tell him how much it meant that he'd believed in me. But this time, words failed me. Kyle looped his arm around my other shoulder, and the four of us stood together in a huddle, grinning ear to ear.

"That's cute," Ray said, speaking to a camera guy. "Make sure you get a shot of this."

We pulled apart at the reminder they were still there. I'd completely forgotten about the interview they did with everyone who got on the show, when they asked how the band got started, what kind of music they liked—that kind of stuff. Hopefully one of the other guys would do all the talking since I'd been in the band for, oh, less than a day now.

Ray arranged us so that Jared and I stood in front, with Kyle and Hector slightly behind us and to the side.

"This will be quick," he said. "I'll ask you some questions and you'll look straight at the camera when you answer. Don't worry if you mess up, we'll edit it together so you look good. Ready?" He launched right into it without waiting for a response. "I'm here with Villain Complex from Los Angeles, who just joined Angel's team after a fierce battle between her, Dan, and Lance. Tell me, why did you pick Angel as your mentor?" He shoved the mic in Jared's face.

"It was a tough decision, but she seemed like she wanted us the most."

"You're the singer, yes? Can you each state your name and what you play in the band?"

"Sure. I'm Jared Cross, and I'm the lead singer and bassist." He flashed his stage smile, and Ray thrust the mic at me next.

"Oh, um." I yanked at the bottom of my dress, worried the

camera was getting a view. "I'm Maddie Taylor, and I play the guitar."

"And sing backup," Jared added, much to my dismay.

The other guys said, "Hector Fernandez, drums," and "Kyle Cross, keyboard."

"Great," Ray said and then asked Jared, "So what does Villain Complex mean? Who came up with that?"

"I did," Jared said. "It's a play on the phrase 'hero complex,' which is when someone always wants to save the day and get recognized for it. I figured someone with a villain complex would crave the opposite—they'd want to be noticed for the bad things they do. Fame through villainy and all that." He laughed. "Basically, we all love comic books, and villains are cool."

I studied his face and wondered if there was a personal reason he'd chosen that name or if they really were just comic book geeks. His comment reminded me of the lyrics in "Behind the Mask," about presenting a certain image to the world but no one seeing the real person underneath.

Before I could ponder it further, Ray continued with his next question. "Can you tell us a little about how long you've been together and how you formed?"

"Sure. Kyle and I started playing music together when we were kids. Our mom's a songwriter and our dad's an entertainment lawyer, so it must be in our blood. Hector was my best friend in high school, and I convinced him to learn the drums so we could start a band." He stopped and glanced at me.

"And Maddie joined us…recently."

Ray quickly rattled off a few more questions to Jared about the band and what we hoped to get out of the show while the rest of us just stood there like we didn't exist. Hector and Kyle kept trying to butt in, but Ray never let them have the mic.

"One last question," Ray said. "Maddie, are you and Jared together?"

"What? No!" He hadn't addressed me for the entire interview and now he asked *that*? Where had that question even come from?

"So no hidden story there?" he asked, and I shook my head. "C'mon, there has to be something. Look at this guy. You like him, right?"

My god, what was this guy's problem? As the camera focused on me, I coughed, trying to find the words to make this moment end.

"No, we're just friends," I finally managed to say. Jared stared at the floor, like he wanted to be anywhere else. Me too, Jared, me too.

"Too bad. Okay, that's it," Ray said, and the interview was over. He left the room without another word, with the camera crew trailing behind him.

"What the fuck was that?" Hector asked. "This isn't the Jared Cross band."

"Huh?" Jared asked. "I didn't ask the questions."

"No, you just answered all of them. And this isn't the Jared and Maddie love story either."

"I didn't—" I started while Jared said, "There's nothing—"

"Whatever," Hector said. "Just keep it in your pants, man."

Jared's face darkened. "What the—"

"Enough," Kyle said, getting between the two of them. "The show is just trying to find an angle they can work. Don't worry about it. Besides, Maddie already promised she won't hook up with Jared."

Wow, thank you, Kyle. As if this moment wasn't embarrassing enough. "Can we please drop this?" I asked.

Jared raised his eyebrows at me and Hector snorted, but no one else said a word after that.

The show gave us all the information about what would happen next, and we were finally sent home. I still couldn't believe I'd made the choice to do this, to give up my internship to join a rock band and compete on a reality TV show. Who was I and what had I done with my former self?

CHAPTER SEVEN

Quitting my internship was harder than I'd expected. Let's just say the LA Philharmonic wasn't pleased to have their carefully selected intern back out at the last minute. I'd definitely burned some bridges there, not to mention with the professor who'd sponsored me. I came pretty close to calling the guys to tell them I couldn't join the band after all, but Carla and Julie assured me I was doing the right thing. God, I hoped they were right.

On Monday, I met the band at the high-rise hotel in LA Live where we'd be staying as long as we were on the show. We were only allowed two rooms, and the guys decided it would be best if they shared one, giving me a room all to myself. I think they just didn't want to argue over who would have to share with me.

I dropped my luggage off in my nice big room and ran into the guys again in the elevator—their room was a few floors up. As the door closed, a voice said, "Going down," and immediately the Fall Out Boy song "Sugar, We're Goin' Down" popped into my head. As if on cue, Jared started singing the chorus of that exact song.

"I heard that, too," I said, and he grinned at me.

"I thought of Aerosmith's 'Love In An Elevator,'" Kyle said.

"Also a good one," Jared said, and belted out the lyrics.

Hector shook his head. "Not me. I heard that Nelly song 'Country Grammar.'"

"What?" Kyle gaped at him. "I think we might have to kick you out of the band."

"No kidding," Jared said. "I'm not sure our relationship can survive such fundamental differences in musical taste."

"Please, we all know you'd be lost without me," Hector said.

"True." Jared grabbed him, and they wrestled until the elevator door opened. I rolled my eyes. *Guys.*

The lobby was all smooth bamboo and stainless steel trim, and my shoes squeaked loudly as we walked across the shiny floors. Some of the people checking in or sitting on the couches were business people or tourists, but the rest had to be musicians on the show, with their dyed hair, faded band T-shirts, and guitar cases. Many of them were sizing us up, too.

"What do you think the other bands on Angel's team are like?" I asked the guys.

Kyle shrugged. "Who knows? Last season she had all kinds of music."

"Yeah, but she tends to go for harder stuff usually," Jared said. "Punk, emo, heavy metal."

"Last season she had one pop band that almost won though," I said.

"True. I just hope she picks a good song for us to play in the battle."

After the auditions, the next step was *The Sound's* Battle of the Bands. Basically, the mentors paired off the six bands on their team and had them compete against each other by performing the same song. The mentors chose the winners and also got one rescue that they could use on any band eliminated from one of the other teams—leaving four bands on each team for the next show.

Usually there were two battle rounds, but this season had been shortened to only six weeks and moved to the summer instead of the spring, probably because ratings had been dropping steadily. Maybe they hoped a shorter season would keep everyone on the edge of their seats the entire time, or maybe they thought the show would have less competition in the summer since there was nothing else on TV.

We found the meeting room for Team Angel just as four

guys with skinny jeans and identical shaggy haircuts walked over. They had that combo of nerd-meets-hipster down, and two of them even had black-rimmed glasses to complete the look.

"Are you on Angel's team, too?" one of the guys asked. He had a boy-next-door kind of face, with broad shoulders and sandy blond hair. Definitely the best-looking one in the group.

"Yeah, we're Villain Complex," Jared said, and we all made our introductions.

"Sweet name," the cute guy—whose name was Sean—said. "Wish we'd thought of it. We're The Static Klingons."

I couldn't help but laugh at the *Star Trek* pun. "That's awesome."

Sean grinned at me. "Yeah? I think you're the only person who's gotten it so far."

"We probably should go in now," their bassist said, scowling at us like we were the enemy. Technically we were, even though we were on the same team.

Sean opened the door and stepped back, waving me inside. "After you."

I smiled at him and entered. The room had identical chairs lined up in rows, facing a podium at the front. A camera crew was already set up so they could film clips for next week's episode. Judging by the clusters of people in the chairs, three bands had already arrived. That meant one more had to show, and Angel was nowhere to be found either.

I picked a spot in the fourth row, and Kyle and Hector filed in next to me, with Jared going around to sit on my other side. The Static Klingons sat two rows in front of us, and Sean turned around and grinned at me before saying something to his band.

Jared leaned closer to me. "He likes you."

"What?" I said it a little too loud, then blushed and lowered my voice. "Why do you say that?"

"I saw the way he looked at you."

"This is the real reason why having Maddie in the band is a bad idea," Hector said, smirking. "Now we're going to have to fight off hordes of horny guys going after her."

"Thanks for the offer, but I think I'll be okay," I said, but I was secretly pleased Hector thought I would attract so much attention. Or that he would actually fight them off for me. Not that he'd need to because one boy smiling at me one time did not equal "hordes of horny guys." Nor did it mean that this one guy was interested in me that way. Sean just seemed friendly.

Jared didn't seem to think Hector's comment was amusing at all. "You said it was a bad idea to let Maddie join because I'd—how'd you put it?—'bone her and then break her heart?'"

"Oh, god, you said that?" I asked Hector.

His face turned almost purple. "You have to admit that is your style."

"Give me a break," Jared said. "One time with Becca and—"

"Knock it off, you two," Kyle interrupted, giving them each a warning look. "This is so not the time for this."

"I wouldn't do that to Maddie anyway," Jared muttered.

"We'll see," Hector said, leaning back and crossing his arms.

Jared turned away but didn't say anything else. Tension created a concrete wall between them, with me and Kyle stuck in the middle. I was relieved Jared wouldn't do that to me, but also a tiny bit disappointed he didn't see me that way, even though I knew it was for the best. I didn't want to mess up anything with the band, and getting involved with Jared would do exactly that.

The last band arrived, with hair spiked into mohawks and chains hanging from their leather jackets. Definitely Angel's type. The one girl in the band wore a chainmail bikini and very short shorts, and I recognized her as one of the people Jared had talked to before our audition. She caught his eye and winked, and I almost threw up in my mouth a little. The rest of her band glared at everyone and sat down.

While we waited, Kyle and I quietly discussed the other bands and tried to figure out what kind of music they played. I started to wonder if Angel would ever show or if we'd all been given the wrong time or what.

Hector was lost in his sketchbook, and I leaned over to ask, "What are you drawing?"

"Just working on ideas for my next graphic novel."

"Can I see?" Kyle had once mentioned Hector went to art school, but I didn't know much else.

"Sure." He passed me the sketchbook, and I flipped through it. There were lots of random doodles, but also rough sketches of comic panels with lots of action.

He was good—like professional-level good.

"Wow, this is awesome," I said. "What's your graphic novel about?"

"It's called *Misfit Squad*, and it's about a group of teens who have really uncool superpowers, so they band together after the other superhero groups won't let them in. Like the main character accidentally breaks things, and at first it seems like a curse, but then she learns to control it." As he talked, Hector's face lit up in a way I'd never seen before, even when he was drumming. "The first one just came out, and we're planning to do two more."

"Okay, I definitely need to read that."

"I'll give you a copy later."

"Hector designed the Villain Complex logo, too," Kyle added. "And did the quote wall in our studio. He's amazing."

Angel finally walked in, nearly an hour after our scheduled time, with her stringy blonde hair and caked-on makeup trying to cover up her wrinkles. Back in the day, she'd had a voice that could go from screaming to sweet to sexy in an instant. But after one of the band members committed suicide, Dark Embrace had broken up, and she'd started bouncing in and out of rehab. Now she was just a washed-up celebrity trying to relive her former glory days. Still, my mom had played her songs all the time, and I'd grown up with her raspy voice and scratchy guitar, so I was a bit star-struck being in the same room with her. Almost enough to forgive her very late arrival.

"Good, you're all here," she said, like she hadn't made *us* wait. "Let's get this over with." She gestured to the two assistants who had walked in with her, and they began passing papers out to all of us. "Here's your schedule, blah blah blah. Read it, whatever."

She leaned against the podium and started playing on her phone. Jared and Kyle exchanged a look, the kind siblings give each other that say an entire sentence without a word, and I got the feeling they were not impressed. I had to admit it was odd how the Angel at our audition had been so excited while this one seemed like she couldn't wait to get out of here.

We spent a few moments looking over our band's schedule for the week. After this meeting, we had to take photos together, but then we were free for the rest of the night. Starting tomorrow we had a six-hour rehearsal slot every day at a local studio. On Friday, we'd record the song so people could buy it on the show's website, and on Sunday, we'd be filming the actual battle round, which would air Monday night.

Angel finally put her phone away and stood up straight. "Are we rolling now?" One of the camera guys nodded, and she tossed her hair and put on a big smile. "Welcome to Team Angel. I'm so thrilled you're all here!"

Silence from all of us. Maybe we were supposed to cheer or applaud or something, but none of us could be bothered. She looked annoyed for an instant and then continued. "All six of your bands were chosen because I believe you can win this thing. I'm confident that this year I have the most talented group of musicians on the show, and I know Team Angel is going all the way!" This got a tiny bit of forced applause. "Unfortunately, only one of you will make it to the final four. You all have talent or you wouldn't be here, but to make it to the end, you need to work hard and want it more than anything. I want you all to ask yourselves: How bad do you want this? What are you willing to do to win?"

Angel had been doing this show for four years, and she gave the same speech every season. I wondered if she knew from the very beginning who had the best shot at winning, if she could tell, just by looking in our eyes now, who wanted it the most. As I glanced around the room, it hit me that we might not be on the show after this week. Out of six bands, only three of us would be staying with Angel. Any band she eliminated might be picked by the other mentors, but there was no guarantee that would happen.

Beside me, Jared's eyes took on a fiery determination I'd never seen before. Jared was in this thing to win it, no doubt. He'd do anything for that chance, but would I? How much did I want it? Or was I only doing this for Kyle? For Jared?

No, I wanted to win, too. Maybe not as much as Jared did, but after hearing that roar of the crowd, feeling the music blasting from the giant speakers, and playing with the band at my side, I wanted to do this for the rest of my life. I wanted that record deal and the tour and the future as a part of Villain Complex. To get that, we had to win *The Sound*.

After an appropriate pause for her words to sink in, Angel continued. "This week we have the battle round, which will be fun." I couldn't tell if she was being sarcastic or not. She waved at her assistant, and he passed her a sheet of paper, which she squinted at while he disappeared against the wall again. "Okay, let's see here…. First up, The Static Klingons will compete against Villain Complex."

I groaned softly. Why couldn't we have been up against any of the other bands on the team? Of course we would be paired with the one band that seemed sort of nice. Now there was a strong chance one of us would be going home next week.

"You're both going to perform 'Somebody Told Me' by The Killers," Angel said. "I think it'll be a good song for your different sounds."

An interesting choice. I liked the song, but I worried it was a bit too peppy for our usual vibe. Maybe that was more of The Static Klingons' thing.

She paired off the other bands and then said, "I'll see you all at your rehearsals." She flicked a hand at her assistants, and they left the room.

"I haven't played this song before," I said to the guys. "Have you?"

"No," Jared said, as the other two shook their heads. "Which means we need to work our asses off this week."

CHAPTER EIGHT

We spent the next couple hours having photos taken of us, both individually and as a band. After that, another camera crew had us walk down a long red carpet outside while they filmed us. Like in the interview the other day, they had me and Jared up front, and the other two guys behind us. We did this multiple times, walking toward the camera and trying to look cool with the wind blowing our hair back, like we were a Serious Band Doing Serious Music. Mostly, I felt ridiculous.

When I returned to my room, my phone was flashing with a bunch of texts from Julie and Carla asking how my first day was and another from Jared telling me to come to their room to watch the show in an hour. I'd forgotten that the first episode of *The Sound* was tonight, and there was a good chance we'd be on it. Even if we weren't on until tomorrow's show, we needed to check out the other bands and see what we were up against.

I wrote the girls and told them my day was crazy but exciting and that I would update them more later. After a quick shower, I pulled on some yoga pants and a tank top, but one glance in the mirror told me that wouldn't work. The tank top was too tight on its own, and this wasn't like hanging out with my roommates in my apartment. I barely knew these guys—other than Kyle anyway. I switched to jeans and threw a flannel shirt on over my tank top. Much better.

When I got to the guys' room, they already had two pizzas sitting on the desk, and my stomach growled. Hector was hogging an entire bed, Jared was on the other, and Kyle took up the only chair, leaving me no place to sit. I hesitated just inside the door, trying to figure out a way to solve the seating problem without it being super awkward.

"Grab some pizza and come sit," Jared said, patting the bed next to him. None of the other guys said anything, so I guessed that was my spot then. Thanks a lot, guys.

I got some food and a beer and sat next to Jared, careful to stick to my side of the bed so we didn't touch. With my luck, I'd probably drop pizza all over his white sheets. Why couldn't they have ordered something less messy to eat? But soon the warm smell of cheese and pepperoni hit me, and I was digging in, too.

"Oh my god, this pizza is the greatest thing I've ever eaten."

"I know. I thought I was going to chew my arm off earlier," Jared said.

"Maybe the show is starving us so we'll lose those ten pounds the camera adds."

He laughed, and I loved the sound of it, how honest and real it was. "That must be it. Though I think you look perfect the way you are." His voice dropped so the other guys couldn't hear the last part, and I swear the room temperature jumped by at least ten degrees.

"Quiet, it's starting," Kyle said and used the remote to raise the volume.

For the first few minutes, the show explained the premise and how it worked and then introduced the mentors. They made a big deal about how Lance had won the last three years in a row and then showed a quick preview of the bands performing tonight, including a one-second shot of us, before it cut away to commercials. I nearly dropped my pizza when I saw it. I knew our audition would be aired one of the nights, but it was still a total shock to actually see us on TV.

"That was us!" Kyle said, slapping his hand on the desk.

"We must be on tonight's show," Jared said.

He got up and dropped his empty plate in the trash and then sank back on the bed. His elbows brushed against my side as he opened his laptop, making me tense up, but when I tried to look at him without actually looking at him, he didn't seem to notice. Had he purposefully sat a little closer to me this time? Or was I imagining it?

The show returned with the first audition from an alternative band I didn't recognize. Lissa was the only one who buzzed for them, which explained why I hadn't seen them yet. The auditions continued, and we all made comments about who was good and who was probably just filler while Jared took notes on his laptop. There were always a few bands that would obviously get weeded out early on. They weren't bad, but they didn't have the skills or experience yet for the show. I really hoped we weren't one of those bands.

I finished my pizza and tossed the plate. This time, my thigh touched Jared's when I sat back down, but he didn't react. I settled against the pillows and watched the show, but left my leg there to see if he'd do anything and—if I was honest with myself—because touching Jared woke up every inch of my body in a way I couldn't resist. He didn't move his leg, but he didn't make any *other* moves either. I must have imagined that he'd sat closer to me earlier. And now that I wasn't eating, I didn't know what to do with my hands. I tried different positions—crossing my arms, leaving them at my sides, and finally settled on lacing my fingers in my lap.

After an hour, we were finally on. We all sat up straighter and Kyle said, "Shh!" even though no one was talking. They showed part of our interview first, when we all introduced ourselves, and then they cut to a clip of us waiting before the audition with the other bands. I hadn't realized they'd been filming us, but there was Jared singing to me in front of everyone and the look on my face of pure longing made me cringe. Was I always that obvious? They followed that clip with the interviewer asking if there was anything between me and Jared and my quick denial and then went to commercials.

"Wow, you looked horrified by his question," Jared said.

"I know!" Kyle said. "Did you see her face when he asked that?"

"Yeah, hilarious," I said, trying to make light of it so they would move on as soon as possible.

"Is the idea really *that* bad?" Jared asked.

"No!" I said, a little too loudly. "I was just surprised when he asked me that."

"I love it." Hector cracked up. "Maddie's the one girl disgusted by the idea of dating you."

"Ha fucking ha." Jared threw a crumpled–up, oil-covered napkin at Hector, who tossed it back at us. Naturally, it landed on my lap. I threw it at Kyle, and it bounced off his head and hit the floor. He gave a mock-growl, and we all laughed.

Our laughs cut off instantly the second the show was back on. The stage turned, revealing me clutching my guitar like it would protect me from the audience somehow, and Jared looking confident and sexy as usual, a man born to be on stage. Hector started us off, and he was an animal on the drums. His muscular arms pounded away while sweat dripped down his forehead, and his energy fueled the rest of our performance. Meanwhile, Kyle bobbed his head to the music, sometimes playing the keyboard one-handed and getting the crowd going. I hadn't seen either of them when we performed, and it was fun to watch them now.

And then there was me. Stiff. Wide-eyed. Looking like I was about to bolt off the stage. It was obvious who the weak link in the band was, and even worse, this was on TV for the entire country to see. I might have been playing the song, but I just wasn't bringing it.

The mentors began buzzing for us, and on the bed, my fingers dug into the sheets, itching to get back on stage with my guitar and relive that moment. Jared's hand slipped between our bodies, and he tangled his fingers with mine, sending a jolt under my skin. I wanted to look at him, to see his face when he squeezed my hand, but then it would make the moment too real. Instead, I kept my gaze on the screen while Jared's thumb brushed against the spot on my wrist where my pulse raced, making my lips part with a silent sigh. None of the other guys noticed, too busy watching the mentors fight over our band on TV. They showed the clip of the guys all hugging after the audition, with Jared pulling me in to join them, before the show moved on to the next band.

Jared finally released my hand and put his fingers back on the laptop, allowing me to breathe again.

"That was pretty good," he said. "Even though I sucked at

bass, and my voice was too pitchy on the third verse."

"You were fine," Kyle said. "I screwed up the bridge though."

"You were both amazing, and Hector, too," I said. "I'm the one who stood there like a deer in the headlights the entire performance. And I was so shocked when a mentor buzzed for us that I lost my place."

Jared leaned against me, nudging me with his arm. "You did great, really."

A conflicting mix of feelings rushed through me. I wanted to rest my head against his shoulder. I wanted the other guys to leave so I could be alone with him. I wanted to escape to my room and forget about Jared completely. That was definitely the safest option.

"That was your first live show," Kyle said, bringing me back to the moment. "You'll do even better next time."

Hector nodded. "Don't stress about it, Maddie. You were really good."

I gave them all a weak smile. "Thanks. I just don't want to let you guys down."

"You won't," Kyle said. "You just need more practice on stage, that's all."

Jared sat up straighter. "Look, it's The Static Klingons."

The four of them wore matching shirts made to look like they were crew members on *Star Trek*. Sean spoke for the group during their interview, describing how they practiced in an old barn in Nebraska.

"Ha! Your boyfriend lives on a farm," Kyle said.

"He is *not* my boyfriend." Sean was cute, but he was so...vanilla. So bland. He reminded me of my high school boyfriend—nice and boring and safe.

Hector smirked. "But he'd like to be."

We quieted down as the band took the stage. Their song got the audience going, though not as much as our performance had. Sean played guitar and had a catchy, high-pitched voice—a little nasally but in a good way.

"They're not bad," Hector said.

"Yeah," Kyle said. "They sound sort of like if Weezer had a love child with Daft Punk."

"They're really good," I said. "And unfortunately for us, their sound is perfect for The Killers' song."

Jared sighed. "I wish Angel had paired us with that punk band. We'd crush them."

"But then you wouldn't have the chainmail bikini girl to flirt with," Kyle said.

"Eh, she lives in Boston anyway."

Hector snorted. "Like that matters. You're not going to *date* her."

"Hey, I already told Jared he's not allowed to bring girls up here," Kyle said.

"Yeah, but that means you can't bring Alexis either," Jared said.

"I'll make that sacrifice to not have to deal with your women the morning after." He made a gagging sound.

Thanks for reminding me, Kyle. And soon, Jared would have even more groupies, more screaming girls who would love to invite him to their rooms for the night. I couldn't let myself forget the kind of guy Jared was, no matter how he made me feel. Especially since he seemed to make *every* girl feel that way.

The guys kept bantering until the show ended. When it was over, Hector went into the bathroom and Kyle went onto the balcony to call Alexis. Leaving me alone in a bed with Jared, our bodies much too close and my hands way too tempted to reach for him again.

"I should go," I said, jumping off the bed. "Early morning and all that."

"Right." He walked me to the door. I stepped outside, and he lingered in the doorway. "Maddie," he said, and I turned back, wanting something I wasn't ready to name yet. But all he said was, "Goodnight."

CHAPTER NINE

The next morning I downloaded "Somebody Told Me" and listened to it on repeat as I got ready. During my elevator ride to the lobby, I got so into picking apart the guitar chords that I nearly crashed into Jared when I stepped out.

"Hey," Jared said, giving me a quick once-over with a smile. "You look great."

"Thanks." I flushed, but reminded myself that Jared always said things like that. It didn't mean anything. He was just a flirt.

Julie had helped me get my wardrobe ready for my time on the show, including an all-day shopping event over the weekend. Everyone had to be prepared to be filmed at any time, so I had to keep up my rocker look for the next few weeks. Today I was wearing a long, one-shouldered top over black-and-white-striped leggings and ankle boots. But I was more surprised by what Jared wore; over his black jeans, he had on a T-shirt with the classic Joker and Harley Quinn on it.

"Oh, wow, I love your shirt," I said.

"Yeah? They're my favorite Batman villains."

"Mine too! They're like the Bonnie and Clyde of comics." I paused before revealing the next bit since it might cross the line, but I decided to let my geek flag fly. "I'm actually dressing up as Harley Quinn for Comic-Con next month."

"Really?" he asked, as we moved to a spot near the revolving doors to wait for Kyle and Hector.

"I know, it's pretty nerdy, but my friend Julie is making all the costumes. She's going to be Poison Ivy and my other friend Carla is going to be Catwoman."

"Gotham City's most dangerous women. I like it."

"That's the idea."

"You know, we're all going to Comic-Con, too. Maybe I'll dress up as the Joker." He winked at me.

That wink was dangerous. It could get a girl in trouble. And was he saying he wanted to go as a couple? Or was I reading too much into that comment? "You're all going to Comic-Con?"

"Yep. Hector's going to promote his graphic novel, and he got me a ticket, too. Kyle is going with Alexis, who's taking photos for the website she works for. I've never been before, so I'm excited."

"We went the last two years. It was amazing."

I told him about it as we waited for the other guys—waking up at 3 AM to get in line for the biggest panels, eating nothing but pretzel dogs and mini-pizzas for days, the unbelievable number of people crammed into the exhibit hall, plus all the incredible costumes and free swag. Jared listened intently and asked questions, and in return, I asked all about Hector's graphic novel. Hector had done the artwork, inking, and coloring, but someone he'd met online had written the script. The band really *did* live up to their geeky name.

Jared's phone buzzed, and I stood close enough to sneak a peek when he checked it. The text was from someone named Michelle and said, *"hey sexy wanna get 2gether 2nite?"* He shot me a quick glance and shoved the phone back in his pants without answering. He probably didn't want me to see what he wrote back. It had to be from one of his many groupies or maybe someone he'd met on the show. One of those girls from the audition perhaps? The girl with the mohawk and chainmail bikini? Did she seem like a Michelle? Whatever. Jared's sex life was none of my business.

When the other guys arrived, we walked the three blocks to the address we'd been given for the studio, and Jared told us how Villain Complex's social media sites had all gained thousands of followers overnight. More people had visited our website in the last day than ever before, and many were even buying the album. It was crazy to think we now had fans all over the country, rooting for us and anxious to see our next performance. Even more pressure to do a good job on this week's show.

We stopped at a brick building that looked like it had once been a factory or something. The windows were all dark so we couldn't see inside, and there was no sign or anything—just a number on the black door.

"Is this it?" I asked, checking the address again on our schedule.

"Must be," Kyle said.

We stepped inside and found a lounge with dark couches scattered around the room, plus an attached kitchen area with coffee and food. A guy at a reception desk directed us to room four, where our gear was waiting for us in a soundproofed studio. Someone from the show had dropped off sheet music, and I studied the guitar tabs, mentally replaying the song in my head. I was already familiar with "Somebody Told Me," but singing along to it on the radio and playing it with the band was a totally different story. I hadn't been lying to Jared, though—I did have an ear for this stuff. I set down the papers after a quick once-over and tried out the opening guitar riff. It was easy but very catchy with the way the chords got higher and higher.

The other guys tried some things, too, testing out their own parts of the song. After a few minutes, Jared turned to face all of us.

"Before we do anything else, we need to figure out a way to differentiate our version from whatever The Static Klingons do."

"Good idea," I said. "They already have a similar sound to The Killers, so they probably won't change the song very much."

"What if we made the song darker?" Kyle asked. "Drop the tuning, make it almost an emo cover of the song."

Jared rubbed the stubble along his chin as he considered. "That could work, and it would sound more like our own stuff, too. Let's try it."

For the next three hours, we worked on getting our version of the song figured out, experimenting with different ways to make it our own. The guitar on the song wasn't hard, but the bass was trickier and Jared had a tougher time with it.

After a particularly bad play-through, we decided to take a break and stretch our limbs before the next three-hour block. I headed to the kitchen to grab lunch and found Sean in there, pouring some coffee.

"Hi," he said. "Crazy day, huh?"

"Very. I'm still trying to catch my breath."

"Me too." He watched as I grabbed a plate and piled on some salad. "I hate that our bands are competing against each other."

"I know, it really sucks." I examined the mini-sandwiches, trying to figure out what they were, and then grabbed two turkey ones and a soda. I was just thrilled the show wasn't starving us today.

"So how's it going for you?" Sean asked, resting his hip

against the counter in front of me. "With the song?"

"We've got it figured out I think. Just need to practice more. How about you?"

"We've done covers of 'Somebody Told Me' before at shows, so we feel pretty good about it. What kind of spin are you putting on it?"

"Um…" I wasn't sure what to tell him, and then I was distracted by the sight of Jared in the lounge, talking to a girl with long copper hair. Was this Michelle? She gave him a flirty smile and put her hand on his elbow, and I wanted to dump my plate of food on her head. Jared flashed her his devilish grin, but when he looked at me and Sean, something crossed his face. He ditched the girl and walked over to us.

"Hey," he said, standing close to me and glaring at Sean. "What do you think of the song choice?"

"We're happy with it. It's a good song for us. You?" Sean's sunny disposition had vanished, and he eyed Jared with an openly hostile look. I wasn't really sure what was going on between them.

"We'll make it work."

"Cool." They stared each other down for a long, painful moment, and then Sean turned back to me. "Hey, it was great to see you, Maddie."

"You too." I pulled my shirt down to better cover my leggings, suddenly self-conscious. The mood had turned frosty ever since Jared had arrived, like they both wanted to stake their claim on me or something, which was ridiculous.

"What was that about?" I asked Jared once Sean had left.

Jared turned to make himself some tea with honey. "He's trying to work you to get info on what we're doing."

I rolled my eyes. "He's just a nice guy, and you're being paranoid."

"Okay, then he wants to get in your pants."

"I highly doubt that." Yes, Sean was the sort of guy I usually dated, but he was also our competition. He lived in Nebraska anyway. "And if he does, what do you care?"

It was a loaded question and Jared's eyes widened for second, but then his cool exterior took over again. "I don't. Just be careful what you say to him."

"God, Jared, I'm not going to tell him anything."

I walked away before he could reply. Did he actually think I would betray the band just because some cute guy smiled at me? And why did it sting so much that Jared didn't care if Sean wanted me? Like the other guys, he only saw me as a little sister. While I found this charming in Kyle and amusing in Hector, when Jared acted like an overprotective big brother, I kind of wanted to kick something.

According to our schedule, Angel was supposed to show up during our final two hours of practice, but she never did.

That night I told the guys I was tired and watched the second group of auditions alone in my hotel room. I couldn't handle another night of awkwardness next to Jared, especially after our conversation earlier.

For the next few days, we spent most of our time in rehearsal, and Angel still never appeared. I was starting to think she was a mentor in name only. Were the other bands on her team being ignored, too, or was it just us? I thought about asking Sean, but Jared's warning echoed in my head. I didn't think Sean was using me for info, but it wouldn't hurt to be careful either.

In the evenings, many of the bands hung out in the lobby of the hotel, mingling and gossiping and flirting, but I didn't join them. I had zero interest in seeing Jared slipping off to some hotel room with another girl. Besides, I felt like an imposter around the other bands, like as soon as I opened my mouth they'd realize I wasn't really one of them. I didn't want them to think, *Why are you on this show, you hack?*

Instead, I retreated to my room and ate alone every night. Being around the guys all day was exhausting anyway, and I needed some alone time to recharge. I sent updates to Carla, who was in New York on some fashion shoot, and Julie, who had returned to the town in Northern California where we'd grown up to see her parents.

On Thursday night, she called me while I was watching TV

and painting my nails a dark burgundy. "Hey, Julie, what's up?"

"I saw your mom today, and she asked how you're doing." Julie paused, and I could feel her judgment in the silence. "You didn't tell her about the show?"

"No, I haven't spoken to her in…" Honestly, I wasn't sure how long it had been. "A while."

"Maddie!"

"I know, I know. I should have told her." I sighed. Everything with my mother was so difficult, it was easier to just ignore that part of my life sometimes. "What did you say?"

"Nothing, and it was seriously uncomfortable. You need to tell her."

"I'm sorry. I'll call her tomorrow." I blew on my nails, debating whether or not to ask the thing I really wanted to know. "How's she doing? Is she…"

"She looks good. Better. She said she's been sober for three months now."

I closed my eyes, relieved. I didn't think it would stick, but at least she was trying. Again. "Where did you see her?"

"At the store. She was buying cigarettes."

"Of course." The only two things my mom would leave the house for: booze and cigarettes. "How's your family?"

"Ugh, all they want to talk about is my sister and how wonderful she is. They'd trade me in for a clone of her in an instant."

I laughed and started painting my toenails while Julie told me all about her time back home. It should have made me homesick, but it didn't. When I'd turned eighteen, I'd gotten out of that place as fast as I could, and I had no regrets.

On Friday, we went to a different part of the studio to record our version of the song so *The Sound* could sell it on the website. The more songs a band sold, the better they did in the live shows; though for this episode, they'd just earn us some extra cash. Angel was supposed to attend the recording session, but, surprise surprise, she never showed up.

The other guys had rented a recording studio before to make their album, but I'd only recorded music for school so a lot of it was new to me. The sound guys advised us from the control room while one of the producers watched—a guy named Steve who wore the biggest watch I'd ever seen, along with a suit that probably cost more than my car.

In the live room, we played through the song together a few times, and then we each recorded our part of the song alone, too. When it was my turn, I played my guitar with the headphones on, just me and the music, the sound clear and beautiful while everything else faded away. Jared went last, recording the vocals while the rest of us watched, his eyes closed as he emptied his soul into the lyrics. I'd never seen someone who could channel emotion like he did every time he sang, like each word was being ripped out of him. His voice stirred something deep inside me, a longing that was almost painful, a desire I couldn't ignore. I ached to pull him into my arms and press my lips to his, to feel him pour that same passion into me.

Saturday was our last practice before the battle, and it was starting to look like Angel would be a no-show for that, too. I grabbed some coffee during our break and prepared to settle in for our last three hours of rehearsal. We'd gotten the song down, and now it was only a matter of practicing until we felt confident we wouldn't make any mistakes tomorrow.

We still had about ten minutes to relax before we started again, so I sipped my coffee and played with my guitar picks. Hector was sprawled across the floor drawing in his sketchbook while Kyle and Jared talked quietly, heads ducked close together. Brother stuff, I guessed.

The door banged open, and a stream of people entered with cameras and other equipment, followed by Angel and her assistants. The four of us just gaped at them as they set up around the room.

"All right," Angel said. "Let's hear what you've got." When none of us moved, she snapped her fingers a few times. "I only have a few minutes, so hurry it up."

Unbelievable. She didn't show all week, and now she acted like we were wasting *her* time? Still, we each scrambled up and got in place while she grabbed a stool and sat in front.

"Any day now," she said.

Jared scowled, but he adjusted his mic and we started the song. We were all off this time, the pressure of the camera crew and of Angel's gaze making us each mess up. When she turned to me, I lost place of where I was in the song, and I had to make my mind blank for a second to find where we were so I could jump back in.

"Stop, stop," Angel said, waving a hand at us. "You on guitar, what happened there?"

"I—I just got distracted, sorry."

"Whatever, just get it together. And you," she said to Jared. "You need to step it up." She flicked a hand at the camera crew. "Okay, let's film this one and get this over with."

Jared gripped the mic so hard I was surprised it didn't break, but he said nothing and we started again. Angel let us finish this time and then plastered on her fake cheer now that the cameras were rolling.

"That was great!" she said with a little clap. "I love the way you've twisted the song and made it darker. I'm so happy you chose me for your mentor!"

Kyle snorted and then covered his mouth with his hand like he couldn't believe that had escaped. Angel's eyes narrowed at him, but then her phone rang—playing her band's most popular song, of course. She held up a finger to us as she raised the phone to her ear.

"You've got to be kidding me," Jared muttered.

My thoughts exactly. Since there was nothing to do but wait for Angel, I picked up my coffee and took a sip, but it had gone cold now. Yuck. I moved across the room to dump the plastic cup in the trash.

"No, you tell him that doesn't work for me. All or nothing!" Angel yelled at someone on her phone, pacing across the room like an angry jungle cat. She waved her free hand as she spoke and backed right into me, knocking into my arm. Coffee splattered all over both of us, and time seemed to slow as Angel looked down at herself and then up at me.

"You stupid bitch!" She wiped coffee off her leather jacket. "Look what you've done!"

"I'm so sorry!" I looked around for some napkins or something, my face burning. All of this was being filmed by the camera guys, who were probably thrilled to have captured some drama. I could only pray some kindhearted producer cut this moment so the entire country wouldn't laugh at me. Kyle ran over and handed me some napkins, but Angel waved him off when he offered her some.

"I don't have time for this shit," she snapped and turned to the door.

"No, you don't seem to have time to be a mentor at all," Jared said.

She spun to face him. "What did you say to me?"

"You heard me." He moved to stand in front of me, like he was going to protect me from her wrath. "And you need to apologize to Maddie."

Angel pointed a finger at Jared. "You ungrateful little shit, you're lucky to even be on this show!"

Seeing her shout at Jared upset me even more than her calling me a bitch. "We should have picked one of the other mentors."

"No kidding," Hector said. At some point, he'd moved to stand beside us, fists clenched at his sides.

Angel looked like she might strangle one or all of us. I was surprised the show didn't intervene, but they probably loved this stuff. "You're done," she yelled. "Tomorrow you're all gone!"

She stormed out, followed by her entourage, who either gave us looks of sympathy or ignored us completely. The door closed, and we were alone again.

"This is all my fault," I said, my shoulders slumping. "She's going to send us home because of me."

Jared ran a shaky hand through his hair. "No, if anything that was my fault. Shit, what have I done?"

"I can't believe you said that to Angel," Kyle said. "Even if it was true."

He sighed. "I know, it was stupid. I just can't stand bullies, and when she yelled at Maddie, I lost it."

There he went, being my big brother again, but this time I didn't mind as much. I placed my hand on his arm. "Thanks."

"What do we do now?" Hector asked. "We're screwed."

There was only one thing we *could* do. We had to nail this song and hope for a miracle.

CHAPTER TEN

We arrived at the Nokia Theater early on Sunday for a quick soundcheck, followed by an hour of hair and makeup. We got to pick our own outfits for this show, and of course we all wore black. I had on a low-cut top with leather pants, of all things, and after about ten minutes, my crotch was sweating and I was cursing Julie in my head. But I had to admit, I did look pretty hot—and we needed every advantage we could get tonight.

We filmed a clip about what it was like being mentored by Angel, and we'd forced smiles and lied through gritted teeth about how great it was. We'd decided being honest wouldn't help us if the show was trying to cover up what she was really like. Now that our battle with The Static Klingons approached, I found it hard not to bite my dark red nails and tear out my extra-volumized hair. We already knew Angel was going to pick The Static Klingons no matter what happened today, and our impending doom hung over us through every step of our prep work.

Our gear had been transported to the theater and carted away, and it made me realize how much we left it in the hands of others. I hated giving up my guitar to strangers and trusting they wouldn't mess it up or misplace it, but bands on tour did it all the time and *The Sound* had this down to an exact science after so many years.

We were shuffled into a waiting area for Team Angel's bands, where we could watch what happened through giant TV screens. The battle rounds weren't live and didn't use the rotating stage; instead, the two competing bands were both set up on opposite sides of the main stage. As the first competitors went on, I found myself munching non-stop on the chips and cookies they'd put out for us while trying not to watch Jared flirt with the mohawk girl from the punk band. The only way to distract myself was to eat my anxiety away, until Sean appeared next to me at the food table.

"You're getting crumbs all over your shirt," he said, trying hard not to stare at my cleavage and failing.

"Ugh, thanks." I brushed off my chest with a sigh. "I thought eating would help, but now I just feel sick."

"Me too. This whole week has been overwhelming. Very different from life on a farm, trust me."

"I bet."

For a few minutes we watched the screen, where two country bands from Team Lissa took turns performing "Need You Now" by Lady Antebellum. The first band was good, but they were missing a certain spark, while the second one, Fairy Lights, was led by a pretty blonde teenager with an amazing voice. When both bands finished and Lissa chose Fairy Lights, it wasn't a surprise at all.

Sean cleared his throat, reminding me he was still there. "So I saw your audition. Your band is really good."

"Thanks, but you don't need to be worried. The song is a much better pick for you." I left out the part about how Angel wanted to kill us, too.

"Maybe, but I'm curious to see what you'll do with it."

Was he trying to get info out of me or just being nice? Hard to tell. Maybe I'd try the same tactic on him. "What do you think of Angel?"

"You mean when she actually shows up?" He laughed but then looked around like he was worried someone had heard him. I didn't think they were filming us now, but you never knew. "She's...okay."

It sounded like The Static Klingons hadn't gotten much more mentoring than we had. Of course, they probably hadn't dropped coffee all over Angel and turned her into a screaming banshee either, but what could you do?

Jared laughed at something Mohawk Girl said, and jealousy sliced through me like a sword to my gut. I shifted my gaze back to the screen as two other bands went on stage, but that only reminded me that we were going up there soon. The walls in the stuffy room began to close in around me, and the urge to bolt grew strong. I desperately needed some air right away.

"I have to go," I said to Sean. "Good luck today."

"Thanks. You too."

I stepped through a door to an outside area, where a few people were smoking, and found an empty spot by the chain-link fence separating the space from the parking lot. I kicked some trash away, sank to the ground, and closed my eyes. My leather pants would probably get all scuffed up, but at this point, I didn't care.

I'd thought I could handle all of this, but the paralyzing fear had crept back in and this time it was mixed with dread. Did it even matter if we performed today? We already knew Angel would never let us stay on her team, even if we blew The Static Klingons away. And odds are I was going to mess up and embarrass the band during our show. I couldn't even remember how the guitar went in "Somebody Told Me." What had been simple in practice now seemed impossible. I'd given up my internship for this show, and now we'd be going home in the second week. It didn't seem fair.

"Hey." Jared's voice made me snap my eyes open. "Are you not okay again?"

His reference to the song he'd sung for me before our audition made me smile—barely—but I wished it had been Kyle or even Hector who had found me. Jared looked especially handsome today, with his hair spiked up and the barest hint of eyeliner making his blue eyes pop even more. Being alone with him was a delicious agony.

"I just needed some air," I said.

"Sorry. Should I go?"

"No," I said, a little too quickly, and then cursed myself for it. It would be better if he left, but I also wanted him to stay. I was a hot mess.

He sat next to me on the ground, his long legs stretching in front of us. "I always get stressed before shows, too."

"You do?" I found that hard to believe. Jared was always so confident on stage, so sure of himself. "You make it look easy."

"That's all an act, but it does get easier every time. You'll be a pro soon, too."

"Assuming we don't get kicked off this week, you mean."

He leaned his head back against the fence and stared up at the clear sky. "Trust me, I'm still beating myself up for that."

"It wasn't your fault."

Jared was silent for a minute, picking at a rough spot on his black jeans. "So you and that Sean guy, huh?"

"What? No. I mean, he seems nice and all, but that's it." I

nudged Jared with my shoulder. "You jealous?"

He flashed me a smile that made my toes curl. "Maybe."

"Don't be." The words slipped out, and I wanted to cover my mouth the instant I said them. I'd meant it as a joke, but it had come out a lot more serious. But he didn't respond or brush it off with another joke. His eyes searched mine, like he was looking for answers in them.

I dropped my gaze. "We should head back in."

"Yeah, Kyle's probably tearing the place apart looking for us."

He jumped to his feet and reached down to help me up. I slid my hand into his, but as I stood, I stumbled into him a little, still unsteady on my new heels. I braced myself on his chest, our hands still entwined, almost like we were dancing and just as close. My eyes caught on the patch of skin just above the buttons on his shirt, and I itched to undo them and see what was underneath. His free hand rested on the curve of my hip, and my gaze traveled up to his mouth, to lips that begged me to kiss them.

"There you are," Kyle called from the door to the theater. "I've been looking for you two everywhere."

I jumped back, hoping Kyle hadn't seen how close we'd been a second ago, and Jared shoved his hands in his pockets. I was equally grateful to Kyle for saving me and annoyed with him for ruining my moment alone with Jared.

"Sorry," I said. "Jared was just giving me a pep talk before the show."

Kyle looked back and forth between us, like he didn't believe that was all there was to it. I'd promised him I wouldn't get involved with his brother, but I wasn't doing a very good job of staying away from Jared. No matter how much I tried to fight it, I was attracted to him. Unfortunately, so was every other girl who laid eyes on him. Being in close proximity to him all week had definitely not helped me get over it either—if anything, it had only made it worse because now I knew Jared a little better. He'd stopped being an impossible fantasy in my head and become a real person I actually liked to talk to, and that was even more dangerous. If I wasn't careful, I'd get my heart broken or get kicked out of the band. Or both.

Kyle informed us were scheduled to go on in fifteen minutes. Commence panic mode. I ran to the bathroom to check my outfit and makeup, and then the band was directed to the edge of the stage to wait for our cue. The Static Klingons were taken to the other side, and Sean waved at me as he walked past. Jared raised an eyebrow at me, but I ignored him. I didn't have time for any more guy drama, not with so much riding on this next performance.

Ray Carter walked onto the stage, this time in a dark red suit, and it was time. "Now we have a battle between two bands on Angel's team! First up, from Nebraska, The Static Klingons!" The band walked out from their side of the stage while the audience cheered. "Versus…Villain Complex, from right here in Los Angeles!"

We rushed out, smiling at the crowd of 7,500 before us—yes, last night I'd looked up how many people the Nokia Theatre held. It was hard to see anything with the bright lights blinding me, so I focused on getting to my spot without tripping. As I threw on my guitar strap, I caught Angel eyeing us from her chair with a smirk, no doubt plotting our demise.

Once both bands were in place, Ray continued. "They're both performing 'Somebody Told Me' by The Killers, and now we'll flip a coin to see who goes first." He flicked it dramatically. "And the first one up is…The Static Klingons! Here we go!"

He hustled off the stage while the lights over us went out, leaving our band in darkness while The Static Klingons were illuminated. Sean gave the audience a boy-next-door smile before starting the opening guitar riff. As the band rocked out, we stood on the other side of the stage and watched, knowing we would be next, performing the same song for a mentor who hated us. And the worst part was…The Static Klingons were good. They'd barely tweaked the song at all, but it worked for them. Basically, we were screwed before we'd even started playing.

The song ended, and everyone cheered. I clapped along too because it seemed like the polite thing to do, and the other guys joined in with me. Sean gave a little bow, and from the center of the stage, Ray said, "And now, Villain Complex!"

The lights flashed over to us, and my heart pounded as I looked out into the theater, at all the faces staring at us. They'd already heard this song once, and it couldn't possibly be as exciting to hear it a second time. Going first definitely would have been better.

Jared grabbed the mic, pulling it close as he surveyed the crowd, and the theater went quiet. "Somebody Told Me" had a killer opening with great build-up, and we nailed it. Our version was darker and edgier, and when Jared sang, he twisted the lyrics into something beautiful and tortured, full of longing and regret.

My focus narrowed down to the guitar in my hands, and the rest of the world faded away until it was just me and the music. We got to the bridge and Jared held the last note, turning it into an anguished cry that rang across the room. We let it hang over the crowd for a heavy pause and then dove back into the chorus, with me singing backup behind him. I loved this song and the way we'd made it our own, and once again I felt like I belonged here, on stage, with these three guys. Playing with them gave me an energy I'd never experienced anywhere else.

We ended strong, and the sound of the audience's cheers washed over us, like a blissfully cold wave on a hot day, but I couldn't tell if they screamed more for us than they had for The Static Klingons. The mentors clapped, too, but it was hard to know what they really thought. None of them had used any of their rescues yet, but that didn't mean they'd use them on us either. Even though, in my opinion, we'd totally owned this song.

Ray Carter moved to the center of the stage again. "That was great! I love that song, and tonight we had two amazing performances of it. Dan, what did you think?"

"I thought both bands did a really amazing job. The Static Klingons got the crowd going, but Villain Complex has such a killer sound and they did something really unique with the song. I'm glad I don't have to pick one as the winner."

"Thanks, Dan," Ray said. "Lissa, what about you?"

"Like Dan said, both performances were strong. I do think the song was a little better for The Static Klingons and their sound, but Villain Complex held their own, too. I'd probably go with The Static Klingons myself, but definitely a tough decision."

Damn, guess we weren't getting a rescue from Lissa tonight. Still, we only needed one.

"Lance?" Ray asked.

"I agree. They're both talented bands. I wouldn't want to let either of them go."

As usual, Lance kept it short. Ray turned the mic over to Angel. "Well, these are your bands. It's your decision, Angel."

"I know," she said with a dramatic sigh. "I shouldn't have paired these two together. They're both so good!" She was really playing it up tonight, like we didn't already know who she would pick. I wished she'd just get it over with already.

"It's time to make your choice, Angel," Ray said. "Which band stays on your team?"

"I don't know." She tossed her bleached hair, her brow

furrowed like the decision was really difficult. "This is just *so* hard."

Here it came. Our final moment on the show. I took Jared's hand for support, then realized everyone would see that on TV and quickly reached for Kyle's hand, too. Jared grabbed Hector, and the four of us all stood linked together on stage, united against our mentor.

Angel's eyes narrowed at the sight of us together, and then she plastered on one of her big fakey smiles. "I choose The Static Klingons!"

I squeezed my hands into a death grip around the guys' as the audience cheered. It was over. Our fifteen minutes of fame were up, and now the entire country would see us get kicked off on week two of the show. If only I hadn't spilled coffee all over Angel, if only Jared had kept his mouth shut, if only we had picked a different mentor at audition, if only we'd practiced more…. I wanted to rewind the last week and do everything all over again.

Ray went over to The Static Klingons, who were all jumping up and down and smacking each other on the back. The mic was thrust into Sean's face, and he grinned at the audience. "Thank you, Angel!"

They left the stage, and Ray made his way back over to us. "Any last words for our mentors and the audience?"

He shoved the mic in my face, but when I opened my mouth, nothing came out. I was frozen, blinking back tears, wishing this wasn't the end. What was I going to do now? I'd given up everything to be on this show, and now we were going home.

Jared leaned in, saving me. "We're really happy for The Static Klingons. They're great guys, and they deserve to be here."

A loud buzzing rang out, and something around us flashed red and blue. The audience erupted into frenzied cheers. What was happening?

"A rescue from Dan!" Ray yelled into the mic.

Dan wanted us on his team! We weren't done yet! I started laughing and wiped at my eyes. Kyle shouted, "Yes!" while Hector grinned and thumped Jared on the shoulder. Jared just looked shocked and squeezed my hand harder. We were still holding on to each other, even though the other guys had let go.

"I think this band has a lot of potential," Dan said. "I wanted them from the beginning, and now that Angel was dumb enough to let them go, I have my shot."

"Hey!" Angel said, glaring at him.

"What? You made the wrong choice." He shrugged, and I already loved our new mentor. "Anyway, they're really talented, and I'm excited to have them on my team."

"Thank you so much!" Jared said into the mic.

"And that's Villain Complex, the newest member of Team Dan!" Ray said, and our time on stage was over.

We ran backstage and had another group hug with lots of laughter, the relief making us all giddy. We had no idea if things would be better or worse on Team Dan, but at least we were still on the show for another week.

CHAPTER ELEVEN

Monday morning we took a shuttle to our new recording studio, which was a bit too far to conveniently walk to. This studio was a big, boxy concrete building, with tiny slits for windows and no other distinguishing features. They sure didn't like to advertise these places. Inside, the lobby was sparse except for modern white furniture and a display of all the awards Dan's band Loaded River had won—Grammys, MTV Awards, and many others I didn't recognize. Along the wall were photos of the band, plus shots of Dan and his husband, who was the drummer in another grunge band.

There were three other bands already there: a folk band with a bazillion people in it, a Christian heavy metal band, and a reggae band. They all gave us the side-eye when we entered. I got it—we were the new kids, the outsiders, taking the spot of someone else on their team. Even though the show liked to pretend there was camaraderie between team members, the truth was, we were competing against each other. With each episode, one band went home from every team, so in a way these people were more a threat to us than anyone else on the show. Until the final episode anyway.

"Tough crowd," Jared muttered while we sat on the last remaining couch.

A camera crew was already set up around the room, and Steve, that producer from our recording session with the giant watch and expensive suits, supervised everything from the side. It still creeped me out that everything we said or did here could be aired on the show.

Dan arrived and handed out our schedules himself. "Everyone welcome our newest team members, Villain Complex." The other bands grunted or let out a weak hello. One older woman with dreadlocks from the reggae band gave us a warm smile, but she was the only one. "Make sure you check your schedule for the week," Dan continued. "You'll notice you have a lot more interviews and all that crap, so don't miss those or the producers will be on my ass. The live shows start next Monday, and each week has a theme. This first one is 'Sick of It All,' whatever that means, so start thinking about your song choice."

"He lets us pick the song?" I whispered to the guys. I thought the mentors always chose.

"Remember for the live shows, it's all about appealing to the audience at home," Dan said. "If you have any problems, let me know. I'm going to meet with Villain Complex now, and I'll see the rest of you in rehearsal tomorrow."

The other bands took off, and we stared at our schedules while Dan talked to Steve for a minute. I could already tell that being on Dan's team would be a very different experience from Angel's. Dan was friendly but direct and acted like a real person instead of a diva rock star. He also smelled like pot and had long hair that looked like it hadn't been washed in a month, but hey, no one was perfect.

"He seems a lot more involved than Angel," Kyle said.

"Let's hope so," Jared said. "Either way, the mentors don't have a say anymore in who stays. From now on, viewers vote for whoever they like the most."

"So we just need to appeal to all of America somehow," I said with a sigh. "Piece of cake."

"All right, let's head into the studio," Dan said, waving us over. We followed him into a soundproofed room where our equipment was already waiting for us, like magic. "This will be your room for the rest of the time you're on the show, so go ahead and get settled in."

"Thanks for rescuing us," Jared said. "We really appreciate

being given a second chance."

"Hey, I wanted you on my team from the start." Dan grabbed a stool to sit on. "Besides, I heard you got in a fight with Angel, and I'm a fan of anyone with the balls to stand up to her."

"Maddie threw coffee on her, too," Kyle said.

I scowled at him. "I didn't throw it. She bumped into me."

"Yeah?" Dan asked. "I need to hear this story."

Kyle told him all about it while we got set up, and Dan laughed along with us. "Damn, I knew she was neglecting her team, but I had no idea how bad it had gotten." He shook his head. "Well, you're on Team Dan now, so forget all that. Today we'll pick your song for the next episode, but mostly I want to talk about who you want to be as a band and how you can be better at that, both on stage and off."

For the next few minutes, we all brainstormed a song for that week's theme of "Sick of It All." Ultimately, we decided on "Uprising" by Muse, since it would give viewers a good idea of our sound and the kind of band we wanted to be. Even better, I already knew how to play it.

"That song has already been approved by the producers, so you're all set," Dan said, as he put on reading glasses and checked some papers in front of him. "I'll have the sheet music sent over tonight, but for now I'll give you some tips I wrote down after watching your other performances again. First, Jared, your voice is incredible, but your bass playing could be better. Did you start out on guitar, by any chance?"

"Yeah. I know I need to work on it."

"It's obvious to anyone who primarily plays bass, but you're not terrible either. Just remember that your job is to bridge the drums and the guitar. You need to provide the groove and the pulse for the entire song. Bass isn't as showy as the guitar, but it's just as important."

Jared exchanged a look with his brother like, "What is happening?" Dan was the bassist in Loaded River, so it didn't surprise me he had tips for Jared. Still, I was impressed Dan knew our names already and that he'd done his homework on us. Five minutes in and he was already a better mentor than Angel. We might actually learn something from him.

"Maddie, you're a strong guitarist," Dan continued. "In fact, from a technical standpoint, you might be the best guitarist on the show. But let me guess—you're a classically trained musician?"

I nodded, still reeling over him saying I might be the best guitarist here. That was so far from the truth I couldn't even consider it.

"I figured. You're too stiff when you play, like you're focusing too much on hitting the right notes and not on the emotion the music is conveying. You have the skills and you know the songs, but you don't *feel* them. You need to work on your stage presence and bring a little passion to your performance. I'll help you with that."

"Thanks." Everything he said about my stage presence was

true, and I was eager to improve. I'd take any advice he had.

He gave the other guys some tips, too, and then said, "All of you need to remember, sometimes less is more. You need to learn to listen to the rest of the band and react to them, instead of just focusing on your own playing. This is what makes the strongest bands: cohesion. We'll work on that this week. But cohesion and raw talent aren't enough to win this show, especially since you're not exactly what the producers or record label are looking for."

"What do you mean?" Jared asked.

"Do you remember Addicted to Chaos? The last rock band that won *The Sound*, two seasons ago."

"They broke up after they won, right?" I asked. "When the singer and drummer got a divorce or something?"

"I remember that," Kyle said. "Didn't one of them get arrested, too?"

Dan nodded. "It was a total nightmare for the show. The divorce ripped the band apart, and they stopped showing up for the tour and bailed on recording their album. When the show sued them for breach of contract, they really went off the deep end, trashing concert halls and hotel rooms, getting in fights in bars…. The bassist even got hit with sexual assault charges. The show had a pretty bad rep for a while because of them, with the network threatening to cancel *The Sound* entirely. Ever since, the producers have wanted a nice, no-risk, low-drama winner. That means, no edgy rock bands and no bands that have any sort of romance angle at all."

"There is no romance angle," I said quickly. "We're just friends."

Jared shot me a sharp look, but said nothing.

"That's good," Dan said. "I know the show has been trying to feel out what kind of relationship you two have. They don't want another repeat of Addicted to Chaos, so don't do anything to fuel those rumors about the two of you being together."

I nodded. Being part of the band and winning the show were the only things that mattered, and I couldn't let my attraction to Jared mess that up. I'd just have to stay away from him as much as possible over the next few weeks.

"Fine," Jared said, though he didn't sound happy about it. "But do we even have a shot at winning if they don't want another rock band?"

"Yes, because it's up to the voters who wins. No matter what the producers want, your band is one of the most popular ones this year. I think you can make it all the way to the end, but you'll need to keep winning the viewers over and not just when you're performing. I'll be coaching you on what to say in interviews, what to wear for the live shows, and how to act when you're in public. You have an image to keep up now. You're not just a band anymore—you're a *brand*, too. "

I wasn't sure how to process all of this. We could work on cohesion and I could try to avoid Jared, but I'd never thought about our "brand" before, other than how I dressed to fit in with the other guys. Now it sounded like everything we did from this point on would be scrutinized, especially if we didn't fit with what the producers wanted.

Dan checked the papers in front of him again. "Jared, from the rumors I've heard and things I've read online, you seem to be something of a playboy, right?"

Jared coughed and stared at the floor. "I guess so."

"Good. Play up that angle for the show. Stay single, flirt with women, make everyone at home think they could have a shot with you. That will prove you're not with Maddie and might get you more votes. Ladies love a bad boy."

Hector smirked. "Shouldn't be too hard for him."

Jared nodded, but his hands were clenched at his side. Dan's advice made me want to punch something, but I didn't know why it would bother Jared since it was the same thing he was already doing now.

"The rest of us don't have to do that, right?" Kyle asked. "Because I have a girlfriend."

"Nah, you're fine," Dan said. "In fact, you should mention that. You have the edgiest look in the band and having a steady girlfriend will make you seem more relatable. And Hector has the diversity angle covered, which is good for attracting a wider audience."

Hector scowled, and I didn't blame him. There was more to Hector than just being Latino.

"Hector's an artist," Jared added. "He has a graphic novel that just came out."

Dan wrote something down. "Okay, we'll see what we can do with that." He turned to study me again. "And to attract the male vote we'll have to make sure Maddie looks hot every week."

"Should I wear my contacts instead of my glasses?" I asked with a sigh.

"No, keep them. The glasses make you seem more relatable, more real, especially to other girls."

I hated this. For the live shows, it wasn't just about being musicians anymore; now we had to look and act certain ways to get votes. I just wanted to play my guitar, not worry about manipulating the viewers to like us, but I had no choice but to go with it for a few weeks. It was a game, and if that's what it took to be on the show until the end, so be it. And unfortunately, my contributions seemed to be "looking hot" and "not getting involved with Jared."

The next few days went by in a blur of practice, and Dan actually showed up for every single one of them for at least an hour while the camera crews filmed from the sidelines. We'd been working on everything he'd told us, and I could already tell we were improving a lot. One day Dan even had us switch instruments to try and give us a better understanding of each other. Turns out, I was terrible at drums (though they were fun), not too awful at bass (maybe I'd learn it next, once this was all over), and playing keyboard was as easy as guitar for me, even if I wasn't familiar with Kyle's setup. Hector was a disaster with anything other than the drums, while Kyle could scrape by on every instrument, even if he obviously never practiced them. Jared was good at everything, of course. It shouldn't surprise me, since he wrote most of the band's music, but it'd be nice if he were bad at something for once.

Our rehearsals were interspersed with photo shoots and interviews about what it was like to work with Dan now that we were on his team, along with questions like why we chose this song and why we wanted to win *The Sound*. Dan had coached us each on what to say, and we repeated his sound bites until they lost all meaning. The show especially loved to ask me and Jared about our relationship status. We both chimed in that we were single and, yes, we would definitely date a fan. Those lines sounded fake when I said them, but Jared was much better at pulling them off than I was. I avoided him entirely outside of rehearsal, which was easy since I kept to my room a lot...until Kyle insisted I come to their room to work on my stage presence.

Jared opened their door, wearing nothing but a towel around his waist. His wet hair hung in his face, and water dripped down his long, toned chest. I'd always wondered if Jared's tattoos continued under his shirt, and the answer was no, except for the word "VILLAIN" inked across his chest, just below his collarbone.

"Hey," he said. "I didn't know you were coming."

"Um...Kyle told me to stop by." Damn, it was really hard not to stare at him. My eyes followed the dark hair that trailed down his stomach and under the towel. *Please let that towel fall*, I thought. I'd never wished for something so hard in my life.

"Ugh, go put some clothes on," Kyle said from behind him.

Jared stood back to let me in, and I was careful not to get too close to his steaming, naked body as I walked past. He disappeared into the bathroom and shut the door, and I remembered how to breathe again.

Kyle rolled his eyes. "Sorry. I thought he was going to the gym with Hector."

There wasn't much room to practice, so we moved the desk and made space in front of the sliding doors to the balcony. Once that was done, I pulled out my acoustic guitar and checked the tuning. It wasn't as exciting as my electric guitar, but it would have to do since my Fender was still in Dan's studio.

Jared emerged from the bathroom wearing black jeans and a T-shirt with Darth Vader that read, "Choking Hazard." If there was anything that could make him sexier to me, it was a geeky shirt. Dammit.

He sat on the bed beside Kyle, and they waited for me to start. I put my hands in position on my guitar, but still I hesitated. I'd played in front of the brothers dozens of times now, but for some reason, I was more nervous than ever today. Maybe because they were both watching me intently instead of playing alongside me. It was like my first night in their garage all over again. Except now I was in their bedroom, which made it even worse.

Jared must have sensed my reluctance because he grabbed his own guitar and plugged it into a small travel amp. I hadn't realized he'd brought his Fender to the hotel, the same one I'd played at his party all those nights ago. He started the opening to "Uprising," and with his music to concentrate on, I joined him on my own guitar. The mix of acoustic and electric sounded odd, but it didn't matter for this exercise.

Kyle examined me for a minute and then jumped up. "Your body is too stiff." He grabbed my arms and shook them a little. "You need to loosen up."

I dropped my guitar pick and then grabbed it off the floor. "I'm not that stiff."

"You look like you've got a piece of wood jammed up your ass," Kyle said.

"You *are* pretty stiff," Jared said. "Try moving your hips when you play. Like this."

He stood behind me and put his hands on my waist, and I sucked in a breath as he showed me what he meant. Heat rushed through my body as I imagined him sliding those hands lower, across my bare skin. He stepped back, and I remembered Kyle was still there, too, which cooled me off a little.

Jared took off his guitar and passed it to me. "Here, use mine. Playing with an acoustic guitar isn't the same."

I flushed as I put it on, remembering the previous time I'd used it. I started up again, trying to keep my arms loose and swinging my hips along with the beat, but I was so focused on moving that I missed notes and got all messed up and had to stop playing. Or maybe I was still flustered from Jared's hands on me.

Kyle squinted. "Well, that was terrible. You looked like you were in pain or something. This time try not to look like you've been set on fire and are trying to put it out."

I sighed and played the opening again, moving less and forcing myself to smile, but Kyle shook his head. "Nope. You look like a creepy doll with that grin."

"Ugh!" I flopped onto one of the beds, dropping the guitar next to me. "This is hopeless. I'm never going to be any good at this."

"We have to find something that works for you and doesn't make you look psychotic or like you're dying. Maybe—" Kyle stopped and fished his phone out of his pocket. "Shit, Alexis is here early. I've got to run. Sorry. We'll continue this tomorrow, okay?"

After his brother left, Jared sat on the edge of the bed near me. "Kyle's only trying to help you."

"I know. I just suck. I'm going to ruin everything for us." I threw my arm over my face. This bed was comfortable. Maybe I could just lie here forever, and then I'd never have to perform again. A perfect solution to this problem.

"You don't suck." He jumped up and grabbed his guitar again. "C'mon, maybe I can help. Kyle spends all his time on stage behind a keyboard anyway."

I sat up to watch him. I was willing to try anything at this point, and let's be honest, I always enjoyed seeing Jared perform.

"For me, the trick is to feel the music and move along with it. Tap your foot, nod your head, whatever feels natural." He started the opening again and leaned back, stretching his long body as he played. I stared at the spot where his stubble trailed off on his neck, yearning to press my mouth there. I imagined the way it would feel to slide my fingers under his shirt and across his toned stomach. I wanted to see that tattoo on his chest again.

He stopped and frowned at me. "What?"

What was *wrong* with me? I dropped my gaze and grabbed my own guitar. "Nothing."

This time I tried to feel the music as I played, but it didn't come as easily for me as it did for him. The truth was, I was still too distracted from picturing all the things I wanted to do to him. It was like avoiding Jared had only made my desire for him increase, and now that we were alone—and now that I knew what he looked like without any clothes on—I found it even harder to resist him.

"That was better," he said. "But I can tell you're still holding back."

No kidding. If I was in this room with Jared for one more second, I might not be able to stop from touching him. Where was Hector? Shouldn't he be back from the gym by now?

"This isn't working," I said. "Maybe we can try again tomorrow." Tomorrow, when the other guys were here, too, and I could focus on something other than being alone in a hotel room with the hottest guy I'd ever met.

"Hang on, I have another idea."

I sighed. "I don't know…"

"Let's try playing something together, something just for fun."

"Like what?"

"Do you know this one?" he asked and then started up "Blitzkrieg Bop" by The Ramones. It was one of those songs most rock guitarists learned since it was simple but a lot of fun to play. I reluctantly joined in when the chords repeated again. When he got to the chorus, I sang along too, and he grinned at me.

As the song went on, I loosened up and let myself get into the music with him, tapping my foot to the beat. We jammed on our guitars and grew louder and more ridiculous, not caring if the people in the rooms next to us complained. It was the kind of song you could easily be silly and over the top with, and by the end, we were bouncing around and belting out the words like we were drunk.

When it ended, I fell back on the bed and laughed, my pulse

racing. Playing with Jared like this, banging on our guitars and singing at the top of our lungs without caring what we sounded like, it was different from playing alone or with the band or even in front of Julie and Carla. With one song, Jared had reminded me why I loved playing guitar in the first place.

He crashed on the bed next to me, and we stared at the ceiling as we caught our breath. After a minute, he propped himself up on one arm to look at me. "I'm impressed you could sing all the words to that one. Who knew piano player Maddie had this hidden punk rocker inside her?"

"No one. Before I joined the band, guitar was a secret, a guilty pleasure. Something I only did when I was alone in my room."

He raised an eyebrow. "And yet you picked up my guitar at a party and played one of my songs like you had written it yourself."

I covered my face with my hands and groaned. "I knew you'd bring that up eventually."

"Hey, I'm flattered. Besides, it worked out in the end." He trailed a finger across my arm, his touch soft, making me shiver. "I saw the real you that night, and just now I saw her again. That's the trick. When you're on stage, play like you do when you think no one's watching."

I dropped my hands to stare up at his face, so close to mine I could smell the shampoo he'd used. I wanted to kiss him so badly my body ached with it. It wasn't just how his hair was still wet, framing his blue eyes and dark lashes, or the way the tattoos on his arms stood out against his otherwise flawless skin or how his voice made me forget everything but him. It was the Jared I discovered every time we were alone together, the one who somehow found the real me and set her free.

His hand cupped my face and his head dipped lower, lightly brushing his lips across mine. Little warning lights flashed in my head. What was I doing, lying on a bed with Jared, about to kiss him? This couldn't happen. Not only because of what Dan had said about the producers and the show, but because I knew if I fell for Jared, I might never recover.

I pressed a hand against his chest. "I'm sorry. I have to go, um, to dinner. With my friends. Right now."

He stared at me while I jumped up and stuffed my guitar back into the case. "Maddie—"

"I'll see you tomorrow." I ran for the door before he could even get up.

Once outside the elevator, I pushed the button a hundred times until it arrived. Only when I stepped inside and the door shut did I allow myself to relax. That had been way too close. Kissing Jared could only lead to heartbreak, and it would ruin everything with the band and with the show. But how was I supposed to resist him for another three weeks?

CHAPTER TWELVE

The crowd screamed as the lights went up and the four mentors walked to their seats, waving at the audience. Ray Carter appeared on stage, his black hair shining, and he flashed a big smile.

"Welcome to *The Sound!* This is the first live show, and tonight's theme is 'Sick of It All.' Starting now, your votes will determine who stays and who goes, and ultimately, who wins *The Sound*. We have some amazing performances lined up, so let's get started! But first, let's talk to the mentors about their bands and what they're hoping to see from them."

I watched from the screens in the lounge and then turned away to get some coffee. After a full day of hair, makeup, wardrobe, and soundchecks, I was already exhausted—and we still had another hour before we went on stage.

Mohawk Girl was filling up on coffee, too, wearing a green plaid skirt with a studded corset and matching choker. "Hey," she said as I grabbed a cup.

"Hey." I wasn't sure what to say to her. We'd never really talked before. I didn't even know her name.

"You're a lucky girl."

"Huh?" Had I missed something? Maybe I was more out of it than I'd thought.

"You and Jared," she said, nodding to where he sat with Kyle. He looked over at us, as if he'd somehow heard his name, and winked.

"Oh. We're not together." I dumped a bunch of sugar and cream into my coffee and stirred it, hoping this conversation would end already. She was not helping with my plan of thinking about Jared as little as possible.

"Yeah?" She leaned against the table, with no intention of leaving. "I tried to get him up to my room the other night, but he wouldn't go for it. I figured it's 'cause he's with you."

"Nope. We're just friends." I was tired of repeating that phrase, but maybe if I said it over and over, I'd start to believe it, too.

She nudged my side with a bony elbow, which kind of hurt.

"Uh huh. He can't keep his eyes off you. If you're not tapping that now, you need to get on it before someone else does."

I was sure my face had turned bright red, despite the layers of makeup on it. "Um…thanks for the advice."

"No problem. Good luck tonight."

"You too."

She went back to her band and I sipped my coffee, going over her words. All the rumors I'd heard about Jared made it seem like he would sleep with any girl who offered, and Dan had told him to encourage this reputation. But to be honest, I'd never actually *seen* Jared do anything beyond flirting, and hearing he'd turned down this girl who had thrown herself at him was a huge relief. But even if Jared *was* interested in me, he and I had to stay apart as long as we were on the show. Besides, I doubted he wanted anything beyond a quick fling, like his former bassist had been.

Bands moved in and out of the lounge as they waited for their sets or recovered afterward, and I admired all of their costumes. Compared to some of them, our band's sleek, futuristic, black-and-red military uniforms looked almost tame. Of course, mine had a short skirt and a low-cut jacket with nothing underneath, while the guys got pants and a jacket that completely covered them. Dan said it was necessary for the "young male vote," but the blatant sexism still made me want to set my costume on fire, even if I did look pretty hot in it—especially with the tall black heels that made my legs look longer.

The Static Klingons took the stage and performed "Pumped Up Kicks" by Foster the People, which the audience seemed to enjoy. When they were done, Sean ran over to me with a giant smile. "Maddie!"

"Hey, Sean. Great performance!"

"Thanks!" He reached out a little, like he wanted to hug me, but then pulled back when I didn't respond. "I'm so sorry about the Angel thing. I just feel horrible about how it all went down."

"Don't worry about it—really." Not this again. I'd seen Sean a few times in the hotel lobby since our battle, and he always apologized for getting us kicked off Angel's team. Truthfully, I should be apologizing to him, since we now had a better mentor and he was still stuck with Angel.

"Are you doing something tonight after the show? Do you want to get something to eat or…?"

While Sean talked, Jared watched us with a scowl on his face. Probably worried I was giving away all our secrets again.

Hang on, was Sean asking me out on a date? I must have waited a little too long to answer because then he added, "You know, to talk strategy and stuff and, uh, just hang out… "

Now I was even more confused. Did he actually like me or was he trying to get info out of me? I couldn't tell, but it didn't really matter because I had no interest in going out with him. "Sorry, I can't tonight. I have a meeting with the band."

"No problem. Maybe later this week?" His drummer called his name, and he turned to wave at him. "I've got to run, but we'll talk later!"

He bounced off to join his band, saving me from further conversation. I'd need another excuse to avoid a date with him later, assuming we both lasted that long on the show. Who knew if either of our bands would still be around after tonight?

The Quiet Battles, the folk band on Team Dan, went before us with a song I didn't know, and there were so many of them they barely fit on the stage. Did they even have enough instruments for all of them to play? I saw a harmonica, a violin, and a banjo, and one guy even "played" a plastic bag, if you could call it that. I'm not sure crinkling it in front of a microphone counted as playing, but I was trying hard not to judge. They also had two complete drum kits. Who needed *two* drum kits? If The White Stripes could be the loudest band ever with only two members, there was just no need for that.

Next it was our turn. Our equipment was already set up on the back of the revolving stage, and we quickly got in place and waited while The Quiet Battles got comments from the mentors. The thrill of going on stage made every nerve in my body tingle. I wasn't scared this time; instead, I was anxious to get back out there and perform again. Playing on stage was my drug, and I was an addict now.

The stage began to revolve, and the crowd swelled in front of us. As red lights flashed behind us and smoke filled the air, the guys started playing. I waited, tapping my foot along with the beat, and then my fingers took off across my guitar with the eerie opening notes. Hector's steady rhythm centered us and Kyle clapped along to get the audience going while Jared's voice filled the theater. I nodded my head with the music and leaned into my mic to sing the backup chant at the end of each verse. The bass line Jared pulled off was almost hypnotic, and as his fingers moved up and down the fret board, I imagined those same fingers playing across my skin. I watched his lips caress the mic as he sang and pictured him doing the same to me. And as his voice rang out from the speakers, I wondered what it'd be like to hear him cry out my name instead.

Damn, I needed to get a grip. I stomped on my pedal to change the tone and forced myself to focus. Jared's advice about playing like no one was watching came back to me, and I tried to let myself fall into the song. Dan and the guys had told me to move more, so I started walking across the stage toward Jared, as if his words were pulling me to him. But when I neared him, I tripped on a cord in my stupid tall heels. I tried to catch myself to prevent a complete face-plant but ended up stumbling off the edge of the stage, on top of a very large security guard.

The audience gasped, and Jared's voice choked on the lyrics. For a second, I just sat there, stunned and horrified by what had happened. I couldn't tell if I was injured or not, my body still in the post-fall adrenaline shock. I got to my feet quickly, the audience pressing around me, on my level now with only the security guards keeping them away. Sweat dripped down my back, under my clothes. I had to escape, from the cameras, from the crowd, from this complete disaster of a performance. I glanced around, looking for an exit, but there was no way out.

Behind me, tiny explosions went off on the side of the stage, and the band kept going. No, I couldn't run. I couldn't abandon the guys, who were still trying to keep it together without me. No matter how embarrassed I was, the show had to go on.

I waved to show I was okay and then hopped up to sit on the edge of the stage. Kyle had filled in for me, but now it was time for the guitar solo. All I could do was go for it and try not to think about how I'd just ruined everything. With my legs hanging into the crowd and the security guards holding people back, I played my heart out. The high notes squealed as my fingers flew, and I blocked the world out, closing my eyes and letting the song take over. Just me and my guitar and an intimate performance with 7,500 of my closest friends. And somehow, it worked.

After the solo ended with the last hard riffs, I jumped back on stage with a little help from the poor security guard I'd tackled, and the crowd went crazy. I returned to my mic and joined in with Jared on the last chorus, and we ended together in perfect harmony.

The audience's cheers shook the theater, and even the mentors looked shocked by our performance. Jared threw one arm around me, holding his other arm out to the audience like I'd just won a prize or something. He whispered in my ear, "Are you hurt?"

"No, I don't think so." I leaned against him while Kyle and Hector joined us, adrenaline still pumping through my veins. Soon we were all holding onto each other, feeling the audience's enthusiasm like tremors coursing under our feet.

Ray sprinted across the stage. "Wow, what an...unexpected performance! That was Villain Complex on Team Dan. Angel, they used to be on your team and you let them go last week. Are you regretting it now?"

"Sure." She shrugged and inspected her nails, like she was bored with it all. Whatever, Angel.

"Lance, what did you think?" Ray asked.

"Great song choice. What I want to know is, what happened with that fall?"

The host shoved the mic in my face, and I froze. This was all live and Jared was so much better at this stuff, but I decided to be honest.

"That was an accident, but I thought, whatever, I'm going to own it. Sometimes I fall down, but I get back up again and keep going. That's life, right?"

The crowd screamed again so I must have said the right thing, and Jared squeezed me tighter.

"Very wise words," Ray said. "Lissa, what did you think?"

"I thought it was brilliant how you turned an accident into a triumph. That's so important in this line of work because things do go wrong sometimes, and you just have to roll with it."

"Very true. Dan, they're the newest member of your team—how did they do?"

"All I can say is, I'm so glad I rescued them from Angel. What were you *thinking*?" He leaned over to smirk at our former mentor, who huffed and crossed her arms. When she didn't respond, he sat back and continued. "They've already improved so much in the week I've been working with them, and I can't wait to see what they do next week. I'm really proud."

My heart swelled at Dan's words, and it sounded like he actually meant them, too. He must think we weren't completely doomed if he was already talking about next week. I prayed my screw-up tonight hadn't cost us our spot on the show.

"Now it's up to you at home," Ray said, staring at the camera. "If you like Villain Complex, download their song and vote for them on the website or by texting or calling this number."

The stage turned so the next band could play, and roadies ran around us and broke down our gear. Kyle wrapped me in a big bear hug as soon as we were out of view. "Are you all right? Are you injured?"

"No, I'm not injured," I muttered into his shoulder, which was pressed against my face. I tried to pull away, but he had me in a death grip. "Really, I'm fine!"

"Are you sure?" Jared asked, when I finally broke apart from his brother. "Does it hurt anywhere?"

"I can't feel anything, but that might be the adrenaline. Tomorrow I might wake up with a broken leg or something, but at the moment, I feel great."

Hector thumped me on the back, knocking all the air out of me. "That was hardcore, Maddie. Not sure I could have done that."

"Um, thanks."

The show had a medic check me out before they let me do anything else. She said one of my ankles was twisted and told me to ice it and stay off my feet for a day or two. Someone found me some flip flops, and then we had another interview with Ray about how we felt about the performance. He said I was really brave, but I replied that I just didn't want to let the other guys down. When he asked them what they thought, Jared leaned into the mic and said, "I nearly had a heart attack when she fell off stage, so I'm just happy she's okay."

We had to return to the stage with all the other bands on Team Dan one more time to wave while Ray reminded everyone at home how to vote, and the other musicians all patted me on the back and asked if I was okay. I may have fallen, but this felt like a victory.

CHAPTER THIRTEEN

By the time we got back to the hotel, I didn't think I could keep my eyes open even a second longer. Plus my ankle had started to throb now that the buzz from the performance had worn off. Even breathing seemed tough. Maybe I was more beat up from the fall than I'd thought.

I wanted to crawl right into bed, but the guys said we should check the Internet and see what people were saying about us. I was too tired to argue and soon found myself in their room again, sitting beside Jared on the bed while he opened up his laptop.

"Don't forget to vote for us, too," Kyle said. "And remind everyone to vote by 10 AM tomorrow."

I checked my phone and saw that Carla and Julie had been sending me panicked texts for the last hour or so. I texted them back that I was okay and reminded them to vote for us. I'd call them both tomorrow and give them the full scoop when I wasn't so tired. That reminded me: I'd never called my mom like I'd promised Julie I would. I'd meant to do it, but things had been so busy these past few days and I'd completely forgotten. Yet another thing to add to my to-do list.

"Holy shit," Jared said, staring at his screen. "Our Twitter account shot up to thirty thousand followers tonight."

"Thirty thousand?" I asked, choking out the words. Last I'd heard, we were at ten thousand. Kyle and Hector crowded around us to see the screen, and Hector whistled.

"That's good, right?" Kyle asked. "That means we're going to get enough votes to stay this week?"

"Maybe," Jared said. "Some of the other bands have fifty thousand. We should post more photos on Instagram and Tumblr. That might bring in more fans."

"I can ask Alexis to take photos of us rehearsing one day," Kyle said.

"Good idea."

"Thirty thousand," I repeated, still in shock. "We have *thirty thousand* fans?"

"Probably more actually," Jared said. "There's a huge segment of older people who watch the show who aren't on Twitter. I'll make sure our Facebook page is updated, too, and the website…" He rubbed his face, looking tired, and for the first time, I appreciated how Jared ran the entire business side of the band by himself. I had no idea how he kept up with it all on top of the rehearsals and other things we had to do for the show. I could barely find time to eat, sleep, and shower.

"What are people saying about tonight?" Kyle asked.

"I don't want to know," I said, biting my nails. "Unless it's good. No, don't tell me. Oh, god, it's probably all over YouTube already."

"Some people seem to think what happened was cool," Jared said. "One girl tweeted, 'I love how she kept playing, she's so fierce!'"

"I don't feel very fierce, but that's nice of her to say. What else?" I leaned over again, trying to get a glimpse of his screen.

"Nothing." He quickly yanked the laptop away, but not before I saw "four-eyed cow" and "she only did that to get attention."

"Is that what people really think of me?" I tried to reach for the laptop, but he passed it to Hector on the other bed.

"Only stupid people who shouldn't be allowed on the Internet," Jared said. "Besides, we're trending on Twitter, so I think your fall off the stage might end up being a good thing."

"The world is full of haters," Hector said. "Don't let them get to you."

"I guess so." Those comments stung, but I was too tired to stress about them right now. I yawned and checked the time. "I should get to bed."

As soon as I stood up, my ankle went out from under me with a sharp pain. I yelped and slammed into the side of the bed, bracing against it for support.

Jared was at my side instantly. "Do you need help?"

Kyle jumped up, too. "Should I get some ice?"

Talk about embarrassing. I didn't need both brothers hovering over me like this. I stood up a little slower this time, balancing on one foot. "I'm okay. I just got up too fast. I'll be fine after I get some sleep."

Jared slid his arm into mine, and every nerve in my body woke up. "Come on, I'll take you back to your room. I need to walk off some of this energy before bed anyway."

"You don't need to do this," I said as we moved to the elevator together. "I can get back by myself."

"I'm not going anywhere until I make sure you get to your room safely. I can't have my guitarist injuring herself again." He winked and hit the elevator button while I leaned against him, taking comfort in his strength. His breath ruffled my hair as he quietly added, "Besides, I'm worried about you."

The elevator door opened, and we stumbled in. "Really, Jared, I'm fine. It's just a twisted ankle, not that big a deal—"

The door shut and his lips were on mine, cutting me off mid-sentence. His kiss was tentative and searching, a question he wanted me to answer, but I was so surprised I just stood there while my brain caught up to what was happening.

He pulled away and ran a hand through his dark hair. "Sorry. I've wanted to do that forever, and when I saw you fall..."

My mouth opened but no sound came out. I swallowed and tried again. "You've wanted to do that forever?"

"I know it's a bad idea. We have to stay single while we're on the show, and the guys would kill me if they found out, and you're into that Sean guy anyway..." His voice trailed off, and he looked away.

I'd never seen Jared be anything but cool and confident, and it sent a thrill through me, knowing I'd done that to him. The elevator didn't move, waiting for us to hit a button, but suddenly I didn't want to go back to my room anymore. I grabbed the collar of Jared's jacket and pulled him down to my mouth, kissing him hard, showing him that he was the one I wanted.

We broke apart long enough for me to whisper, "It *is* a bad idea, but I don't care."

"Good. Because I can't resist you any longer." And then our mouths met again.

We kissed like we were drowning and our only hope of living was each other. He devoured my mouth with his tongue and lips while I tangled my fingers into his thick hair, drawing him closer. Knowing we shouldn't be doing this only gave our passion a desperate edge, a recklessness that had us gasping and clawing at each other, like we had to cram everything into this one brief moment we were alone. His hands slid down to cup my butt and lift me to his height, my back slamming against the side of the elevator, my skirt riding up to my hips. While he pinned me to the wall and teased me with his mouth, I smoothed my hands across his rough jaw, down his neck, along his broad shoulders. After weeks of fighting my desire for Jared, I needed to touch every inch of him, with my fingers, with my lips, with my entire body.

The elevator started moving, though neither of us had pushed a button. It said, "Lobby," and reality came crashing back, like a bucket of water had been tossed on us. We broke apart to opposite corners, breathing heavily. I yanked my skirt down just as the door opened.

Lacey, the blonde country singer from Fairy Lights, stood there wearing the sexy school uniform she'd performed in when she'd sung "Mean" by Taylor Swift tonight. Her eyes honed in on Jared as she sauntered in and hit the button for her floor.

"Hey there," she said, her voice accented with a Southern twang.

"Hey." Jared's hair was messy, but otherwise you'd never be able to tell he'd just been kissing me.

She touched his arm with a pink fingernail after the door closed. "I heard you're the guy to see if a girl is lonely at night."

Her words spread like ice in my blood, cooling my passion instantly. Did Jared get this a lot? How many girls' rooms had he visited in the few weeks we'd been here?

"That's me," Jared said, but he sounded tired. "How old are you anyway?"

"Seventeen."

He took her hand off him. "Sorry, we only serve eighteen and up here."

"Don't worry. I won't tell anyone." She flicked her hair and looked at him from under her long, fake eyelashes. "It'll be our little secret."

"I'm sure your mother would love that. She has to be here while you're on the show, right?" He moved around her to stab the button for my floor, like he couldn't wait to get away. I accidentally let out a faint chuckle, and she glared at me. Oops.

"Whatever." She crossed her arms and turned her back to us, and it was a very long ride to her floor.

After she got out, Jared let out a long breath. "What she said…just ignore her. That's not me."

I met his eyes but didn't respond. Jared had a reputation he had to maintain for the show, but I couldn't tell how much of it was based on truth and how much was an act. I didn't know what to believe anymore. Was the real Jared the one I saw when we were alone or the one I saw flirting with other girls and getting texts from them wanting to hook up? And now that I'd stopped kissing him, all my reasons for staying away from him came back to me. There could be no *us*; there could only be me and Jared, two separate entities, as long as we were on the show.

We made it into my room, and he leaned against the

doorframe, not stepping inside but not leaving either. He dipped his hands into his pockets, fixing me with a smoldering gaze as he waited for me to make the next move. I could invite him in, but I knew where that would lead. Despite how much I wanted him, we couldn't let things go any further tonight.

"Do you need anything else?" he asked, with a quirk of his lips that hinted at a hidden offer behind his words.

"No, I think I'm okay. Thank you." But I couldn't stop myself from moving until our bodies were only an inch apart, his breath on my skin as I looked up at him. He drew me to him like a magnet, and there was only so much attraction I could resist.

He dipped his head, crossing the space between us. His mouth brushed my ear as he whispered, "Don't forget to ice your ankle."

God, he drove me crazy in the best way when he got like this, the way he was always looking out for me. "Yes, doctor."

His hand slipped into my hair, and he kissed me slow this time, tender, tilting my head back to explore my mouth without the frenzy of before. He teased one finger under the bottom hem of my shirt, burning a line across my skin, and I gasped. Our kiss grew deeper, and I pressed myself against him, gripping his jacket to draw him closer. I couldn't get enough of him, of the taste of his soft lips, of his masculine scent, of the way he felt under my hands.

"I need to go," he whispered between kisses. "Kyle is going to wonder why it's taking me so long."

I sighed. "I know."

He kissed me one last time, and I clutched his jacket and held him there, not wanting him to leave but unable to ask him to stay. I dreaded the reality of tomorrow, when we'd have to face what had happened and what it meant for the band. But finally, I let him go.

CHAPTER FOURTEEN

The next morning I was bruised and sore all over, my ankle was the size of a small country, and my mouth felt like it had been rubbed with sandpaper. All signs pointed to last night not being a dream, which meant today I had to deal with the aftermath of what I'd done.

Okay, technically Jared had kissed me first, but then he'd given me the chance to end it right there. I could have walked away and laughed it off later, but instead I'd crossed the line, passed the point of no return, and all those other clichés. There was no going back to the way things were before unless we both admitted it had been a mistake. Except…it hadn't felt like a mistake. It had felt like fate, like every moment since I'd met Jared had led me to this surprising, yet inevitable, conclusion.

I never wanted to get out of bed because then I'd have to face him again and figure out what to do about us. Luckily, the show's medic had told me to rest with my foot elevated until we had to be at the Nokia Theatre for the results show. The bands didn't perform tonight, so we only had to show up and pray we'd gotten enough votes to move on. They'd probably want to interview us again, too, because they never seemed to have enough interviews of us saying how great being on the show was.

I called Julie and then Carla to give them the update, but I didn't mention kissing Jared. I'd tell them eventually, but for now it was too new, too raw, too uncertain. Maybe last night had been a fluke, a one-time thing. Maybe today he'd regret it ever happened. Maybe tonight he'd be with someone else.

I shoved those thoughts to the back of my head. There was one other call I couldn't put off any longer, no matter how much I dreaded it.

"Hey, Mom," I said when she picked up.

"Madison, I was just thinking about you. How are things?" I heard the TV on behind her, with noises that sounded like a game show.

"Things are…good." I wasn't sure how much she knew about, well, anything. Even when I told her something important, she often didn't listen or forgot it soon after. It was easier to keep silent about my life most of the time. "There's something I have to tell you. I'm not doing that internship I mentioned before. I'm actually um…in a band. And we're on that TV show, *The Sound.*"

She sighed. "I know."

"You know?" Why hadn't she called me? Never mind—that would have taken effort on her part.

"Of course. I watch the show. I didn't realize you still played the guitar."

"Oh. Yeah." I paused for her to say something else, to tell me how I was wasting my talent and how guitar wasn't a real instrument, but it never came. "I'm sorry I didn't tell you sooner, about the band and the show and…everything. It just happened so fast and everything got crazy and I've been so busy…"

"Hmm. I saw you last night. Looked like a bad fall."

"I twisted my ankle, but otherwise I'm okay. I'm icing it now."

"Good, good." Another pause. She sounded far away, like she was barely listening. Probably distracted by her show and her cigarettes. This is why I never called her; neither of us knew what to say to the other. "How's school?"

That was it for her interest in the show, aka the biggest thing that had ever happened to me. No words of encouragement, questions about how it was going, or good luck wishes. Why was I even surprised? And this question sounded like something she felt obligated to ask, rather than actual interest. "School is good.

One more year and all."

"Is that all?"

"Yep, just one." Did she really not know that? Mother of the Year, for sure. I adjusted the ice on my ankle, but I needed a new pack. Perfect—an excuse to hang up. There was one last thing I needed to talk to her about, but I hated this part. Julie had said my mom looked better, but I had to hear it for myself. "How are you doing? With…you know…"

"I'm not drinking again, if that's what you're asking," she snapped. "Sober for three months now, thank you very much."

"That's great, Mom."

"Yes, well, it's not a big deal." There was another long pause. "Did you tell your father about the show?"

My fingers dug into the side of my phone. She always did this. I'd ask her about her drinking, and in return, she'd bring *him* up. Even though I'm sure it brought her just as much pain to talk about him. "No, and I don't plan to."

"He's your father."

"Tell that to his real family."

She huffed into the phone. "Suit yourself."

Neither of us said anything for a minute, and I tried to think of a way to end this on a better note. Nothing came to mind.

"I voted for your band last night," my mom said.

"You did?" It was a small gesture, and yet, for a mother who thought anything more than changing the channel was a chore, it was huge. Maybe it was her own way of saying she supported me. "Thanks, Mom."

After we hung up, I found my father's contact info in my phone. I probably *should* tell him about the show at some point. But as my finger hovered over the CALL button, I just couldn't do it.

By the afternoon, my ankle was good enough to walk on, so that medic did know what she was talking about. I headed to the lobby to meet the other guys, my stomach heavy with dread. I hadn't heard anything from Jared since last night. Not that I'd contacted him either, but still. He was the one who'd initiated this mess. He could have texted me at least.

I spotted him the second I walked out of the elevator, sitting at the lobby bar with a blonde leaning close to him, hands pressed against his chest. Typical. He met my eyes and something crossed his face, but I'd seen enough. I walked out of the revolving doors and stood under the warm summer sun, hoping it would burn away the jealousy swirling through my veins like poison. What had I expected really? That's who Jared was—the guy with girls all over him, who slept with one and then immediately moved on to the next. Kyle had warned me, and Dan had encouraged it, so I couldn't even say I hadn't known what I was getting myself into. I was mostly angry with myself, since I'd let myself fall for Jared's easy charm and good looks. Last night I'd been drunk on the moment, still high from the performance, half-asleep and delirious, but during the light of day everything was clear again.

I checked the time. The other guys were running late and Jared might walk out any moment, and I wasn't ready to deal with him yet. Screw it, I'd walk to the theater by myself. They could catch up. It wasn't far—just a short walk across LA Live past the restaurants, shops, and the Staples Center. It was empty this time of day with most of downtown's population still at work, and a faint breeze blew my hair back, helping cool me down by the time I got to the theater.

Even though we weren't performing, we still had to go through hair and makeup, plus a brief run-through so we'd know where to stand on stage at various points. The winner of last year's show was performing tonight, followed by a duo between Angel and Lance, along with recaps of last night's show and eliminations from each team. That gave us a lot of free time to sit around and wait for Team Dan to be called up.

As the night went on, I managed to steer clear of Jared by hiding in the bathroom whenever we might be alone together. Kyle must have noticed something was off though because he cornered me when I finally came out.

"Everything okay?" he asked.

"Just checking the ankle and all that." It was throbbing a little from all the walking around, but not too bad. Still, it was the only explanation I had for spending all night in the bathroom.

"That's not what I meant." He combed his black hair back, forehead creased. "Did something else happen last night with Jared?"

"Nope. Nothing happened." I hated lying to him, but I couldn't tell him the truth about me and Jared. Best case, he'd say, "I told you so." Worst case, he'd want me to leave the band when the show was over. Besides, kissing Jared had been a brief moment of weakness, and it wouldn't happen again. There was no reason to bring it up.

"Are you going to be able to rehearse tomorrow?" he asked.

"Yeah, but remind me to not fall off a stage ever again."

"I thought that would be obvious, but sure." He grinned, and my shoulders relaxed. I didn't want anything to be weird between us. Before I'd joined the band, we'd been the kind of friends who always sat next to each other in class and did homework together, but we'd never hung out much otherwise. Everything had changed that night after his show, and even if this thing with Jared was a mess, I was still happy I'd gone to that party.

"I'm really glad you joined the band," he said, echoing my thoughts.

"Me too." And there was the guilt again.

I was this close to spilling everything, but he led me back to the lounge. "C'mon, it's almost time for the Team Dan elimination."

Jared frowned as we entered together. "Everything okay?"

"Fine," Kyle said, shooting his brother a dark look. He must suspect I wasn't telling him everything, but there was no time to worry about that now. We had bigger things to stress about, like whether or not we'd still be on the show after tonight.

We joined the other bands backstage and waited until it was time for Team Dan to go on. Team Lissa went before us, and when Fairy Lights was saved, Ray yelled, "And America's sweetheart continues to the next round!" Ugh, when had they started calling Lacey that? She gave a pageant wave and dashed off the stage, where she was met by an older woman with big Texas hair. Her mother, I guessed.

When Team Dan was up, the show's people arranged it so Hector and Kyle would walk out first, with Jared and me behind them. Ray's voice echoed from onstage, preparing for our arrival.

"Maddie, can we talk?" Jared whispered, his mouth close to my ear.

I flushed with the memory of those lips on me. Dammit, I wanted to kiss him again. Must. Resist. "Later."

"How about coffee after the show?"

"I can't. My ankle—" I started.

He raised an eyebrow. "Would you rather I come to your room?"

"No!" They started waving us onto stage, but Jared didn't move, still waiting for my answer. I couldn't think of a good excuse, and I couldn't avoid him forever either. "Fine, we'll have coffee. Now can we go?"

We followed the other guys on stage, waving and smiling at the audience. This was the real trick to being an entertainer: pretending everything was great while your life was falling apart around you. Our lives were covered in gold foil, but if you scratched hard enough, you'd see the rust underneath.

We lined up with the other bands just as we'd practiced earlier, and Ray opened an envelope. "The first band to be saved is…The Quiet Battles!" Everyone clapped, and the many members of the folk band hugged each other. The wait was killing me, and I nearly grabbed Jared's hand but restrained myself. Instead I wrung my hands over and over while Ray took his sweet time announcing the next name.

"The second band is…As We Die!"

That was the Christian heavy metal band—leaving us and the reggae group for the elimination. *Please don't let us go home yet*, I silently prayed.

"And the final band is…Villain Complex!"

Relief swept through me, and I almost jumped up and down, except that would be bad for my ankle. Instead we cheered and hugged each other, and the three bands still on Team Dan left the stage in a whirlwind of applause and bright lights while the reggae band said their goodbyes behind us. We were safe, for one more week anyway.

Jared and I agreed to meet three blocks from the hotel at a small hole-in-the-wall coffee shop where no one would see us. He was already sitting at a table in the corner when I arrived, playing with the lid from his cup and gazing out the window. I ordered a coffee and sat across from him. I didn't know what to say or think or even what I hoped would come out of this conversation. When his blue eyes met mine, I was torn between wanting things to go back to the way they were and recklessly wanting to kiss him again.

"Maddie, about last night…"

In that pause I heard it all. I clutched my cup so hard the lid popped off and coffee spilled over the edge and onto the table. Jared handed me a napkin, and I mopped it up.

"Sorry," I said. Did these kinds of things happen to other girls, or was the universe just mocking me now?

"It's okay." He sucked in a breath, but I cut in before he could start again.

"I already know what you're going to say, and it's fine." If I said it, it would feel less like he was rejecting me and more like I'd decided this myself. Which I had. Really.

"You do?"

I nodded while I formed a pile of wet napkins on the table. "And I agree. Last night was a mistake, it can't happen again, and we should just be friends." His eyes widened and he opened his mouth, but I went on. "It's fine. Really." I gave a short laugh that sounded more like a choking sound. "We both got caught up in the excitement from the show. Don't worry about it."

"Yeah." He fidgeted with the heat protector on his cup and cleared his throat. "Kyle and Hector would lose their shit if anything happened between us anyway."

"I know, right?" This time it was easier to laugh.

He ran a hand through his hair and stared out the window. I thought he'd be relieved, but he looked as tortured as I felt and it tugged at my heart.

"Not okay?" I asked, trying to keep it light, yet also hoping it would remind him of all the times he'd asked me that.

"Of course I'm okay." He smiled at me, but it was missing the normal luster.

We both played with our cups and looked at anything but each other. Our usual easy banter had vanished, and my chest ached with everything I really wanted to say. I didn't know if I could go back to being friends with Jared. Just being near him made me sick with longing, and every time I saw him with another girl, I felt violent. But ending it now would be better for both of us and for the band.

After a few minutes of uncomfortable small talk, we finished our drinks and walked out. The late summer sun had set while we'd been inside, and now the streets were packed with cars and bathed in the glow of headlights. Jared kept his hands shoved in his pockets, and neither of us spoke. I just wanted this night to be over already. Why was the hotel so far away?

We passed between the thick pillars of a tall office building, and Jared stopped. "Maddie, wait." I turned to see his eyes pleading with me. "Back there—that wasn't what I was going to say."

"It wasn't?"

"No." He moved closer, and my breath caught. "Last night *wasn't* a mistake. I *want* it to happen again. And I *don't* want to be friends." His head bowed, and his lips hovered near mine, tempting me with how close they were. "Do you?"

"No, I don't want to be friends." Lady Gaga's "Bad Romance" popped into my head as I said it. That's what happened when you thought in music. "But what about the show? And...your reputation?"

"We'll figure something out. But Maddie, I swear, you're the only one I want."

I'd been dying to hear those words for weeks. Our mouths met, forced together by the unstoppable release of pent-up desire. He pressed me back against a pillar, using one arm to shade us from anyone who might see. With his other hand, he gripped my hip, digging his fingers into the fabric of my dress while he kissed me long and hard until I was practically moaning for more. I slid my hands down his chest and under his shirt, running my fingers across his bare stomach like I'd fantasized about for weeks. He tugged at my bottom lip with his teeth, driving me crazy, making me forget all the reasons we couldn't be together. I didn't know what we were doing or where this would lead, but I didn't want to stop.

"We should go to the hotel," I said, breathing heavily.

"I like the sound of that."

We walked side-by-side, stealing glances and smiles whenever we could. I still found it hard to believe that, out of all the girls he'd flirted with, he'd chosen me. He was just so different from the normal guys I went out with. I usually dated guys like Sean—friendly and nice, safe but not particularly exciting. But I was done with safe.

Suddenly, Jared belted out the chorus to "Bad Romance," which was still playing on a loop in my head, too. I laughed, and when he continued with the next line, I sang along with him, right there in the middle of the street while cars drove past and people in suits walked by. They probably thought we were crazy or drunk, but whatever. Jared was the first guy who truly got me, who understood that music coursed through my blood and crept into every single thought—because he was exactly the same way.

"Singing Lady Gaga might be the sexiest thing you've ever done," I said.

"Is that so?" He pulled me close, singing the next line of the song against my lips.

I pushed him back with a smile. "Stop or we won't make it back to the hotel."

"Is that a promise?" he asked, his arms circling my waist.

We turned the corner and froze when we saw Kyle and Alexis walking out of the hotel, on their way to dinner. We ducked out of sight and broke apart, returning to a friends-only distance.

The magic vanished, leaving us with only questions and doubts.

I leaned against the wall and combed my fingers through my hair until my heart slowed down. "What are we going to do? We have to stay single for the show, and the guys will kill us if they find out."

Jared frowned in the direction of the hotel, rubbing the stubble on his neck. Finally, he sighed. "We'll have to be careful. Keep this under wraps until the show is over."

I bit my lip, considering. I didn't want to lie to the others, but I had to be realistic, too. Staying away from Jared for the next few weeks would be impossible. We couldn't ignore our attraction while spending almost every waking moment together. If we tried, eventually we'd combust from the sparks. Even now, with the threat of discovery so close, I wanted to touch him. But if anyone found out about us, it could ruin everything for the band.

"This is a really bad idea," I said.

"I know." He fixed me with an intense gaze that took my breath away. "But I can't think of any other way."

"Me either." We were really going to do this, to carry on a secret relationship under the other guys' noses and try to fool the entire world that we weren't together. And meanwhile, Jared would continue flirting with other girls in front of me. But the only other choice was to end it now, and that wasn't an option. "We should return to the hotel separately to avoid suspicion."

"Do you want me to stop by your room later?"

God, yes. But I shook my head. I might have agreed to a secret relationship, but I wasn't ready to go further with it tonight. And as much as I desired Jared, I didn't want to be just another hook-up either. If we were going to do this, I'd want something real. Problem was, I didn't know if Jared could give me that.

CHAPTER FIFTEEN

People thought being in a rock band was glamorous and exciting, but in reality, it was often pretty tedious. We spent most of our time rehearsing or doing other business for the show, and finding a moment alone with Jared was near-impossible now that I badly wanted one. Hector and Kyle were always around, and when they weren't, the cameras were.

Alexis showed up to a few rehearsals to take photos of us for the website and make out with Kyle between songs. It was torture watching them be so open with their love, not caring who saw them together. Meanwhile, Jared and I were forced to duck into closets, sneak into empty studios, and steal quick kisses when no one was looking. It was hard to keep the charade up, but I couldn't invite him to my room yet. I knew where that would lead, and I wanted to take things slow for now. Something had shifted between us when we'd moved from friends to something else, and we were still figuring out the rules of this new situation.

This week's theme was "Neon '90s," which meant we had to pick a song from 1990 to 1993. We settled on Depeche Mode's "Enjoy the Silence" after listening to the remix Linkin Park had done, along with the covers by Breaking Benjamin and Anberlin. There wasn't much for me to do during this song, but maybe that was better—less chance of falling off the stage and making a fool of myself again. Instead, it was Kyle's turn to shine on keyboard.

During our final rehearsal before the live show, Jared wore a T-shirt with a bunch of X-Men villains on it, like Magneto and Mystique. Seeing him embrace his inner geek made me want to rip his clothes off right there in the studio. He kept grinning at me like he knew exactly what I was thinking, but the other guys were too busy practicing to notice.

After we finished, the guys headed back to the hotel, and I made an excuse about wanting to check out the piano in one of the other practice rooms. I'd hoped Jared would stay behind, too, but unfortunately, he left with them. Oh, well. Just me and the music. But I was used to that after a lifetime of practicing alone.

It wasn't completely an excuse either; I'd been itching to get back on the piano. I hadn't touched one since I'd joined the band, except for that brief moment with Kyle's keyboard. Guitar had completely taken over my life, and while I didn't regret it for a second, I did miss other instruments, too. Okay, not so much the clarinet.

I sat in front of the piano and ran my fingers along the smooth black-and-white keys. Without thinking, I slipped into my usual warm-up routine, as if I was practicing in my old living room or in one of the music rooms at school. The nostalgia should have been comforting, but instead it made me feel trapped, like I was shoving my true self back in a box.

I shook off the feeling and placed my fingers back on the keys. I wouldn't play anything I'd practiced in school. If I had only a few stolen minutes with a piano, I would play the music I loved most: movie scores. I'd lose myself in an epic piece, letting the melody paint a scene in my head, from romantic to action-packed to bittersweet.

To get into the mood, I played through a few different themes, from *The Godfather* to *Harry Potter* to *Inception*. Jared walked in at the end of the *Jurassic Park* theme, and I barely managed to keep my cool while I finished the piece, trying not to show how much his presence affected me. He could have returned to the lobby to flirt with other girls and keep his reputation going, but instead he'd come back to me.

He slid onto the bench, fitting against my side in a way that was deliciously distracting. "I should have known you'd sneak off to spend time with John Williams."

"I can't help it. He's just so dreamy," I said with an overly dramatic sigh.

"There you go, making me jealous again."

"How about this instead?" I started a fun piece while Jared watched my fingers dance across the keys.

"I know this," he said. "*Nightmare Before Christmas*, right?"

I nodded. "Danny Elfman is my hero. He sang for Oingo Boingo—"

"Who did the best '80s song ever, 'Dead's Man's Party.'"

"Yes! He also writes movie scores, like for all the Tim Burton films. I basically want to be him when I grow up."

"He does make some great Halloween music." He nudged me with his elbow. "Kyle told me you're from the Bay Area. Why didn't you go to the San Francisco Conservatory if you're such a musical genius?" My hands froze over the keys, and he said, "Sorry if that's too personal a question…"

"No, it's fine." I took a moment to consider my next words. "I picked UCLA so I'd be far enough away that I couldn't go home all the time, but close enough to hop on a quick flight if there was an emergency."

His eyebrows shot up. "Everything okay?"

"My mom's an alcoholic. Sober at the moment, but she's told me that before, so who knows. She's also just…a mess. It's a rare day she gets out of bed. And my father…" I used my sleeve to wipe fingerprints off the music rack, keeping my eyes fixed in front of me. "He had an affair with my mom. She had no idea he was married and had kids, a whole secret life he kept from her, but when she got pregnant, he confessed everything."

"Damn. That's messed up."

"Yeah. Most of the time I forget that part of my family entirely, until he does something like buying me a guilt car for my sixteenth birthday. He paid for all my music lessons and instruments as a kid, too, like he thought he could make up for not being a real dad by throwing money at us." I tried to shrug it off. "What about you? Kyle told me you both grew up in LA, and I know your mom is a songwriter and your dad a lawyer, but that's it."

Jared stared at the keys and didn't answer, and I worried I'd crossed some line by asking him something personal, even though I'd just spilled something myself. Finally, he said, "My parents split up when I was seventeen and Kyle was fifteen. Nasty divorce."

"Oh, I'm sorry."

"They'd fought for so long I was relieved at first—until they started trying to get information out of me and Kyle, using us like pawns in their never-ending battle. They even wanted us to testify that the other parent was 'unfit' to get custody of us, too."

"That's horrible." All these years, Kyle had never mentioned any of this. Though, in retrospect, he'd never mentioned any of his family except Jared. I could understand why.

Jared trailed his fingers along the keyboard, staring at nothing while he spoke. "When I wouldn't play their games they focused on Kyle, and it really messed with his head. He started doing drugs, he was sent to therapy—it was bad. I was supposed to go to Columbia but switched to UCLA at the last minute and rented us a place so Kyle could live with me while he finished high school. He got better once my parents gave him some space, and I think being in the band helped a lot, too. Since then it's just been the two of us, except for the obligatory holiday dinners with one of our parents."

No wonder the brothers were so close. I'd never known Kyle had such a dark past—he'd always seemed like the most balanced one in the band. I placed my hand over Jared's, entwining our fingers together. "You're a good brother."

He was silent for a moment and then cleared his throat. "So have you started applying to grad schools yet?"

"Not yet. But now, with the show…I don't know." I removed my hand from his. My future used to be crystal clear and I'd known exactly what I wanted and how to get there, but joining the band had changed everything. Something had shifted in me over these past few weeks. I still wanted to write movie scores someday, but I wanted to focus on being the guitarist for Villain Complex, too. If we managed to win the show, there'd be tours and albums to record, and I didn't know if there was room in that life for grad school, too. But I didn't want to quit the band or leave behind this new part of myself. Or Jared.

"If you wanted to focus on school, we'd understand," he said, as though he could read my thoughts. "I mean, we'd all cry and eat a lot of ice cream and listen to 'Everybody Hurts' by REM for days, but we'd eventually find *some* way to keep going."

"Good to know." I leaned against him, his body warm and comforting at my side.

"Don't get me wrong, I don't want you to leave." He brushed hair away from my face, his touch gentle. "But you can't let anyone hold you back. Not your parents, not the band, and definitely not me. In the end, all we have are our dreams."

"What if I don't know what my dreams are anymore?"

"You'll figure it out."

I thought he would kiss me, but he turned back to the piano and started playing something. I became transfixed by the sight of his long fingers moving across the keyboard and his perfect wrists and tattooed forearms arching over it. When he started singing, his voice raspy and full of emotion, I recognized the piece as "Stay" by Rihanna. Was he singing this in response to what we'd talked about? Or was I reading too much into it?

I needed to kiss him, but his voice was so beautiful I didn't want him to stop either. Instead, I pressed my lips to his collarbone, just above his shirt and his hidden VILLAIN tattoo. While he played, I trailed kisses along his neck, his skin humming against my mouth as he sang the chorus. I nibbled his earlobe and slid a hand along his thigh, trying to see how much of a distraction I could be. But still he kept playing.

As soon as he finished the song, he yanked me against him with a groan and pressed his mouth against mine. I moved to straddle him, my knees on either side of the piano bench, pushing my hips against his hard body. I didn't care that anyone could walk in and see us. Knowing how wrong this was, how dangerously close to being caught we were, only made this more right. I clutched his unshaven face as we kissed, and the rough feel of his stubble against my fingertips made me wild. His hands dipped under my shirt and traced patterns along my back, sending shivers down my spine.

Now that we were finally alone, we couldn't get enough of each other. His lips kissed down my neck like he needed to taste every inch of me, and the way he pressed his mouth against my pulse made me gasp. I tilted my head back, arching against him, digging my fingers into his shoulders. His hands smoothed up my stomach, along my ribs, inch by inch until he found my breasts. He circled my nipples through my bra, and I closed my eyes, losing myself in his touch. I couldn't focus on anything but Jared and how badly I wanted him, without all these clothes in the way. But when I moved my hands to the button of his jeans, he stopped me.

"We can't. Not here," he whispered, glancing at the door.

I sighed, remembering there was another life outside of this room, outside of us. "I know."

He pressed his forehead against mine while we tried to regain control of our breathing. "Trust me, I want to. God, you have no idea."

"Oh, I have some idea," I said with a slight smile. "But you're right. And we have that interview with that website tonight, too."

He groaned. "Yay, another interview."

"You know you love them."

"Maybe a little." He gave me one last lingering kiss. "But I'd rather be alone with you."

We reluctantly broke apart, and I knew I wouldn't be able to go slow with Jared any longer.

The show really was trying to starve us. By the time we finished the interview, it was close to midnight, and no one had fed us since lunch. Once we got back to the hotel, the four of us immediately piled into the band's van and headed out to find a late-night drive-thru. We ate burgers in the backseat, shoving food in our faces and laughing at the stupid questions we'd been asked earlier. "Which mentor would you want to date?" (Dan, obviously) and "what color would your music be?" (duh, black) were our favorites.

Once we were stuffed, we drove to the nearest supermarket,

since we'd been living in a hotel for weeks and needed to stock up on basic things like toothpaste and deodorant. We stepped into the harsh fluorescent lights and I reached for a shopping basket, but Kyle stopped me.

"You'll need a cart for this," he said with a devilish grin. Wait—how much stuff were we getting?

"All right," Jared said, rubbing his hands together. "Time for another round of Supermarket Treasure Hunt."

"What's that?" I asked.

"Only the greatest game ever," Kyle said. Hector nodded solemnly, like this was serious business.

"Since Maddie's new, I'll go over the rules," Jared continued. "We each grab a cart and split up. You have ten minutes to find three bizarre items anywhere in the store, and bonus points if they all follow a theme. The person with the most ridiculous treasures wins."

"What do we win?" I asked.

"Bragging rights, of course," Hector said.

"Um, yay?"

"Meet in front of the bananas in ten minutes," Jared said. "Okay, go!"

The guys all shoved each other out of the way as they grabbed their carts. I followed behind them at a slower pace, laughing as they rammed their carts into each other's and made race car sounds before darting down the aisles. I studied the signs and chose the pet supply section, figuring this downtown supermarket probably catered to all sorts of rich people living in lofts with their pampered pets. Luckily, the place didn't let me down. I grabbed the three oddest things I could find and rushed back to the produce section.

Kyle and Jared turned a corner ahead of me, racing to get in front of each other and nearly knocking stuff off the shelves. Kyle arrived at the finish line first and seized a banana in each hand to do a victory dance, making me laugh.

"You totally cheated," Jared said.

"Did not."

Jared grabbed his brother and wrestled with him, their unshaved faces squished together while Kyle stuck out his tongue like he was dying. They had such a strong bond, and I loved seeing my two favorite guys being silly like this.

"Ow, beard friction," Kyle said, rubbing his cheek.

"We're so hot we're starting fires with our faces." Jared ran a hand along his matching dark stubble, and it took all my effort to not reach for him, too. Sometimes this secret romance thing was pretty damn frustrating.

Kyle grinned. "Hey, that can be our next song."

Jared belted out, "Fire in our beards / Ice in our hearts / You'll get seared / Here in the mart."

I laughed. "Sounds like a hit."

He gave a dramatic bow while Hector wheeled his cart over. Once we were all together, Jared announced, "Time to see what we all got. Kyle, as reigning champion you go first."

"My theme is 'candy fail,'" Kyle said and held up each item to show us. "Lollypops with spiders in them. Bacon-flavored breath mints. And mushroom-shaped gummies that look like dicks. Bam!"

"Ew," I said, not sure which of those things grossed me out the most.

"Nice finds," Hector said. "But I'll see your dick gummies and raise you my Crunchy Nude Balls." He held up a box of Korean rice candy with that name.

"Hector, there are ladies present," Kyle said, in an overly shocked way.

I held my hand over my heart. "It's true. I'm a delicate flower who is easily offended."

Hector snorted. "Of course you are. I also found these." He showed us his other two items: a Tea Bag Buddy for mugs and a bottle of something called Head Lube. For shaving, maybe?

Jared nodded. "The 'unintentional sexual innuendos theme.' Always a good one."

"I knew you'd approve."

"My turn," Jared said. "The theme tonight, ladies and gentleman, is 'strange things in your bathroom.' First up, garlic shampoo, so you can ward off vampires at all times and probably everyone else, too. Next, men's grooming wipes in 'boardroom scent,' for when you need to feel both clean and extra-manly down there. And finally, drumroll please...lightsaber-shaped lip balm."

"Um, I kind of want that," I said.

"I figured." He grinned and tossed it into my cart. "You're up, Maddie."

"This theme is 'crazy pet owners,'" I said, as I pulled each item out of my cart. "Number one: fruit smoothies for all those health-conscious dogs. Number two: water for turtles and tortoises, for the ones too spoiled to swim in regular water. And number three: a book called...*Crafting With Cat Hair.*"

"What the shit," Hector said, taking the book to page through it. "I think you win with this alone."

Kyle leaned closer to look inside. "Agreed. Nothing can top fingerless gloves made out of fur balls."

Jared grabbed my arm and raised it over my head. "I'm proud to introduce our new champion, Maddie Taylor!"

"Woo!" I yelled, and the other guys applauded and hooted. Thank god the store was empty at this hour.

"Good job, everyone," Jared said. "Let's put this stuff back before the people who work here kick us out."

We split up to return our treasures and grab the things we actually needed. While I was deciding which snacks to get, Jared's arms slid around me from behind and he placed a kiss on my neck.

"Hey, stop that." I glanced around quickly, but we were alone in this aisle. It was only the thought of Hector or Kyle walking over that kept me from kissing him back.

"I couldn't resist." He let me go, and we pulled apart to an innocent distance but did the rest of our shopping together.

While we grabbed some beer, a girl about our age with bright pink extensions swayed down the aisle and stopped in front of us. She stared at Jared with narrowed eyes and then asked, "Are you famous?"

"Nope."

"You look like that guy on that show. Um, that one show on TV, you know? In that band?"

He waited for her to get it out, smiling the entire time. "Oh, yeah?"

"Wait, you *are* that guy! Right? You're, like, totally famous!"

He laughed. "Yeah, I am that guy."

"Oh my god, I love you, I love your band. Can I have a hug?"

"Sure." He held his arms out, and she rushed into them. Over her shoulder, he raised his eyebrows at me, an amused expression on his face. I covered my mouth to suppress a laugh. This was just too surreal, being attacked by a drunk fan in the middle of the night in a supermarket. I wondered if this sort of thing happened often to Jared. The girl didn't even seem to notice I was standing there, too, but that didn't surprise me. Jared was the face of this band for good reason.

"My friend is never going to believe this. She knows, like, all your songs," the girl said. "Can I get a photo so I can make her jealous?"

"Of course. But you have to include my lovely guitarist too." He dragged me in, though I scowled at him, and took a selfie of the three of us with her phone. "There you go."

"Oh my god, thank you, I love you!" She grabbed him again, pressing her face against his shoulder. I'd be jealous if this wasn't so hilarious.

"This has been so much fun, but we have to run," Jared said when the girl wouldn't let go of him. He mouthed, "Help!" but I shook my head and grinned.

As soon as we managed to escape across the store, we burst into laughter. "Does that happen a lot?" I asked.

"No, that was new. And very weird. I kind of want a shower actually."

"Better get used to it. You're 'famous' now. Soon you'll have fangirls ripping off your clothes every time you go out."

He moved closer, a teasing smile on his lips. "The only one I want ripping off—"

He cut off as Kyle and Hector rounded the corner and joined us, but I knew what he meant. We returned to friend mode and told them about the girl, and the other guys all laughed with us. It was a new kind of agony, being near Jared but being unable to actually *be* with him. But at the same time, I didn't want to do anything to jeopardize this new family I'd become a part of either.

CHAPTER SIXTEEN

Carla hopped out of her '67 Mustang and grabbed me in a hug, and Julie dashed around to join us. With Dan's help, I'd been able to score VIP tickets for tonight's live show for my two favorite ladies, who were both back in town.

"I'm so happy you're here!" I hugged them back hard. After being surrounded by nothing but testosterone for weeks, I really needed my girls again.

"I demand to see everything," Julie said. "Dazzle me with your rock-star lifestyle."

Carla shook her head, her dark curls bouncing. "She's been

talking nonstop the entire drive over. I kept turning the music up, but she just got louder."

"What? I'm so freaking proud of Maddie I could scream." She shrieked to demonstrate, and it echoed across the open-air parking lot.

"How are things going?" Carla asked me.

"Things are great. The show is amazing, and I've improved so much in these last few weeks, and playing with the band and on stage…there's nothing like it in the world."

"You do seem a lot happier than you've been in months. Maybe years."

As we headed toward the Nokia Theatre, we passed the massive line of people hoping to get into tonight's show.

"Thank god we don't have to wait in that mess," Julie said.

"Nope, you get the VIP treatment tonight. Backstage tour and—" I slid to a halt when I saw Jared ahead of us, near the front of the line. Groupies surrounded him, taking pictures with him and having him sign everything from their phones to their bra straps to their bare skin. He wore dark sunglasses and a black leather jacket, and with his hair spiked up, he looked every bit the bad boy rock star. A girl in a slinky dress pressed her red lips to his cheek, and he never dropped his smile. I wondered if any of his groupies could tell it was his stage smile and not his real one or if I was the only girl who knew that.

"Maddie?" Carla asked. She followed my gaze and then said, "Ah."

I tore my eyes away after another girl squeezed her body against him for a photo, and he whispered something in her ear. It was actually really cool of Jared to take the time to meet our fans. I didn't know of any other musician on *The Sound* who did that, and there was no doubt all those people would vote for our band now. But these women were so much more aggressive than the one in the supermarket, and I wanted to shove them all aside and prop a big sign on him that said, "MINE." I knew he had to keep up his reputation for the show, but god, it hurt to see him do it in front of me.

Julie clucked her tongue at me. "Still obsessed with him, I see."

"I'm not obsessed." Okay, maybe a little. For good reason. "Besides, we're just friends."

She nudged me with her hip. "Yeah, but you'd like to be more, right?"

"So nothing's happened with him?" Carla asked.

"No," I said, and my chest tightened up at the lie. I never kept anything from them, but there was too much at stake with the show and I didn't know if the girls would be able to stay quiet tonight if I told them what was really going on. Especially Julie. She meant well, but she was terrible at keeping secrets. I'd tell them when our time on *The Sound* was over, assuming my whatever-this-was with Jared lasted that long.

I led my friends around the crowd, away from the Jared Cross Fan Club, and into the backstage area of the theater. I hoped giving them a behind-the-scenes tour of *The Sound* would keep all our minds off of my love life, but no such luck.

Near the rotating stage, Sean was talking to one of the roadies, and he perked up when he saw us. "Hey, Maddie. Are these your friends?" He held out his hand to each of them. "I'm Sean. Nice to meet you."

Both Carla and Julie grinned at him like he was a giant chocolate cake, and I introduced them. "They're here for the show tonight," I added.

"You're in The Static Klingons!" Julie blurted out. "I love you guys!"

He laughed and turned to me. "You didn't tell me your friends were not only beautiful, but had great taste in music, too."

I grinned. "They're here with me, isn't that obvious?"

"Good point. Hey, do you want to grab that bite to eat sometime this week? Assuming we're both still around after tomorrow, that is."

The girls nodded frantically at me, and I plastered a smile on. "Um, sure. Let me get back to you on when I'm free."

"Great! Good luck tonight." He saluted my friends. "Ladies, have fun."

He walked off, and the girls checked him out from behind. "Holy hotness," Julie said, with a low whistle.

"He seems to like you," Carla said to me. "He asked you out in front of your friends—that's pretty bold."

"I know. He's cute and nice but…" I shrugged. "He just doesn't do it for me."

"How is that possible?" Julie asked.

Carla set her hand lightly on my arm. "Maybe you're so focused on Jared that you're ignoring the guy practically throwing himself at your feet."

"I'm not—" I started to protest. Was she really giving me guy advice when she was *still* with Daryl? I took a deep breath and started again. "Sean's just not my type, that's all."

"He's exactly your type, and he seems like the perfect guy to help you forget Jared," Julie said.

"You're the one who told me to go after Jared in the first place!" I blurted out, and then I glanced around quickly, hoping no one had heard me. Here they were, teaming up against me again. I loved my friends, but not the way they always wanted to run my life for me. I'd definitely not missed this over the last few weeks.

"Yeah, at the party. But you've known him for weeks, and if he hasn't seen how amazing you are by now, he's hopeless."

"But—" I bit my lip. I couldn't very well tell them the truth about Jared now. They'd just say he was going to hurt me, that this was only going to end badly, and a dozen other things I knew in my head but didn't want to hear in my heart. "Let's just drop this, okay?"

Carla gave me a pitying look. "We just don't want you to get your heart broken, that's all."

I assured the girls I wasn't interested in Jared and resumed the tour, but I didn't think they believed me. And a nagging feeling in my gut told me they were probably right about him. This thing between us could only end badly, but when I was alone with him, I didn't care.

For this week's show, some of the other bands had completely embraced the "Neon '90s" theme, but we'd decided to go in a different direction, with all white outfits for the guys and a short white dress and matching boots for me. The makeup people had gone a little overboard though, and my eyes were watering so much I darted into the bathroom to check them. I set my glasses on the counter just as Lacey walked out of the stall behind me.

"Nice dress," she said, in a tone that implied she meant the opposite. She wore a sparkly hot pink dress with a neon green cowboy hat and matching boots, so she wasn't really one to talk.

I dabbed at my eyes with a paper towel, but stayed silent. The producers loved to parade her around like she was some sort of Disney princess, and on the Internet, her band Fairy Lights was already an early favorite for the win. The only other band with as much attention was ours, but I suspected that was due to Jared's sex appeal more than anything.

"Don't think I'm not on to your little game," she said with her strong Southern accent. "Winning the audience over with your 'fall' and all those lies about how you and Jared aren't seeing each other. Soon all of America will know what you're doing."

I blinked at her. Was she threatening us? "I'm sorry?"

"I'm going to win this thing. You'd best be staying out of my way."

She left the bathroom before I could come up with a witty comeback. I didn't know what that was about or why she suddenly had such a problem with us. Was it because we were potentially her band's biggest competitors? Or because I'd seen Jared shoot her down in the elevator? Whatever, I couldn't afford to let her get into my head before I got on stage.

I reached for my glasses, but they were gone. I checked the floor and then looked in all the stalls, in the sinks, even in the trash and the toilets, but my glasses had disappeared.

No, not disappeared. Lacey must have taken them.

I ran out of the bathroom to go after her and crashed into Jared. "Hey, it's almost time for our set." His eyes swept over my face. "What's wrong?"

"Lacey stole my glasses. I can't see anything. I can't play. We have to find her, we have to delay the show, we—"

"Slow down." Jared placed his hands on my elbows, holding me steady. "Are you sure she took them?"

"She was the only one in the bathroom with me, and I had them when I went in, and I've looked everywhere but they're *gone*." I closed my eyes to stop the hallway spinning around me. I couldn't deal with this right now, not when we were about to go on stage. Not when my friends were in the audience, ready to cheer me on. Not when our entire future rode on how we did tonight. "I'm going to kill that sparkly cowgirl."

"We'll tell the producers and they'll deal with her. For now, do you have another set of glasses or contacts you can use?"

"Back at the hotel, but we don't have time to get them."

"How bad is it without your glasses?"

"Um, bad. I can barely see anything." I covered my face with my hands, trying not to cry. I didn't need my eyeliner to be even more of a mess than it was. "This is a disaster."

He pulled me into his arms and kissed the top of my head. "It's not that bad. You don't even need to see to play the guitar. You could do it blindfolded. And maybe it'll be better if you don't walk around the stage. Less chance of falling off, right?"

"Very funny." But his calm demeanor was helping a little, and his words made me think. He was right; I didn't *need* to see. Maybe I *could* play the guitar blindfolded. "I have an idea."

When our stage turned, I was already standing in place, my guitar hanging from my shoulder, my pick clutched in my fingers. I couldn't see anything—not the rest of the band, not the audience, not even my guitar or the mic right in front of me. All

I could make out were the lights shining on us, tinted red from the strip of fabric across my eyes. Hector had a matching one across his mouth, Kyle had one covering his ears, and to make our group complete, Jared had one tied around his neck. The red was a sharp contrast to our white outfits, and hopefully got across the Hear No Evil, See No Evil, Speak No Evil message we were going for.

The audience cheered as we rotated in front of them, and my nerves kicked up to high alert at all the sounds without the visuals to accompany them. As Kyle began, I thought my skin might jump right off me, and I prayed I could pull this off. What if I was wrong and I couldn't actually play blindfolded? In theory it didn't seem too hard, but I'd never actually tried before. I was doing it for the first time in front of a huge crowd, plus everyone watching live on TV.

But once I started, my fingers knew what to do. I forgot seeing and focused on hearing, feeling, being. On Hector's steady beat and Jared's baseline vibrating through my bones. On Kyle's clear tones tying it all together. Our version of "Enjoy the Silence" sounded like we'd dipped the original in black ink and razorblades, and Jared's voice was perfect for it. And with nothing in the world except me and the music, I could easily imagine he was singing the words only to me.

When the song ended, his arm took mine to help me move across the stage to the center. I pushed my blindfold back, grateful for his help since everything around me was a blurred mess of faces and lights. By the roar of the crowd, I could tell the audience loved our version, and I knew Julie and Carla were somewhere out there, cheering me on. The mentors praised our unique take on the song and on our interesting performance, and I hoped Lacey was watching this moment. *Suck it, cowgirl.*

The stage turned for the next band, and as soon as we were backstage, they wanted us to do an interview right away. On the way to the interview area, I stopped to ask producer Steve if they'd found my glasses yet.

"No, but we're on it." He had a rapid no-nonsense way of talking. "Don't worry. Let us handle this, and we'll get your glasses back to you in no time." He checked his massive shiny watch. "Now if you could just hurry to your interview, that'd be great. Ray has to be back on stage in six minutes."

Thanks for being no help at all, Steve. I rejoined the band, and we were hustled over to speak with Ray.

"That was a fun performance," Ray said. "And what a statement! Dan said it wasn't his idea—whose was it?"

"It was Maddie's," Jared said, leaning into the mic. "Her glasses vanished right before we went on, and she came up with this solution."

"Talk about quick thinking." Ray shoved the mic in my face. "We've never had anyone play guitar blindfolded on the show before."

"It was really Jared's idea," I said, blushing like crazy, like I always did when the focus was on me. "He said he knew I could play even if I was blindfolded, and a light bulb went off."

"You two are a great team." He grinned at both of us. "And it seems like there's some chemistry there, too. The fans want to know: Is there anything between you?"

"No!" we both said, too fast.

"We're just friends," Jared added. My least favorite phrase these days.

Ray laughed. "That's too bad, though you'd both break some hearts if the fans knew you were off the market."

"Don't worry. Jared is still available," I said and hated myself.

When the interview was over, Hector said, "He didn't even look at me or Kyle. All they care about is the Jared and Maddie will-they-or-won't-they bullshit."

"Sorry," I said. "I didn't mean for that to come up."

"It's not your fault," Kyle said, shooting Hector a look. "It's the producers trying to test us again."

"I just wish they'd remember we're part of the band, too." Hector shook his head. "Forget it. I need to get some air."

He took off down the hallway, and Jared frowned. "I should talk to him."

"He's pissed at you right now," Kyle said. "I'll handle it."

He left us alone or as alone as we could be backstage with other bands and people who worked on the show. Jared rubbed the back of his neck, and even without my glasses, he was beautiful. I wanted to press my mouth to the stubble along his jaw and trace his tattoos with my tongue. I licked my lips and his gaze lingered on them, and I knew he was thinking along the same lines.

"Let's get out of here," he said, his voice husky.

"Where?" We didn't have much time before we had to get back on stage at the end of the show, but a few minutes alone with Jared were too tempting to pass up, even if it was risky. Or maybe, *because* it was risky.

"Anywhere. I don't care, as long as we're alone."

We sneaked out the back door, and Jared took my hand as soon as it closed. I still couldn't see much without my glasses, but he guided me through the parking lot for the trucks with the show's equipment until we found a secluded spot against a chain-link fence between buildings, where it was unlikely anyone would see us.

I leaned back against the fence and slipped my fingers under the red sash at his neck, using it to pull him to my mouth. He yanked my blindfold down to cover my eyes, and I gasped into his lips.

"Do you have any idea how hard it was not to kiss you on stage tonight?" he asked, as he grabbed onto the chain-link fence above me, fitting his body against mine.

He claimed my mouth with his before I could answer. With the blindfold on, my other senses exploded with Jared. The taste of his skin, slick with sweat and desire. His smell, like soap and leather and something unmistakably male. The feel of his stubble against my cheek, his hard chest pressing against my breasts. His voice as he groaned my name, like I was chocolate and he wanted to take a bite. My entire world was Jared's lips and hands and breath and body.

"Jared, you're making me crazy."

"Tell me what you want," he said against my neck.

"I want you," I whispered. "Here. Now."

Jared gripped my hip with one hand, the other still holding the fence. His fingers slid lower, inching down my dress and then under it, moving along my bare skin and igniting a fire within me. Without warning, he lifted one of my legs, hooking it around his body. I clutched his shoulders for support while his hand smoothed up my leg and eased between my thighs. He teased along the edge of my panties in a way that made me moan and beg for more. No more going slow. After weeks of pent-up desire, I needed him now.

When I thought I'd die if he didn't touch me where I burned, he pushed my panties aside to slip one long finger inside me. I gasped and arched against him, but his mouth covered mine and swallowed my wordless cries. He slid his finger in and out slowly and then added another while he began to rub me with his thumb, circling my sensitive skin in a way that sent flames through me. He kissed me the entire time, his tongue matching his fingers as they darted into me, faster, harder.

Anyone could walk out and see me blindfolded against a fence and catch him fingering me, but that only made it hotter, knowing we could be discovered at any moment. Jared's touch wound me tighter and tighter, his mouth never leaving mine as my cries grew more desperate. My fingers tensed around the sash at his neck, holding him close as he brought me to climax, my every nerve springing free. He didn't stop touching me, and the pleasure went on for an eternity while I trembled against him. If not for the fence behind me and his body holding me up, my knees would have given out. Jared made my body weak in the best way possible.

"I'd love to continue this," he said, pushing up my blindfold so I could see again. "But we need to get back."

I nodded, unable to speak, my whole body warm and fluid from what he'd done to me. I wanted to return the favor, to make him as delirious as I was, but we didn't have time. We made our way back to the theater, and I was already counting down the minutes until we could be alone again. He'd brought me release, but instead of satisfying me, it just made me want more. I craved Jared like an addiction, and I was starting to wonder if I'd ever get enough.

CHAPTER SEVENTEEN

I wanted to invite Jared back to my room that night, but I had dinner with Julie and Carla after the show so we could catch up and we ended up drinking too much for them to drive back. They crashed on the extra bed in my hotel room, and I spent the night tossing and turning, partly stressing about whether our performance would be good enough to keep us on the show another week, but mostly replaying those stolen minutes against the fence with Jared.

My friends didn't have tickets for the results show, so I returned to the theater alone the next afternoon. I'd slept in late and hadn't spoken to the guys at all, so I had no idea what kind of reception our song was getting online. It was actually nice being oblivious; people on the Internet could be pretty damn cruel sometimes. But at the same time, it made my stress levels shoot through the roof. Had anyone liked our version of "Enjoy the Silence" or was it too different from the original? We'd picked such a classic, well-known song, and it was hard to know if people would love or hate our darker take on it.

I met the rest of the band in the lounge. Jared wore his black leather jacket again, and the wicked smile he gave me filled my head with naughty thoughts.

"Tonight," I whispered to him as we walked to the stage. "After the show, my room."

In response, he set his hand on my back, moving lower to rest on the curve of my butt. I sucked in a breath, heat building between my legs at his touch, but he released me before anyone saw. Or so I hoped.

We waited while Dan and Lissa finished their duo, their two distinct voices meshing surprisingly well, and then our team was rushed on stage. I held my breath as Ray called the names, but our band was saved first, followed by The Quiet Battles, leaving the Christian heavy metal band to be kicked off this time. Safe for another week, and now we were in the semi-finals. I never expected to get this far, and it only made me want to work even harder to make it to the finals next week.

We all ran off the stage and hugged, and when Jared's arms

wrapped around me, I had to restrain myself from kissing him in front of the other guys. It was getting harder and harder to keep up this friends-only charade in public, and I worried we were too obvious with all of our secret looks and quick touches. How could anyone miss the fire smoldering between us every time we were in the same room?

The show continued with a performance from a pop band whose song played every five minutes on the radio, followed by Team Lissa's elimination. Naturally, Lacey and Fairy Lights were still safe. Ray talked about how sweet and wholesome she was while she ran off the stage, and I wanted to gag. I had a few choice words for the viewers about the real Lacey, not that anyone would believe me over her.

Last night, my glasses had been waiting for me on top of my guitar case at the end of the show. When I asked producer Steve, he said he'd talked to Lacey but she'd denied everything, and there was nothing he could do. I couldn't tell if he was lying or if he thought I'd just misplaced my glasses. But I knew it was her.

Team Angel went up next, and The Static Klingons were safe, too, which meant I'd have to deal with Sean sometime this week. Instead, the punk band was kicked off her team.

Mohawk Girl and I ran into each other in the lounge after the elimination.

"I'm sorry," I said. "I can't believe you're going home."

She gave a one-shouldered shrug, like it wasn't a big deal. "It's fine. We knew we wouldn't win."

"You're not upset?"

"Not really. I'm thrilled we got this far. I mean, a punk band with mohawks and spikes? No way the producers would let us win the show. But we knew we'd get more exposure and bring in a lot of new fans, maybe even get some gigs out of it. That's all we wanted."

I was impressed by how calm she was. If we'd been kicked off tonight, I'd be hiding in the bathroom and sobbing. "I hope things work out for you."

"Thanks." She leaned close and lowered her voice. "We never had a shot at winning this thing, but you do. Don't let that Lacey bitch win, even if the show is practically handing it to her."

"I'll try." I was floored she thought we could actually win. But beating Lacey, America's sweetheart? That might be tough.

Thirty minutes after I got back to the hotel, there was a knock on my door. I opened it to find Jared leaning against the frame. His eyes drank me in, skimming up and down my body, and then he gave me a slow smile. "Room service."

He definitely looked good enough to eat. I shut the door behind him, and he pushed me against it, digging his fingers into my hair while he kissed me. I slid the leather jacket off him and ran my hands across his broad shoulders, down his hard back, along his strong arms. I pushed his shirt up, splaying my fingers across his stomach. Last night had given me a taste of how good it would be with Jared, and now he was wearing far too many clothes.

He pulled his shirt off, and I paused to stare at his toned chest and the dark hair trailing down into his jeans. I dragged a finger across his rough jaw and lower, tracing each letter of VILLAIN inked below his collar. When I saw him like this, tattooed and gorgeous and forbidden, I couldn't believe he was real and in my room and taking his clothes off for me.

He unbuttoned my shirt slowly, like he was savoring each new reveal of skin. When it fell to the floor, he pressed his lips to the hollow of my neck, making me gasp. He tugged down my bra straps and his mouth moved to my shoulders, kissing a line along each one. I threw my head back as he continued lower, down my chest, to the spot between my breasts. He unhooked my bra with one easy gesture, reminding me again how experienced he was. As his eyes swept over my chest, I had to resist the urge to cover myself. He'd been with so many other girls—how could I possibly measure up? And was I just another in his long list of flings?

"God, you're so beautiful," he whispered, and then his mouth was on me again and all my worries were forgotten. He took his time with each breast, circling and licking each nipple, while I tangled my fingers in his hair and whimpered for more. His fingers dipped into the waistband of my jeans, tugging my hips to him, while his lips and tongue continued their exploration of me. He moved slowly, worshipping my body, and I couldn't decide if I wanted to savor every second of this or if I just wanted to rip off his clothes and devour him.

He unbuttoned my jeans, his knuckles brushing against my waist. When he pushed them down, I stood before him in nothing but the lace panties I'd worn on purpose, knowing he might see them. He took me in with hungry eyes, lightly trailing his hands along the backs of my thighs, making me shiver.

"Beautiful," he whispered again.

His mouth moved lower, across my stomach and the curve of my hips. He tugged my panties down slowly, until I stood naked in front of him. Completely exposed and on display while he still had most of his clothes on. And somehow that brought back all my worries, all my fears, all my insecurities about the two of us.

I dug my fingers into his shoulders. "Jared," I said, my voice hesitant.

He pulled back to scan my face. "What's wrong?"

I bit my lip and looked away. Kyle's words came back to me: how his brother didn't do serious relationships, how I'd promised not to get involved with Jared. Next came Lacey's proposition to Jared in the elevator, followed by that text message from the girl wanting to hook up, and a never-ending stream of other girls I'd seen flirt with him. Jared might be mine tonight, but would he be mine tomorrow? And if not, was this night together worth the risk when it could cost me everything with the band and cost us all the win?

"We don't have to do this," he said when I didn't answer.

"No, I want to. It's just…" I tried to figure out how to word my thoughts without sounding completely lovesick and pathetic. If we weren't in my room, this would be the point where I would run away. Instead, I moved to the bed and pulled the covers up to my chest, so I wasn't quite so bare in front of him.

I took a deep breath and tried again. "I know you've probably been to a dozen other girls' rooms while on the show and that you don't want anything serious, but I don't know if I can do a casual hook-up, and I don't want this to ruin things with the band and the show and…"

He raked a hand through his hair, his mouth twisting. "Is that what you think this is? A casual hook-up?"

"No!" This was spiraling out of control fast, but now that it was out there, I couldn't take it back. "I don't know. You're always surrounded by girls, and there are so many rumors, plus that whole thing with Becca… Even Kyle and Hector joke about all the girls you sleep with. What am I supposed to think?"

"All of that is an act, just part of the image for the band. I know what other people say about me, but I thought you saw past all that shit." He shook his head, his voice pained. "Maddie, I haven't so much as kissed another girl since I met you."

"You…what?" Warmth rushed through me, a relief so strong it almost knocked me back.

Jared sat beside me on the bed. "Yes, I used to mess around a lot. But that's over now. That's not me anymore."

I wanted to believe him, I really did. Maybe I was too damaged from my own parents or maybe it would be different if Jared and I could be together openly, but it was just so hard for me to trust him. He said he'd changed, but how could I know for sure?

He must have seen the hesitation on my face because he sighed. "In freshman year, I caught my girlfriend in bed with our first bassist. Between that and the thing with my parents, I just lost it. I did whatever I could to forget, to feel nothing, to escape myself. I slept around, I drank too much, I got in fights. It was so much easier to be the villain, and after a while, everyone just expected me to be that guy. Girls started coming to our gigs or hiring us for parties because they thought I'd sleep with them, and the band grew more popular as long as I kept up that image. But after Becca, I knew I needed to get my shit together."

He'd never mentioned any of this before, and it made me ache for him. Suddenly I understood his obsession with villains and the meaning of the band's name and the lyrics in "Behind the Mask." He was wrong; the band wasn't popular because of his image, but because of how much passion he put into everything he did.

I wrapped myself around him, dropping the covers, my breasts pressing against his bare chest. "Jared…"

He touched my lips to silence me. "That night at the party,

when I saw you playing my guitar, there was something so raw and honest about the way you sang my lyrics, like you really felt them. Not like the girls who came up to me after a show and said they loved my music but didn't know what any of it meant. You got it." He circled his arms around my back, holding me tight against him. "From that moment, you were the only one I wanted."

His words ignited something deep inside me. I did understand his lyrics. I knew all too well what it was like to keep a part of yourself hidden for years, pretending to be what everyone else wanted while you died a little inside. Jared had freed me when he'd invited me to join his band.

I lightly traced his forehead, his dark eyebrows, his jaw with its permanent five o'clock shadow. He was so beautiful, and I couldn't believe he'd had feelings for me all this time.

"Jared, I've been crazy about you since I saw you perform at the Battle of the Bands. Or even before that, from the first time I heard you sing, when Kyle gave me your album. That's why I know how to play all your songs."

His eyebrows jumped up. "Really?"

"Oh, god, does that make me sound obsessed?"

"No, I'm just surprised. It always seemed like you were avoiding me. You've known Kyle for years, and yet we somehow never met. And once we did, you kept running off, like you were scared of me or something."

"Of course I was scared of you. You're the bad boy rock star, and I'm the awkward piano player who likes movie scores and geeky stuff."

"I like geeky stuff, too." He cupped my face in his hands and whispered, "I like everything about you."

Our kiss was slow and tender, a caress instead of a demand. I poured everything into his lips, all the pent-up frustration, jealousy, and longing, all the misunderstandings and worries. With this kiss we wiped the slate clean. The past was over, and all that mattered was us, here, now. Together.

As our kiss grew deeper and more intense we sank onto the bed, our limbs tangling together. His chest pressed me down, and I loved the feel of him on top of me, the weight of his body, the brush of his soft hair against my breasts. He was still wearing far too many clothes though. I reached down and ran a hand along the front of his jeans, trying to unbutton them with fingers clumsy from lust. He stood up, and I watched with hungry eyes as he slid his jeans down his hips and off. His boxers fell next, leaving him as naked as I was, giving me a view of his entire, delicious body. And damn, it was a nice view.

I pulled him down on the bed, on top of me, and there was nothing between us now. Our bodies fit together, skin to skin, and it hit me that we were really, finally doing this. He kissed my neck and slipped a hand between my thighs, touching me where I ached the most. That fever overtook me again, the madness that Jared always brought out, making me want more and more of him. I was already so turned on by everything he'd already done to me, it didn't take long before his talented fingers created a frenzy in me.

"I need you," I breathed into his neck. "Please."

"Are you sure?"

"Very." I grinded my hips against him, and he groaned. I couldn't wait another minute. I'd lose my mind if I didn't have him inside me this instant.

He pulled a condom from his jeans, and after it was sorted, I wrapped my arms around his neck and pressed my lips against his, showing him without words I was ready for this. He spread my legs wider and pushed inside me, and I moaned from the satisfaction of finally getting what I'd been craving. He moved slowly at first, a delicious torture as his long length glided in and out, inch by wonderful inch. I lifted my hips to meet him, urging him faster, sliding my hands down his back to his butt to pull him deeper into me. We were as close as two people could be, and yet it wasn't enough. I wanted Jared to own me completely, to capture my body just as he'd already captured my heart.

"More," I breathed into his shoulder.

He grabbed my hips and rolled us over, pulling me on top of him with a teasing smile. "Show me."

I sat up and took a moment to appreciate the way he filled me completely in this position. He watched me, eyes drunk with desire, while I began to move, rolling my hips and making us both cry out. He let me set the pace, and I moved against his body at the perfect angle to drive me higher and higher. His fingers smoothed along my thighs, up my stomach, to coax my nipples in a way that sent pinpricks of pleasure to my core. My back arched while I rode him, my movements growing faster and more frantic, our breaths turning to gasps. Waves of pleasure crashed through me, and he gripped my hips and bucked under me while every part of my body trembled in sweet release.

When the tremors passed, he rolled us over again in one smooth gesture. "My turn."

I couldn't believe he was still going. All the other guys I'd slept with would have been done by now, but clearly all of Jared's experience was paying off. With one hand, he took my wrists and forced them above my head, holding me down while he rocked into me, hard and fast. He crushed my mouth with his and tugged at my lower lip with his teeth until I was whimpering for more.

"Yes," I cried, "Yes, yes, yes." This was what I'd wanted: a frenzy, a bonfire, a torrent of Jared pounding into me and claiming me as his own.

I wrapped my legs around his hips, drawing him deeper into me, and with his powerful thrusts he brought me close to the edge again. It seemed impossible so quickly after my last climax, but my entire body tensed up, from my fingers down to my toes. It was too much, it wasn't enough, and I never wanted it to end. I let go, losing myself in Jared the way I lost myself when I played guitar, when the music took over and made me whole. I broke apart into a million pieces, and he shuddered inside me, emptying himself with a few last thrusts.

We clung to one another, our naked bodies rising and falling in sync with each breath. His face was so close I could count the gold specks in his blue eyes, the dark lashes above them, the rough hairs on his chin. I was sure he could even feel the pounding of my heart through his skin.

He brushed sweat-soaked hair off my face and then kissed me, soft and gentle this time. "That was amazing," he said in a sleepy, content voice I'd never heard before. I hoped I'd soon come to know it as well as his real smile.

"Mmm..." I kissed him softly. "Even better than I imagined."

He raised an eyebrow and grinned. "So you thought about this a lot? With me?"

"Oh, stop." I covered my face with a hand. "As if that's a surprise. You know what you do to me."

"Nope, maybe you should show me." He nuzzled my neck, and I wanted him all over again. Jared really had become my addiction.

"When do you need to get back?"

"I told the guys I was seeing someone tonight, so I'm yours as long as you want me."

"Good." I wrapped my arms around his neck, kissing him hard. I didn't plan on letting him leave for many, many hours.

CHAPTER EIGHTEEN

Jared kept me up most of the night, and even though I arrived at Dan's studio the next morning bleary-eyed and barely coherent, it was totally worth it.

As I headed into the kitchen area, I overheard Hector say, "I was starting to wonder if you'd lost your game, man."

"Me?" Jared asked. "Never."

The guys all greeted me, and when I met Jared's eyes, my pulse raced, knowing the secret we shared. I felt like I was wearing a giant neon sign that said "SLEPT WITH JARED LAST NIGHT." He'd returned to his room early this morning, and now wore a T-shirt with a stylized outline of Loki's helmet from *Thor* and *The Avengers*. He must have a never-ending closet full of villain shirts.

"What are you talking about?" I asked innocently while I poured my coffee into a disposable cup.

"Jared spent the night with someone," Hector said, in a singsong voice. Whoever said guys didn't like to gossip clearly had no idea what they were talking about.

"First time since we've been on the show," Kyle added. He raised his eyebrows at me, but I couldn't tell if he was suspicious or giving me a warning or what.

I focused on adding sugar and cream to my coffee. "Good for him."

"It's been so long I was worried about him," Hector said, slapping Jared on the back. "Thought he was getting soft in his old age."

Jared coughed into his cup of tea. "Do any of you find it odd we're standing here talking about my sex life? No?"

"Nah, everyone talks about your sex life."

Jared flipped Hector off, and the guys all laughed. I felt bad that he had to keep up this act with his two closest friends, but they'd also just confirmed that he hadn't been with anyone else in weeks too. Thank you, guys.

Jared caught me yawning and gave me a knowing grin. "Tired?"

"I'm just stressed about the show, that's all."

"I hear that," Kyle said while he refilled his coffee. "Hard to believe there are only two weeks left."

Two weeks and two bands per team. We'd made it into the semi-finals, and win or lose, soon all of this would be over. This week's votes were crucial, though, since if we made it to the finals, we'd get a spot on the tour across the country. But the competition was also stronger than ever, since only the best bands remained at this point.

"The Quiet Battles are pretty popular, so we really need to bring it this week," Jared said.

"Can we beat them?" Kyle asked.

"I think so, but it'll be close."

Hector grunted. "We've come this far. We are *not* going home now."

I hoped he was right. Being sent home now, when everything we wanted was within our grasp, was impossible to consider. It just couldn't happen; my brain rejected the idea completely. Of course, The Quiet Battles probably felt the exact same way, but only one of us would be on Team Dan a week from now.

We finished up and headed to our practice room to get started. My hand brushed Jared's hip as I walked past him, and it sent a little thrill through me, touching him right under the other guys' noses without them knowing. Even though I wished we could be open about our relationship, I couldn't deny that having a secret romance was pretty damn hot, too.

Dan was already waiting for us, reading something on his phone.

"Oh, hey," he said, when we entered. "Great job on Saturday. I just heard from Steve that your version of 'Enjoy the Silence' was the most downloaded song this week, so congrats on that."

"No shit?" Hector asked, and the rest of us made similar, shocked comments. Being number one was huge. Not only did it mean more money in our pockets (granted, not much after the show took its massive cut, but still better than nothing), but all the downloads translated to votes. That made our chances of staying to the finals even better—assuming people loved this week's song, too.

"We'll have to find some way to top it for the next show," Dan continued. "The theme is, 'Tainted Love,' so I guess they want some messed-up love songs. Any thoughts?"

"Bad Romance," Jared said immediately.

"The Lady Gaga song?" Kyle asked, looking at his brother like he was crazy.

"We can do a rock version of it, make it dark and twisted." He grabbed the mic and sang the chorus, his voice rough and sensual. The same voice that had cried out my name only hours ago. It nearly turned me into a molten puddle right there in the studio, and when he winked at me, I knew he'd intended that.

"Interesting choice," Dan said. "It will definitely stand out."

"I like it," I said, and Jared gave me a smile full of naughty thoughts. Yes, he was definitely doing this on purpose.

Not that I was complaining.

Hector tapped a drumstick against his hand. "I don't know…"

Dan pulled up the song on his phone, and we discussed how we could tweak it for our style. There was no actual guitar in the song, so we could interpret it in different ways. I played the main melody for them with some heavy distortion on my guitar, and that finally convinced Kyle and Hector.

"One other thing," Dan said. "For this week's show, the mentors have to do a performance of one of our songs with each band still on their team. Pick a Loaded River song you want to cover, and I'll join you for practice every other day."

We let Kyle choose, since he was the biggest Loaded River fan. He wanted "Nothing Breaks Me," a song I'd heard a million times growing up, with grungy guitar riffs and gritty vocals that would sound great with Jared singing them. It shouldn't be too hard to learn, but now we had two songs to perform, not one. Dan bumped our rehearsal time to eight hours a day, and combined with all the added publicity we had to do for the semi-finals, that meant we'd barely have any time to breathe this week.

We spent the rest of the day rehearsing the new songs and then dragged ourselves back to the hotel. We had tonight off for a rare change, and I couldn't wait to take a nice, hot shower and relax. Preferably with Jared.

As soon as we walked into the lobby, we could tell something was wrong. Everyone turned to look at us and not in a friendly way.

"What's going on?" Hector asked.

"I don't know," I said.

Laughter broke out at the bar, the kind you could tell is laughing *at* instead of *with*. The source seemed to be Lacey, who sat with the banjo player from The Quiet Battles and the busty singer of Brazen, a pop band from Team Lance. They stopped and gave us fake smiles as we passed by and then started giggling when our backs were to them.

"Why do I feel like I'm in middle school again?" Kyle asked after we got into the elevator.

"Oh, shit." Jared stared at his phone, and the expression on his face worried me more than anything.

"What is it?" I asked.

He waited until we were in their room and then held his phone up to show us. There, on his tiny screen, was an image of me in Jared's arms, my face pressed against his shoulder as he kissed the top of my head. We were in our white outfits from the last live show, the photo taken after my glasses went missing while he was comforting me. It was an intimate, private moment when we'd thought we were alone—and someone had plastered it all over the Internet.

Lacey. It had to be her.

"What the fuck is that?" Hector asked.

Kyle's head snapped back and forth between me and his brother. "Are you two together?"

I opened my mouth to confess everything, but Jared said, "No! This isn't what it looks like."

"Then who were you with last night?" Hector asked, crossing his arms.

"Just some groupie I met after the show. I don't even remember her name."

"Maddie, is this true?" Kyle asked, looking me right in the eye.

Behind him, Jared shook his head at me. I was torn between the two brothers, one a friend and one something more. I'd have to betray one of them no matter what I chose. I didn't want to keep this a secret from the guys, but I couldn't call Jared on his lie in front of them either. And, if I was honest with myself, I was afraid to admit the truth to them, too.

"He's right. It's not what it looks like. This was taken right after my glasses were stolen, when I was having a panic attack. Jared was helping me calm down, that's all." That part wasn't a lie, at least.

Hector poked his finger into Jared's chest. "Swear to us. Swear right now you're not together and we'll drop it."

Jared raised his hands and said, "I swear."

I nodded and kept my face blank, but inside I was breaking in two. When the show was over, we'd have to tell the guys the truth, and I could already imagine how angry they'd be.

Kyle frowned, but he blew out a breath and nodded slowly. "Well, how bad is the damage?"

"Bad," Jared said. "The photo's all over the Internet, and they have quotes from Becca saying I do this kind of thing all the time."

"That's because you do," Hector growled.

Jared glared at him, and I jumped in before this got any worse. "Lacey must have done this," I said. "When she stole my glasses, she threatened me, something about how we shouldn't get in her way or else."

"We have to tell Dan," Kyle said. "She can't get away with this shit."

Jared sank onto his bed and grabbed his laptop. "It doesn't matter. We're screwed. No one is going to vote for us now. The producers will make sure of it."

I wasn't sure I agreed with him. Just like he thought the band had only become popular because of his bad boy image, now he thought we were doomed because of one photo of us together. Still, we couldn't afford to lose even a single vote at this point in the show. I just hoped there were no other photos of the two of us floating around. We'd been so stupid and hadn't been careful enough, and now our reckless passion was coming back to haunt us. God, what had we been thinking?

My phone buzzed, and I was almost too afraid to look.

Messages from Carla and Julie, asking if the photo was real, asking if I was okay, asking more questions I couldn't answer.

"Damn," Jared said. "Do not read any of these articles. Especially the comments."

"What?" I leaned over his shoulder to read his screen. The photo was on one of the most popular blogs about the show with the headline: "*The Sound's* Secret Affair." Below, the article called Jared a playboy and made him out to be some horny asshole who slept with women as some sort of power trip. They described how this had led to Villain Complex losing their bass player, with a few harsh quotes from Becca to back it up, and compared our band to the show's former winner Addicted to Chaos—exactly the thing we'd been trying to avoid.

According to this article, I'd abandoned my internship with the LA Philharmonic to chase after him like some sort of star-struck groupie. They brought up how my father had cheated on his wife with my mom and my mom's subsequent alcoholism, like that explained everything about me. Like I was just reliving her mistakes all over again with Jared. I couldn't believe they would post stuff like this, shedding light on all the things in our past we tried to keep hidden. Things no stranger had a right to know about us. How did they even get all this info about me?

In the comments, I caught a glimpse of, "I knew it," and dozens of people calling me a slut. One even said I was probably sleeping with every guy in the band. Another said we'd only been rescued by Dan because I was screwing him, too. My eyes watered with tears, and I barely managed to blink them back. How could people be so cruel? And what was with these double standards—Jared could sleep with dozens of women and no one batted an eyelash, yet one photo of me hugging a guy and I was a slut? I hated the Internet.

Jared clicked away to a different screen with a sigh. "I told you not to read them."

I knew I shouldn't take the attacks personally, but it was hard. I wanted to ignore the slut comments, but the underlying sentiment behind every word was that I didn't deserve to be in the band or on the show. That I was a talentless hack, I'd gotten in the band by accident, and I was bringing the rest of the guys down with me. And it killed me because, deep down, I suspected all of that was true.

"I have to go," I mumbled, stumbling to the door.

Jared opened his mouth like he wanted to say something but then shook his head and dropped his eyes. I fled their room and ran down the stairs to my floor. No elevator this time. I couldn't risk running into anyone from the show right now. I had to get away—from the guys, from the show, from this life.

An hour later, someone knocked on my door. Jared stood outside, hands shoved in his pockets. He didn't move to kiss me, and any hope that things would be the same between us quickly slipped away.

"Not okay?" he asked softly.

"Not really." I stepped back to let him in, and he checked the hallway to make sure it was empty before he entered. He stood just inside the door—close but not close enough—and every inch of my body strained to throw myself into his arms. I needed him to kiss me and tell me everything would be okay, but he didn't make a move.

"We talked to Dan. He said the photo was no big deal and that we shouldn't worry about it."

"No big deal? Has he seen what people are saying about us?"

"He says this kind of shit always happens and it will blow over soon. He doesn't think it will hurt our chances on the show."

"I hope he's right."

"Me too…but maybe we should cool it for a while. Stop seeing each other, at least until the show is over. We don't need any more bad publicity."

How was I supposed to cool it with Jared when I saw him every single day? He was the guy I thought about when I couldn't sleep, whose touch set my nerves on fire, whose voice haunted my every step. The guy who always believed in me and made me want to reach for more. I didn't want to give him up. And maybe the article had struck a nerve or something because for the last hour all I'd been able to think about was my father and what he'd done to my mother and how I refused to become her. I didn't want to be Jared's secret anymore.

"Can't we just tell everyone the truth?" I asked. Yes, the producers didn't want us to be together, but it wasn't up to them who won the show. People liked our music, and some of the viewers might even be happy we were together.

"You already saw what they're saying online about us after one innocent photo. If we admit that we've been lying and sneaking around, the backlash could be huge. Not to mention, the guys will completely lose their shit, and you know what Dan says about cohesion and all that." He shook his head, his face pained. "We're so close to the finals and the spot on the tour. We can't afford to mess things up now. If nothing else, we owe it to the other guys to focus on the band for the next two weeks."

I wanted him to pull me into his arms and tell me he didn't care what anyone thought, that he was tired of the lying and sneaking around, that he'd do anything to be with me. But he was right; the truth would only make things worse right now. If we could just get through the rest of the show, win or lose, we might be able to have a real future together when this was all over.

"All right." I stared out the window at downtown LA sparkling with lights, at the Hollywood sign cresting the hills, at anything other than his pleading eyes and the lips I longed to kiss.

He cleared his throat. "Maybe you should go out with that Sean guy, too."

"You want me to date someone else?" I'd spent the night in his arms, and now he was pushing me toward some other guy?

"No, of course not." He drew a ragged breath. "I can't stand the idea of you with him. I just think it might throw people off, make them less focused on the two of us."

Maybe or maybe it would just fuel the slut rumors about me. I didn't want to lead Sean on, but I supposed one dinner couldn't hurt, as long as I was up front with him about only wanting to be friends. But Jared would have to keep up his reputation, too, and the thought made me sick.

"Fine." *Only two weeks*, I reminded myself. I could do anything for two weeks.

"I'll see you at rehearsal tomorrow." He hesitated and leaned in a little, like he was about to kiss me. I held still, waiting, wanting, anticipating, but he pulled back and slipped out the door without another word.

I wrapped my arms around myself and went over his words again. No matter what he said, I couldn't help but wonder if this was more than a temporary split. Suddenly our secret romance seemed a lot less sexy and a lot more like a mistake.

CHAPTER NINETEEN

At the crack of dawn, we went on a national radio show and assured everyone that the photo was just an innocent moment of one friend comforting another. The entire band laughed off the bad headlines, acting like everything was normal, but I didn't know if anyone would buy it. Especially when the fracture in my heart got wider every time I looked at Jared.

After that we went straight to rehearsals, and I suffered for hours hearing him sing "Bad Romance," followed by a photo shoot with The Quiet Battles where we pretended to be one big happy family on Team Dan. When I finally collapsed into bed, I was too exhausted to stay up all night missing Jared, though I couldn't shake his ghost from my sheets.

The next two days were a repeat, with different publicity events and long hours rehearsing and recording both songs while the producers and camera crews watched us like hawks. Being on a break with Jared was easier than I'd expected since we never had a free minute alone together. Hell, if we got a chance to sit down and eat a real meal, we were lucky. Was this how musicians on tour lived? Sprinting from one thing to the next, pushing their bodies to the limits, giving up a normal life for one in the spotlight…. I almost questioned if I really wanted it that bad. Almost.

"We have a problem," Dan said on Saturday morning when he showed up for rehearsal. "I just talked to Steve, and he said the producers have changed their minds about 'Bad Romance.' Now they're saying you can't use it after all and have to choose something else."

"What?" I must have misunderstood him. No way could we have worked on this song for all those hours and now be unable to use it. Not with only two days until the live show. Nope. Not happening. Denied.

Jared gripped his bass so hard his knuckles went white. "But we've been practicing it all week. And we've already recorded it!"

"Did Steve say why?" Kyle asked. "Is there anything we can do to change the producers' minds?"

Dan shook his head. "He just said there was a problem, and

no one can use that song anymore. It really blows, but they've done this before in previous seasons. I'm bummed, too. Your version sounded great."

"Shit. What are we supposed to do now?" Hector asked.

"How are we going to get another song ready by the live show?" I asked, breathless and jumpy, like the walls were closing around me.

Dan yanked over a chair and put on his reading glasses. "We'll pick another song right now, and I'll give you the keys to the studio so you can practice as much as you need. I'll cancel your interview tomorrow, too, so you can use that time to record the new song. I'm really sorry, but that's the best I can do."

He suggested we cover another pop song, something unexpected that we could do a rock version of, but none of us knew what to choose. We were still too excited by our version of "Bad Romance," too in love with the changes we'd made to think about any other song. With that thought, Carla's words came back to me about how I was so obsessed with Jared I couldn't think about another guy, and they sparked an idea. She adored Bruno Mars and I'd learned some of his songs to play for her, and I could definitely relate to one of them right now.

"What about 'Locked Out of Heaven' by Bruno Mars?" I suggested. The guitar in it sounded like something by The Police and I demonstrated for them, busting out the twangy chords from the verses and then the faster chorus riffs.

"That's a good one," Hector said. "It has almost a punk rock beat to it at times."

"Perfect," Dan said. "And the ladies at home will love Jared singing it, too."

Jared scowled, no doubt thinking of why I'd chosen this song. Maybe it was cruel, but I hoped every time Jared sang it he thought about me and what he was missing. He might have argued for a different song, but Kyle and Hector loved it. Dan got it quickly approved by the producers, and it was decided.

We worked late into the night and returned early Sunday for another long day, rehearsing in the morning and recording in the afternoon. By the evening, we all wanted to kill each other.

"The vocals in the second verse are still not right," Jared said, as we listened to the recording for the hundredth time. "I need to redo them."

"They're *fine*," Kyle said. "We don't have time to do them over."

The sound guys were taking a break, and Dan had left an hour ago. I rested my head on the table, too tired to move. When you played the same song nonstop for that many hours, it became like a word you'd repeated too many times: It didn't make sense anymore. That's the point we were at.

Jared continued on as if he hadn't heard his brother. "And the beat in the pre-chorus is off, too."

"Are you kidding me?" Hector asked. "I've recorded it three times already!"

"Well, do it again. We need to get this right."

"There's nothing wrong with it!"

Jared played the section again. "Right there! How can you not hear that?"

"Why don't you go in there and play it then?"

"Maybe I will!"

"Right, because this is the Jared Cross band, and you can do *everything*!"

"You want to trade places? You think it's so easy, getting in front of thousands of people and baring your soul on stage? Or answering the same stupid questions over and over again in interviews? Please, be my guest!"

"Guys, stop," Kyle said, raising his hands between them. "We need to call it a night."

"Seriously," I said. "We've been here since 7 AM. I can barely see straight, I'm starving, and my hands are killing me." Not to mention, this was starting to get ugly. Hector and Jared often bickered and then quickly made up, but never quite like this.

Jared rubbed his face, visibly exhausted. "No, the song isn't done until it's perfect. You can leave if you want, but I'm staying."

I had no doubt he would, too. Jared was not only a perfectionist, but he was hardest on himself. If we didn't stop him, he would work on this all night, and then he'd be a wreck at the live show.

"Jared, please." I placed my hand on his shoulder. "The song sounds great. If we stay any longer, we won't have any energy to perform tomorrow."

"She's right," Kyle said. "Your voice already sounds like you've been swallowing glass. You need to rest more than any of us."

"One more hour," Jared said. "Let me tweak a few things, and then I'll be done."

"Whatever, I'm out," Hector said and banged through the door. So much for our band's "cohesion."

I sighed, resigning myself to a long night in this cold, stuffy room. "I wonder if there are any more of those sandwiches in the kitchen."

"I already checked. There aren't," Kyle said. "Go get something to eat. I'll stay with him."

I hesitated. I didn't want to abandon them, but Jared had already put his headphones back on and was in the zone again, and there wasn't much I could do at this point. All my parts were recorded, and I didn't have the energy to do them over another time. Kyle had studied sound mixing in school, so he was more of a pro at this stuff than me anyway. Besides, Kyle knew how to handle his brother better than anyone.

"All right, but I'm going to check on you both later to make sure you get some rest. Don't let him burn himself out."

"I won't." Kyle gave me a quick squeeze, and I left. Jared never even looked up.

Sean ran over to me the instant I walked into the lobby of the hotel. "Maddie!"

"Hey," I said, with as much enthusiasm as I could muster. Naturally I'd run into him when I hadn't slept, showered, or eaten anything other than coffee and bagels over the last forty-eight hours.

"I saw that whole thing with the photo. I can't believe what people said about you. Are you all right?"

"Oh, yeah. It's just a big misunderstanding." I hadn't even had time to think about that drama, not with the new drama of the song change, but his words reminded me I was supposed to go out with him. I wanted nothing more than to pass out in my bed, but eating real food sounded pretty good at this point, too. And maybe Jared was right, and being seen with Sean would dispel some of the rumors about us.

"Hey, do you want to grab that dinner I promised you?" I asked.

"Yeah, totally. Right now?"

"If you're free," I said, and he nodded. "But before we go, I want to be up front with you, so this doesn't get weird. We're just going out as friends, okay?"

"Of course." He burst into laughter. "Oh, did you think I was asking you out on a date before?"

"No! I mean, I wasn't sure, and I think you're great and all, but with the show and..." This was getting super awkward. Time to shut up.

He grinned. "Hey, I'd totally be interested, but I have a girlfriend back home."

"Oh, okay. Good." It was a relief to know I wouldn't be leading Sean on and that he didn't expect anything from me other than a friendly dinner.

"Besides, Jared would kill me," Sean added.

"I doubt that," I muttered.

"You're really not together?"

"Nope." And this time, it felt like the truth when I said it.

We went through the revolving doors and debated the merits of the different restaurants at LA Live, finally settling on a brewery that blasted rock music and had good burgers. Perfect for a casual dinner with a friend, and since it was popular with people from the show, we'd definitely be seen together. A part of me hoped Jared would stumble back from the studio and catch me with Sean, run to my arms and kiss me in front of everyone, and say he didn't care who knew about us as long as we could be together. Yes, that level of cheese actually ran through my head. What could I say—I was running on four hours of sleep.

Though Jared never showed up to offer declarations of love, I still had a good time with Sean. We laughed about what a bad mentor Angel was, and he told me she'd shown up completely wasted for all her rehearsals this week.

"I have no idea how our song with her is going to go tomorrow," he admitted.

I whined about how the producers had changed our song at the last minute, but he didn't seem surprised. He said they'd denied his band from doing "Some Nights" by fun. for the first live show and that he'd heard about bands having other problems, too. Recording times getting switched without notice, interviews getting cancelled at the last minute, photo shoots that just never happened. We were lucky we had Dan keeping on top of these things for us, but it sounded like the other mentors weren't quite as hands-on.

Sean and I argued over which band on Team Lance would make it to the finals, since it was obvious Fairy Lights would be the last band on Team Lissa. I told him all about how Lacey had stolen my glasses and probably leaked that photo of us, but I wasn't sure he believed me. She'd been perfectly friendly with him, so maybe it was only me she hated for some reason.

Being with Sean was easy, and there was no need to sneak around or lie to anyone about spending time together. I had zero romantic feelings for him, but it was a relief to talk to someone going through a lot of the same things I was. I hadn't realized how much I needed to spend time with someone who wasn't in my band either. I loved the guys like family, but after spending every waking minute with them, I also kind of never wanted to see them again.

After our meal, we walked back toward the hotel but were stopped by a small group of people.

"Oh my god, you're the guitarist who fell off the stage!" one of them said, and the others chimed in with, "Yeah!" and "Whoa!"

I was taken aback for a second. No one had ever recognized me in public before; it was always Jared who got mobbed by fans. Would they call me a klutz? A slut, especially since I was with Sean? Or one of the other horrible things people were saying on the Internet?

"You're so cool," the first girl said. "I freaking love Villain Complex."

"Me too," the guy with them said. "Your band is killer."

"Can we get a photo with you?" a third girl asked.

"Um, yeah. Of course." That was not what I'd been expecting to hear. I wasn't anyone special, and these people acted like I was a celebrity. I couldn't wrap my head around it. But Jared was always friendly with the fans, and I needed to follow his example even if the whole experience was really strange.

They each gave their phones to Sean to have him take photos of us. I hoped he wasn't upset that they didn't seem to have a clue who he was. I posed with the group, smiling for a dozen shots, and then signed random pieces of paper for them. I'd never signed anything for someone in my life before that wasn't a legal document. It was amazing to meet real live fans of our band, but it was also a bit unsettling how they all acted like they knew me when they really didn't.

After they left, Sean said, "Wow, you're really famous now."

"I guess?" I shook my head. "That's never happened before."

"Clearly I need to cause some sort of drama, too, to bring in more fans."

I laughed. "If you do, make sure you never Google yourself. You can never unsee those things."

CHAPTER TWENTY

On the day of the live show, my nerves were so frayed I was barely hanging together. I hadn't been this anxious about a performance since the Battle of the Bands round. We'd practiced "Locked Out of Heaven" as much as we physically could, but it was still not as smooth as we'd like. We were at a disadvantage from the other bands who'd had all week with their songs, and even if we nailed it tonight, I didn't know how many people would vote for us after the photo disaster. Clearly, we still had fans who liked our band, but would they be enough?

Tonight we'd gone for a classier look to shake things up from our normal hard rock image. I wore a strapless, black-and-white sheath dress, while the guys all wore black suits, thin ties, and white shirts. Each of them looked striking, from Kyle with his black hair slicked back and tattoos peeking above his collar, to Hector with his dark curls and broad shoulders filling out his jacket. And then there was Jared, looking almost—but not quite—a gentleman tonight. His blue eyes had a touch of dark liner, his shirt was open just enough to give a glimpse of his neck, and his tailored pants showed off every perfect angle. He looked amazing in a suit, and it killed me that I couldn't have him.

Our Loaded River song with Dan was the first performance of the night. Our mentor played bass, and though he normally sang "Nothing Breaks Me," he only chimed in on the chorus and let Jared take over. Without an instrument, Jared was free to flirt with the crowd and make love to the mic, and it took all my effort to not throw my guitar down and drag him off stage so we could be alone together. I knew what Jared looked like under those clothes, how his touch felt on my bare skin, how it sounded to hear him moan my name. Being so close and yet so far from him was pure torture.

I focused on the audience instead, and as they sang along with each word, I realized how lucky I was to be there, standing on stage with Dan Dorian of Loaded River. No matter what happened tonight, playing beside one of my idols would always be one of the greatest moments of my life.

After the song, Dan returned to his seat in front of the stage with the other mentors. We all glowed with sweat and excitement, like some of the dark clouds hanging over us had dissipated. Maybe, just maybe, we'd make it into the next round.

The guys went to the lounge to relax before our next song, but I needed to cool off away from Jared. On stage, The Static Klingons performed their song for the "Tainted Love" theme of the night, Gotye's "Somebody That I Used to Know." Sean's vocals and the band's faster tempo made it a bit more upbeat than the original version, but I liked it. I cheered for them with the audience and waited for Sean backstage when they finished.

"There you are!" he said. We moved out of the way of the roadies setting up for the next band, and a camera crew followed us. Never a private moment, not this close to the end of the show.

"That was so good," I said. "You're definitely getting into the finals."

"Thanks, Maddie."

He placed his hands on my shoulders and kissed me, right in front of the camera. For a second I could only stand there, so shocked by his soft lips on mine, while my mind screamed that it was all wrong.

I pushed him away and choked out, "What are you *doing*?"

He shot a glance at the camera crew. "What? I thought we had a great time last night."

Wait—had I not been clear that I only wanted to be friends?

I replayed our conversation in my head, and yeah, I'd been pretty damn clear. "You said it wasn't a date! You said you have a girlfriend!"

"I do, but…" His voice dropped, like he hoped the cameras wouldn't catch his words. "I thought if I kissed you I might get some extra attention for my band, get a few more votes, you know? And maybe make my girlfriend back home jealous at the same time. She, uh, didn't really approve of me going on the show."

"So you were *using* me? I can't believe you!" If I had something in my hands, I'd have thrown it at him. Maybe I could find something. A glass of water. One of my shoes. His guitar.

He ruffled his sandy hair, looking embarrassed. "I guess I thought you'd be okay with it."

"Why would you think that? Because of what everyone is saying about me?" Did he think I was a slut, too? Forget throwing something, now I wanted to punch him in the face.

"No! I don't know. Gah, I'm really sorry."

I shook my head and walked away without another word. Jared had been right about Sean all along. Even if the specifics had been wrong, Sean did have ulterior motives for spending time with me. Yes, technically I'd been using Sean, too, but he'd crossed the line by kissing me when I'd said I wasn't interested. And even worse, he'd made me the other woman against my will, just like my mom had been. If people thought I was a slut before, I couldn't imagine what they would call me now.

Jared stared at me from the other side of the revolving stage, where he must have seen everything. He disappeared into the crew unloading gear for the next performance, and I sprinted after him.

"Jared, stop!"

He halted, fists clenched at his side, and I caught up to him. His face was a blank mask, but pain flickered through the eyes I knew so well. I couldn't stand to see him like this, but there were too many people around to talk safely. I took his elbow and led him through the back of the theater to the out-of-the-way women's bathroom no one used, where I'd had my glasses stolen. We slipped inside, and I checked under the stalls to make sure they were empty and then locked the door.

Jared leaned over the sink, his head dipped down as he stared into the mirror. Under the dim fluorescent lights, he looked like a black-and-white photo—dark hair and smoldering eyes, white shirt and fair skin, black jacket and tie. I wished he would say something. I smoothed my hands down my dress to stop myself from reaching for him, fighting the invisible tether pulling me to him at all times.

"He kissed me against my will, I swear," I finally said to break the silence. "We went out last night, but I told him from the beginning it wasn't a date. Nothing happened."

He closed his eyes and drew a long breath but still didn't answer me, and a flicker of frustration made me continue.

"I don't know why I'm even explaining this to you. You're the one who wanted to cool things off until the show ended. *You* told me to go out with him. *You* flirt with other girls every single day. You have no right to be upset!"

He spun around to face me. "What do you want me to say, Maddie? That hearing you went out together makes me want to strangle him? That it nearly killed me to watch him kiss you? That every time I see you, I want to fuck you until you forget all other guys?" He spread his arms wide. "There, are you happy now?"

The passion behind his words nearly undid me. I slipped my fingers around his black tie to pull him to me. "Yes, that's exactly what I wanted to hear."

Our mouths and bodies crashed together, and after being denied Jared for days, his kiss started a riot within me. I dragged my teeth along his bottom lip and scraped them across his neck, making him gasp. His fingers tightened in my hair, tugging my head back so he could return the favor. The other night we'd taken our time together, discovering and savoring each other's bodies, but not now. We only had a few stolen minutes before we had to perform again, and our kisses had a frenzied, reckless edge, two addicts desperate for their next hit after going through days of withdrawal.

I gripped the lapel of his suit and searched his eyes. "You said we should take a break."

"You know we have to," he said, before pressing his mouth to mine again.

"Then why are you kissing me?"

"Because I can't stop myself."

He bowed his head to show me, tasting the curve of my neck and my bare shoulders. I arched my back, and he flicked his tongue between my cleavage, darting inside the top of my dress. When I moaned, his lips brushed against my nipples, already straining through the thin fabric. There was too much clothing between us, but we didn't have time to remove them. We shouldn't even be doing this here, in the middle of a show, when so much was on the line, when the producers and everyone else were only a door away. But we couldn't stop ourselves either.

His hands slid under my dress and along my thighs. I reached for the front of his pants to free the top button, urging him on without words. With one quick movement, he lifted me onto the bathroom counter, putting me at exactly the right height. My knees parted to straddle his hips, and I drew him closer, fitting him against my body. He bent down to drag my panties off me and placed a rough kiss on the curve of each knee. I gasped and tangled my fingers in his hair while his lips burned higher up my legs, along the inside of my thighs. He pushed my dress up to my hips, spreading me wider, kissing me everywhere except where I needed him most.

Only when I whimpered his name did he finally press his mouth to my core. He teased and licked and sucked every inch of me, driving me crazy, darting his tongue inside me. His mouth devoured me, his expert strokes making my entire body weak, and I threw my head back and planted my hands on the counter to steady myself. It was too good, the pleasure too intense, but his strong hands held me in place so I couldn't move away. I strained toward him, never wanting it to end, and he brought me right to the brink. But then he pulled back, leaving my body a spark about to burst into flames.

"Jared, please." I was so painfully close. He couldn't leave me like this.

He moved up my body again, mouth nuzzling against my neck, hands sliding along my waist. A condom wrapper crinkled, and then I felt him, hard and smooth against my sensitive skin. With one smooth thrust, he was inside me, and I groaned, digging my fingernails into him. As he drove into me, I wrapped my legs around him, my bare skin brushing against the back of his pants. I yanked open the collar of his shirt, needing more of his skin on mine, burying my face in his chest to breathe him in. No matter how close we were, I could never get enough of him.

He thrust in and out at a relentless, feral pace, like he was claiming me as his own. I was already so close, but he shifted angles to move deeper, making me cry out and completely lose control. I clenched around him as the orgasm ripped through me, but he didn't let up, pounding harder and faster, making the ripples of pleasure continue on and on. He gripped me tighter and moaned my name into my hair and then joined me in oblivion.

For a few minutes, we could only hang on to each other, hot and wet and shaking from the aftermath of our frenzy. When we could move again, he kissed me tenderly, stroking my cheek with his thumb.

"I missed you," he whispered.

I'd missed him too, so much. I sighed and pressed my forehead against his. "I don't want to go back out there."

"I know. But we have to."

Once we left this room, we'd have to turn off our feelings for each other again, put on our stage personalities and continue on like nothing had happened tonight. People were probably already wondering where we were, and our next performance was the most important one so far. As much as I wanted to stay with him, the charade had to continue.

I slid to the floor, and in silence, we fixed our clothes. We had another song to perform.

When I returned backstage, our gear had already been set up on the back of the revolving stage while Brazen played Maroon 5's "Wake Up Call" for the audience. One of the roadies rushed over to me with a horrified look on his face. "Maddie, there's an issue with your guitar."

I blinked at him. "What do you mean?"

He started to speak but then shook his head and gestured for me to follow him. There, inside my guitar case, was my beautiful sea foam green Fender, the one I'd bought with my own money when I went to college, the one I'd lovingly strummed every night in my room, the one I'd used for each performance on *The Sound*. It was the one instrument that was solely mine, and I knew every dent and chip on it. Only now its neck was snapped, too.

My mouth hung open, tears pricking my eyes, and I carefully lifted my guitar out of the case. The head dangled back, the wood completely splintered, held on only by the strings still attached. It was my baby, and now it was broken. Unplayable. Dead.

"It was like this when I opened the case, I swear," the roadie said, his words hushed. He knew how bad this was. "The other guys can vouch for me."

I clutched the guitar against my chest and sank to the floor, choking back a sob. I'd played it less than an hour ago, so someone must have done this while I was with Jared. If only we hadn't sneaked off...but how could we ever imagine this would happen? And who would do such a thing? We were all musicians here, our instruments were practically sacred to us.

"Maddie, what—" Kyle asked and then kneeled beside me. "Oh, shit. What happened?"

I held it out to him, unable to form words. He took one look and gathered me in his arms. I cried against his shoulder, and he just held me on the floor without saying anything. That guitar had become an extension of my body after so many hours playing it, and a part of me had been destroyed with it. And with only minutes before our next performance, we were screwed.

"Kyle, what am I going to do? The song—"

"It's okay. We'll get you another guitar."

"Where?" I gave a bitter laugh. "Who would let me use their guitar?" The only person I'd feel comfortable asking was Sean, except that was out of the question now.

"Maybe the show has one you can use?"

"It won't be the same, I won't know the guitar, and we've barely practiced this song as it is, and oh god, we're doomed. We're going home now, I know it."

Jared and Hector showed up, and Kyle and the roadie explained what had happened while I tried to pull myself together. Lacey must have done this. She'd stolen my glasses and leaked the photo, and now she'd broken my guitar, too. I knew she hated me for some inexplicable reason, but I still couldn't imagine she'd stoop so low. But I couldn't think of anyone else who would do this either.

While the guys argued about what to do, I rose to my feet, set my guitar back in its case, and stormed off. After a quick search, I found Lacey in makeup, wearing a poofy red dress and cowboy boots. One look at my face and the guy touching up her lipstick split. Lacey, to her credit, stood her ground.

"Why did you do it?" I asked, hands clenched at my sides.

"Pardon?" she asked.

"You broke my guitar. How *could* you?"

Her big blue eyes widened a fraction. "Your guitar is broken?"

"Don't play innocent. I know you did it!"

"Honey, I would *never* lay a hand on another girl's guitar. Not in a million years. I'd sooner steal your wallet or kiss your man."

"Is *that* what this is about? That time Jared turned you down in the elevator?"

Her nostrils flared a little. "I didn't touch your guitar, but maybe this is a lesson that you should keep an eye on your things instead of making out with every guy on the show."

It took all my control not to murder her right there under the vanity lights. "So you admit you stole my glasses?"

"I borrowed them for a few minutes." She gave a little shrug. "Just a bit of harmless fun between competitors, that's all."

"And the photo? Was that you, too?"

"Sorry, but no. Though I'm flattered you think I care that much."

My gaze swept over her for any hint she'd broken my guitar—chips of wood in her clothes, a broken fingernail, a bit of sea foam green paint—but there was nothing. I didn't want to believe her because that meant someone else was intentionally sabotaging me and the band, but unfortunately, I did. She'd been surprised when I'd mentioned my guitar, and no matter how horrible she was, I truly didn't think she would do something like this.

"Shouldn't you be on stage now?" she asked, twirling one of her blonde ringlets.

Did it matter? Without a guitar, we wouldn't be able to do the song. And even if we could find another guitar, I was too rattled to perform. The show might as well send us home right now.

Back at the revolving stage, Kyle and Hector were arguing with Steve, but I didn't see Jared anywhere. No one was performing up front, which was a bad sign. They'd probably had to cut to commercials or something to delay, but that would only give us a few minutes before it was do or die.

Dan rushed to my side. He never came backstage during the live shows, so this must be really serious. "Maddie, I'm so sorry. This has never happened before, but we're going to get to the bottom of this, I swear."

"Thanks," I said with a sigh. "Is there a guitar I can borrow for the song?"

"We can get you a Gibson, I know it's not the same, but—"

"No need," Jared said behind me, sounding out of breath. Sweat beaded across his forehead, his suit jacket was missing, his tie hung on for dear life, but he held his guitar case at his side and he'd never looked more handsome in his life.

"Did you go to the hotel?" I asked.

"Yeah. I figured this was better than some guitar you didn't know." No wonder he was out of breath. He'd gotten back so quickly that he must have run the entire way. Without even asking, he'd instantly jumped into action and known exactly what I'd need to get through this next performance.

He popped open the case and handed me his guitar. His black Fender was nearly identical to mine in weight and shape and felt almost as natural on my shoulder as my own guitar did. Plus, I'd already played it twice before.

"Thank you." I placed my hand over his for a brief moment, and when he gave me his real smile, it hit me: I was in love with him. And not like before, when I'd loved the idea of Jared, the tattooed rock star who could have any woman he wanted. Now I was in love with the *real* Jared, who sang to me in public, raced through supermarkets with his brother, and had a different villain T-shirt for every day of the week. Somehow that made everything worse because I had no idea if he felt the same for me, and either way, I still couldn't be with him. *One more week*, I reminded myself.

"Good thinking," Dan said, bringing me back to the moment. "Now get out there and win this thing."

The four of us looked a bit ragged, our hair and clothes messy like we'd just had sex (for good reason), but that worked perfectly for "Locked Out of Heaven." Jared made every girl in the audience swoon with his sultry vocals, and I stalked across the stage, my feelings for him making it all too easy to connect with the emotion in the song. It wasn't our best performance, but it was still pretty damn good. I just prayed it was good enough to get us into the finals.

CHAPTER TWENTY-ONE

The results show was the longest hour of my life. In between performances from some of the previous seasons' winners (minus the band that had caused so much trouble, Addicted to Chaos, of course), the different teams were called up for eliminations. Team Angel was first, and everyone was shocked when The Static Klingons were sent home. I wasn't that sad to see Sean go, though The Static Klingons were a lot more talented than the remaining band on Angel's team, Not Too Calm. The show hadn't aired our kiss last night, thank god, so I'd never know if it would have helped Sean's band get more votes or not.

And frankly, I didn't care.

Fairy Lights was picked for Team Lissa, of course, and Lacey blew kisses at the audience when she strolled off stage. I still wanted to strangle her a little, but I knew in my gut she hadn't broken my guitar. It was back in Dan's studio now, but I had no idea if it was fixable. Not only had the producers been unable to find who had done it, they'd said it wasn't their responsibility to pay for the repairs, even though it happened while my guitar was in the show's care. Dan knew a guy who would look at it, but I wasn't optimistic. It would be expensive to repair, enough that I could buy a new guitar for the same price or less—but that was *my* guitar. I *had* to get it fixed.

Brazen won the final spot on Team Lance, and then it was Team Dan's turn. We stood on stage with the many members of The Quiet Battles (I finally counted them—eleven!), and I rocked back and forth on my heels, unable to stop moving. Kyle linked his arm with mine, probably to get me to stay still, but then we dragged the other guys in, too. *Please, please, please,* I chanted in my head as the band clung to each other. We couldn't go home now, not when we were so close to the end.

"And the band representing Team Dan in the finals is…" Ray Carter opened his envelope at sloth speed. "Villain Complex!"

The audience roared and lights flashed around us. Did Ray really say our name? Oh my god! We were in the finals! The four of us exploded with a burst of jumping, hugging, and laughing. We'd made it, we were going on tour, and we were one step closer to winning the record deal. My arms were shaking, and I could barely catch my breath. I wanted to let out a happy scream and kiss the guys and tell them I loved them. Hell, I loved everyone in the entire theater right now. And when Jared picked me up and spun me around, I grabbed his face and kissed him.

He stepped back, yanking his hands off me like he'd been burned. "What the hell, Maddie?"

Behind him, Kyle and Hector both stared at us like they weren't sure what they'd just seen. Oh god, what had I done? I hadn't meant to kiss him, I'd just been so caught up in everything, and with his arms around me, my body had taken over and done what felt natural.

"Wow, that was some reaction," Ray said. "We'll talk to Villain Complex in a minute. Let's give a hand to The Quiet Battles, who did a great job, too. We'll miss them."

We hugged the other band and said, "Good luck," but the entire time I was thinking about how I'd just kissed Jared in front of all of America. The show rushed us straight into an interview with Ray, so we didn't even get a chance to talk about what had happened before we were back on camera.

"Congrats on making it into the finals," Ray said. "Are you surprised you made it this far?"

"Definitely," Jared said, perfectly calm and collected again. "I mean, we hoped we would, but we never expected this to happen. We're so thankful for our fans who voted for us and downloaded our songs. We wouldn't have made it to the finals without them."

"Well, it's definitely well-deserved. 'Locked Out of Heaven' was a great song choice." He leaned a little closer to Jared, like he was going to let him in on a secret. "But there's something we have to discuss or the fans will kill me. That kiss." The crowd screamed, and I realized this interview was being shown on TV right now and on screens above the stage. "Now be honest—is there something going on between the two of you?"

Here it was. The moment it would all come out. I found myself strangely relieved. No more secrets, no more lies, no more sneaking around. After we came clean, this thing between us could finally be real.

"No, we're not a couple." Jared said, without any hesitation. He even gave a little laugh. "I was just as shocked as you when she kissed me."

"Maddie? Any response?" Ray shoved the mic in my face, but I could only stare at Jared with my mouth open. Was he really going to keep pretending? Even though our kiss had been live on TV in front of millions of people?

When I didn't answer, Ray turned back to Jared, ignoring Kyle and Hector like usual. "Everyone saw that photo of the two of you together, and now the kiss—but you're still saying you're *not* a couple?"

"No, I'm very single." He gave the camera a little shrug. "I can't help it if Maddie is into me though."

"You do have a reputation of being a ladies' man…"

I couldn't take it anymore. I walked away, not caring that my sudden exit was on camera or that everyone backstage was staring at me. The instinct to flee took over, and I shoved the back door open, stomped past the roadies on their smoke breaks, and ducked around the corner of the theater for some privacy. Only when I was out of sight did I lean against the wall and take big, gasping breaths of cold night air.

How dare he act like our relationship was all one-sided, like I was some groupie obsessed with him, following him around and begging him to love me. He'd been the one who had kissed me first, after all. The other night he'd held me in his arms and told me I was the only one he wanted, yet he still wouldn't admit to being with me. No matter what he said to me in private, he would continue to tell the world he was single and flirt with every girl in sight. I thought I'd uncovered the real Jared, the one behind the stage smile and the player reputation, but that was all a lie. Maybe Kyle had been right all along; Jared didn't want a serious relationship and this was a way for him to keep his options open while sleeping with me. He was just like my father, living two different lives, destroying everything with his secrets and lies.

"I think she went out here," Hector said, around the corner.

I stiffened, straining to hear if they were coming closer. There was nowhere for me to escape, and I didn't want to talk to any of them at the moment.

"Leave her. She needs some time to cool off."

Thank you, Kyle.

"This is what she does," Jared said. "She runs away when she's upset."

"You *are* together," Hector said. "I knew it!"

"No—"

"Then what was that back there?" Kyle interrupted, his voice quiet but sharp as a blade.

"I don't know. *She* kissed me. Why don't you ask her?"

"I don't need to ask her. It was written all over her face when she walked off!"

"It's nothing, I swear. Can we let it go already?"

"Stop lying to us!" Kyle suddenly yelled. I'd never heard him yell before, and it made me jump. Kyle *never* got upset. He was always the one who kept the peace, who calmed the other guys down, but not tonight.

"Fine, we hooked up!" Jared said. "Happy?"

"I fucking knew it!" Hector said. "First Becca and now Maddie!"

"This is *nothing* like what happened with Becca!"

"No? You slept with her and then dumped her, nearly breaking up the band in the process. How is this *any* different?"

Wow, when Hector put it like that, it was obvious I really had become a copy of Becca. Despite what Jared had said, he hadn't changed one bit.

"How could you do this?" Kyle yelled. "She's my *friend!*"

Jared said nothing in response. I peered around the corner

and saw him staring at the street, head down and hands shoved in pockets, while his brother raged at him.

"I knew this would happen! Why do you think I didn't introduce you to Maddie for *three* years? Girls throw themselves at you every day, but no, you had to go after the *one* girl I said was off-limits! And it's my fault, too, because I knew Maddie was into you from day one, and I *still* let her join the band!"

I hadn't realized Kyle had kept me away from his brother for so long. I assumed we'd just been school-only friends who didn't really move in the same crowd. When we did hang out, it was always on campus or in a coffee shop or something. Once I thought about it, it made perfect sense. It must be tough having Jared as your brother sometimes. And I'd done the one thing I'd promised Kyle I would never do: fall for his brother.

"I said from the very beginning this was a bad idea," Hector said. "Not because of Maddie, but because of your inability to keep your dick in your pants. And the worst part is, you went behind our backs and lied to us for *weeks!*"

Jared finally spoke up again. "Only because we knew you guys would be pissed, and with Dan's talk about the producers and—"

"Don't give us that shit!" Hector shouted. "We're supposed to be a team! This isn't the Jared Cross band, despite what the show thinks, and you don't get to make decisions for all of us!"

"I'm sorry, okay?" Jared replied, his voice strained. "The whole thing was a mistake, and if I could go back and redo it, I would."

Was that how he really felt? It was all clear now. I was nothing more than a mistake, another notch in his bedpost he'd like to erase, another girl whose heart he'd broken. I squeezed my eyes shut, but a tear trickled down my face anyway and I swiped it away.

"I can't even look at you right now," Kyle said. "I'm going inside."

"Great, now we'll have to find *another* guitarist or bassist," Hector muttered.

"I know," Kyle said, as they went through the door.

I covered my mouth to hold back a cry. They were already talking about replacing me. I was going to be kicked out of the band, and the life I'd come to love would be gone forever. Jared was right—this had all been a mistake.

I waited a few more minutes in the hope I could escape to the hotel without running into any of them. But when I rounded the corner, Jared was still there, holding onto the chain-link fence and staring at the street.

He heard my footsteps and turned, face falling when he saw me. "Maddie…did you hear all that?"

"When you called me a mistake? Yeah, I heard it." I'd wiped away my tears, but my eyes watered all over again. No, I would not cry in front of him. I refused.

He sighed. "I didn't mean it like that. And what I said to Ray in there, that was all part of the act, you *know* that. We both agreed we had to do this."

"But when will the act end?" I asked. "When the show is over? What about the tour? What if we win? When will I be good enough to not be a secret anymore?"

"It's not like that! The show—"

"It's *always* the show or the band or some other excuse! How am I supposed to believe anything you say? You had no problem lying to your brother and your best friend for weeks. As far as I know, everything you told me is a lie, too, and you just don't want to give up your infamous player lifestyle!"

He stepped back, like I'd punched him in the chest. "Wow. I thought you saw the real me, but I guess I was wrong. I've been with no one else since I met you. No one!"

"So tell everyone right now that you lied, that you do care about me, that we do have something between us. Tell the whole world we're together, and I'll believe you."

He was quiet for a moment and then said, "You know I can't do that."

"Then I have nothing else to say to you." I started to walk away, but he moved to block my path, pleading with his eyes for me to listen.

"Maddie, you don't understand. This band is my *entire* life. It's all I have. If we fail, you and Kyle will go back to school and on to other things, and Hector has his graphic novels and his art. Me? I'm a fucking bartender. Oh, wait, I'm not even that anymore because I quit my job to come on the show. I put everything I have, everything I *am*, into this band. We have to win, or all of that is for nothing."

"How can you say the band is all you have? Even if we lose the show, you're talented, and you have money and connections. You have a brother who would do anything for you, you have a best friend who sticks beside you no matter what…and you have *me*. Isn't that enough?"

"That's not what I meant," he said, tearing at his hair. "Music is the only thing I've ever been good at, and if I don't succeed at that, I'll have nothing, I'll *be* nothing. I thought you, of all people, would understand that. And if I have to pretend I'm single and that I'll sleep with every girl in the world to keep people voting for us, to keep them coming to our shows and buying our albums, then that's what I'll do."

I did understand, on some level, because that same passion for music and that same drive to succeed urged me on, too. But Jared's words made it clear that this would never stop. Not even when the show ended because there would always be something else: the tour, the album, future shows. As long as we were *this* band, with Jared's "villain" image, we could never be together.

"I love you, Jared," I said, my voice breaking. "But I can't do this anymore. I can't pretend we're just friends and sneak around and watch you flirt with other girls. I just can't. And you're wrong—people will buy our albums and come to our shows because they like our music, not because of your stupid reputation. But if this is what you think the band needs, then I'm done and this is over." The words were torn from my chest, burning my throat on the way out, but I couldn't stop them.

His mouth fell open, but he didn't answer. I supposed his silence *was* my answer. I darted around him as the tears burst free. I couldn't look at him, couldn't be near him, couldn't hear another word from his mouth. I'd bared my heart to him, and he had nothing to say in return.

"Maddie, wait!" he called. But it was too late, and I was already through the door. Because that's what I always did when life got to be too much for me: I ran.

I dashed inside the theater, tearing past the roadies and other bands, heading for the exit so I could return to my hotel room and sob my heart out in private. But before I could get to the door, I bumped into Steve.

"Maddie, everything okay?" he asked.

I wiped at my eyes but couldn't answer him. No, everything was very much not okay. I'd just lost everything, and I didn't know what to do now.

"Let's talk somewhere private." He led me to his office, with a desk and a computer and a mountain of paperwork. I didn't know what he wanted, but at least there was no one watching me here.

He sat in his desk chair and gestured for me to sit. "I saw the interview, and I heard the band had a big fight outside. If there's a problem, I can try to help."

I sank into one of the chairs. How could he help me? He couldn't fix things with Jared or the band. God, how was I supposed to face any of the guys again after tonight? They'd already been talking about replacing me. I'd turned out to be exactly what Hector predicted, and even worse, I'd probably destroyed my friendship with Kyle in the process. And Jared…I couldn't even think about Jared right now.

I dropped my head. "I just…I can't do this anymore."

"I completely understand. You've been through a lot. This can't be easy for you." He folded his hands on the table. "We don't usually do this, but in light of everything that's happened, maybe it would be a good idea for you to leave the show." My eyes widened, and he quickly added, "I'm not saying we're kicking you off or anything, don't worry. Just that if you felt you had to leave, we wouldn't stop you."

Would they really let me leave? It was tempting, more tempting than I wanted to admit. Being on the show for weeks, trying to keep up a certain image while putting everything into the band and our performances, only to have it all fall apart tonight…. I was just exhausted. I wanted to go home and sleep for the rest of the summer.

"What about the contract? It says I have to stay for the duration of the show."

"It has a provision that band members can leave in emergency situations. Say, if they're injured or ill or if a family member passes away, things like that. This doesn't technically qualify, but I'm willing to bend the rules a tiny bit. We don't want you to be miserable, after all."

"But what will happen to the band? Who will play guitar for them?" Even if the guys were mad at me, I didn't want to screw them over.

"We'll find someone to fill in for you, don't worry." He gave me a sympathetic smile. "Trust me, they'll be fine. Let me handle everything. And if you change your mind and want to come back, that's okay, too."

I didn't *want* to leave, but I couldn't continue in the band either. That was clear after everything Jared and the other guys had said. Maybe the best option *was* for me to go home. Besides, it sounded like they would be okay without me. They could still win the show, and they could find a new bassist when they were ready, one who wouldn't sleep with Jared and ruin everything.

I made my decision, and that night I packed my bags and left the hotel for good.

CHAPTER TWENTY-TWO

My apartment was empty when I returned, and the mail had piled up. Julie and Carla must both be out of town again. They'd probably told me at some point, but I'd been a terrible friend to them. We'd barely spoken more than a few words in weeks, and when we had, I'd lied to them.

I'd lost myself in the show, in Jared, in the impossible dream and the beautiful lie. No more. Rock Star Maddie had been a total failure. Time to return to Normal Maddie. I'd been a fool, thinking I could be anything more than that. I'd been perfectly happy with my life and my plans for the future until Jared had invited me to join his band and gotten me off-track. He'd tempted me to want a louder life, one where he and I could be together, but we'd been doomed from the start. That life was over, and now I remembered who I really was: the geeky piano player who dated safe guys, practiced guitar in secret, and watched from the sidelines while others went after their dreams.

Maybe if I begged the LA Philharmonic, I could get my internship back for the rest of the summer. No, that would be impossible. But there were plenty of other things I could do until school started. I had enough laundry to last a lifetime. I could start applying to graduate schools. I could lie in bed all day and get really, really drunk.

Guess which one of those I did.

The less that's said of the next few days, the better. I turned off my phone so I wouldn't have to deal with the outside world at all. I raided our alcohol supply and forgot about personal hygiene entirely. I ate nothing but ramen and ice cream and watched a ton of Netflix.

In my darkest moments, I watched videos of us performing on the show and cried about how I'd never be on stage with the guys again. In my rush to leave the show, I'd left my guitar at Dan's studio, not that it mattered since it was broken anyway. Besides, it held too many memories now. It would be a long time before I could touch a guitar again.

I tried to watch some of the interviews we'd done, but all I heard were our lies and all I saw was Jared's fake stage smile.

Even worse, someone had recorded the entire fight between the two of us with their phone and posted it online. One of the roadies, it had to be. I watched it over and over, alternating between regretting everything I'd said to Jared and getting angry at him all over again. This time I didn't read the comments under the video though. I'd learned my lesson on that at least.

But the videos that hurt the most, and the ones I watched a thousand times, were the ones capturing behind-the-scenes moments of all of us. The guys joking around in rehearsal, being silly on our breaks, wrestling and grabbing each other for goofy man-hugs. That time when we'd switched instruments and I'd banged on Hector's drums. Dan coaching me on my stage presence and my wardrobe.

And Jared—laughing at something Kyle had said or bent over his bass with a look of concentration or practicing the same lyric a hundred different ways to get it right. Those videos were the only ones that showed the genuine Jared, and I couldn't stop torturing myself with them. I missed the way his true smile lit up his face, the way his real laugh burst out of him like it was a surprise every time. But I doubted I'd ever see that Jared again.

I heard one of the girls wheel her suitcase into the apartment, but I couldn't get out of bed. What was the point? Besides, moving sounded like a lot of effort, and my head pounded like someone was kicking me in the skull over and over. Last night I'd discovered a secret stash of vodka in the kitchen and might have gone a little overboard. Not that it mattered, since I had nowhere to be anyway.

"Maddie?" Julie called.

"Here," I replied. Ow, too loud, so much pain.

"Why are you here? Isn't there a week of the show left?" Her voice got closer as she moved through the apartment. "Hey, since you're home, I need you to try on your Harley Quinn costume so I can do the final adjustments. Comic-Con is only in two weeks. Can you believe it?"

I covered my face with a pillow and groaned. I couldn't wear that costume now; it would only remind me of Jared. Not to mention, I was never getting out of bed again.

"Maddie?" She knocked on my door. "Can I come in?"

I gave a noise that sounded like "unngghh," and she opened the door and sat beside me on the bed.

"Wow, you reek. Have you been drinking?"

I moaned under the pillow. "I'm never touching vodka ever again."

"Hang on." She left and returned a few minutes later with some water and pain meds. "Take these."

I did as she said and then closed my eyes, leaning back against the headboard. Julie smelled faintly of vanilla, and her familiar scent gave me a small amount of comfort. She'd been my best friend since we were in eighth grade, but I'd barely seen her this summer. I missed hanging out with her. I even missed her getting on my case all the time.

"What's going on?" she asked.

"Didn't you see the show?"

"No, I was flying back from Seoul. What happened?"

Oh, right. She'd been visiting her grandparents. I should have remembered that. Further proof I was the worst friend ever.

I sighed. "It's over. The show. The band. Jared. Everything."

"What? Tell me."

I spilled everything, and she listened without judging or interrupting, letting me vent and cry. When it was over and I'd let it all out, she wrapped me in a tight hug. "Maddie, I'm so sorry."

"I ruined everything," I said, grabbing a tissue and blowing my nose. "My place in the band, my friendship with Kyle, my relationship—or whatever it was—with Jared, and even things with you and Carla. I've ruined it all."

"Okay, now you're being silly. You definitely didn't ruin your friendship with us. We'll be friends forever, no matter where life takes us, so don't worry about that. And I'm sure Kyle feels the same, too."

"I guess." I pulled my knees up and rested my head on them.

"Maddie, you know I love you, but when things get hard, you always run away. You ran from your mom and her drinking, you ran from Jared when he invited you to join the band, and now you're running from this, too. Maybe it's time to stop running and fight for what you want."

"I don't know what I want."

"Don't give me that. You know *exactly* what you want." She stood up and moved to the door. "Think about it. I'm going to unpack, but I'm here if you need me. And take a shower. You're disgusting."

She closed the door behind her. I sat there, digesting her words, until my headache faded enough that I could move again. I took Julie's advice and got in the shower, and the hot water slowly washed off the gloom of the last few days. My god, what was I doing? I'd turned into my mother, staying in bed all day, drowning my life in a bottle, and giving up guitar because a guy had broken my heart. That wasn't me. I didn't want to become her. My life didn't have to be one big repeat of her mistakes.

What did I want? I wanted Jared, but I wasn't sure I could ever have him the way I wanted. But even if we could never be together, I wanted to be part of the band again. I wanted to be *myself* again—my true self, the one I'd uncovered these past few weeks, who went after her dreams, who played guitar blindfolded, who fell off the stage and got back up again.

I wanted to fight.

CHAPTER TWENTY-THREE

It was Saturday, which meant the live show was in two days, and if I wanted to perform with the guys, I had to patch things up with them and learn the new songs as soon as possible. I found them rehearsing at Dan's studio, but I couldn't face them all yet. I texted Kyle and asked him to meet in the room where The Quiet Battles used to rehearse.

When he walked in, he immediately grabbed me in one of his bear hugs. "Maddie, I'm so glad you came back."

"I'm sorry, Kyle," I said into his shoulder, fighting back tears. "For lying, for sneaking around behind your back, for breaking my promise, for quitting the band, for being the worst friend ever. For everything."

"It's okay. Did you get my messages?"

"Yeah. Eventually."

After I'd sobered up, I'd turned on my phone and found both texts and voicemails from Kyle, Hector, and Dan, all begging me to come back. There'd even been one from my mom, asking if I was okay. And four from Jared that I still couldn't face. I'm not sure I'd ever be able to listen to those. But I'd checked all the others and had slowly come back to the world.

Kyle sighed. "I was really mad at first, at both of you, and I couldn't believe you just left like that. But I don't blame you for what happened, and I'm over it now. And since you left, Jared's been a wreck. He spends every waking moment rehearsing this week's songs, even long after Hector and I are done for the day. On those rare moments he does take a break, he just listens to this one My Chemical Romance song over and over."

I sucked in a breath. I knew exactly which song Kyle meant: the song Jared had sung to me before the audition, the one he still referenced all the time. "Is it 'I'm Not Okay'?"

"That's the one, and I swear if I hear it one more time I'll shoot myself." He tugged at the gauges in his ear, like he was annoyed.

The door opened and I froze, worried it was Jared, but instead Hector slammed into me. It was like being hugged by a mountain, squeezed between his hard chest and his muscular arms. "Maddie!"

Hector had never hugged me before, except when we'd been celebrating our on-stage victories, not like Kyle and Jared who gave their hugs freely. I held him for a minute, my eyes watering up again. It seemed like the guys had missed me as much as I'd missed them.

He finally let me go. "Thank god you're back. I've been barely keeping this band together without you."

"It's true," Kyle said.

I laughed at the idea of Hector, of all people, keeping them together. "You're okay with me staying in the band?"

Hector grinned. "Hell yes. We need you."

My shoulders slumped with relief. "I wasn't sure after the other night..."

He groaned. "Jared said you heard all that. Listen, I didn't mean I *wanted* to replace you. I just assumed you'd leave like Becca did."

"And you were right."

"Yeah, but you came back."

Someone knocked on the door, and Kyle slipped out to talk to whoever it was, leaving me alone with Hector. Was Jared on the other side? I wasn't sure I could deal with him yet.

"I'm really sorry about everything that happened," I said.

"Don't worry about it." He grabbed a drumstick from the back of his pants and twirled it in his fingers. "You know, I wouldn't be in this band if not for Jared."

"Oh, yeah, he made you learn the drums in high school?" I remembered Jared saying that in our first interview for the show. Why was Hector bringing this up now?

"Sort of. He and Kyle were always playing music, and one day I tried out their drums and was hooked. I spent every day at their house after that, just so I could play with them. When we started the band, I was living with my grandmother and we didn't have much money, so Jared bought me a drum kit for my eighteenth birthday."

"Wow, that's a pretty big gift."

"It was nothing to him. Changed my life though. And you know their mom is this famous songwriter and their dad is a big shot lawyer for, like, every big musician out there, right? But Jared refuses to let them pull any strings for him. He said if we succeed, he wants it to be on our own, without any handouts. He wants to know we earned it. That's just the kind of guy he is."

A lot of things about Jared clicked into place. How hard he worked, how much he pushed himself, how he would do anything to make sure we won. Not that it excused his actions, but I understood him a tiny bit better. "Why are you telling me this?"

He rubbed the back of his neck. "I know I get on his case a lot and complain about this being 'his' band and all that, but I honestly couldn't do all the things he does for us. Jared makes me crazy sometimes, but he's also the best guy I know. Don't give up on him yet, okay?"

I wasn't sure how to answer that. I didn't *want* to give up on Jared, but I couldn't continue with things the way they were either.

The door opened, and Kyle returned. "That was Dan. He wants to know what's going on."

I drew a long breath and stood up straighter. "Well, I'm back, and I'm ready to rehearse. What songs are you working on this week?"

"The new one is 'Radioactive' by Imagine Dragons. Dan chose it because none of us could agree on anything after the results show."

"What's the theme?"

"No theme since it's the finals. We also have to play our song from the audition again."

I nodded. I hadn't practiced "Behind the Mask" in weeks, but that song was branded on my soul. I'd never forget how to play it. I didn't know "Radioactive," but I would learn the guitar for it by Monday even if I had to stay up all night tonight and tomorrow.

"Who's been playing guitar?" I asked. "Or did you get someone to play bass?"

The guys exchanged a look. "Jared's kind of doing both," Kyle said.

"What do you mean?"

"On Wednesday we all assumed you'd come back after you blew off some steam, so Jared learned the bass for the song. But by Friday, it was clear you were gone for good, and Jared switched to the guitar."

"He learned *both*?"

"Yep. And recorded both parts himself, too."

No wonder he was spending all his time here; he was doing the work of two musicians instead of one. "Didn't the show get someone to fill in for me?"

"They did, but the guy was terrible, and Jared flipped out and scared him off. Dan's been filling in as needed until we figured out what to do."

I hung my head. "I'm so sorry I bailed on you guys. I just went a little crazy, and I couldn't deal with anyone. But I won't abandon you again, I promise."

"Hey, we all lost ourselves a little that night," Hector said. "But that's over now."

"Have you talked to Jared at all?" Kyle asked me.

"No." I glanced at the door again. Jared must be in this studio somewhere, only a few walls separating us. "I'm not ready to face him yet. I know I'll have to, but I just need a little more time."

Kyle nodded. "I'll tell him what's going on. For today, why don't you practice in here while you learn the song?"

"That sounds good." At some point I'd have to talk to Jared, but no matter what happened with him, I was a part of this band and I deserved to be on the show with them. I wanted to be by their side whether we won or lost and for everything that came after.

By some miracle, my hotel room was still mine. I'd never checked out, but I'd assumed the producers would cancel it after I'd left. But Dan wouldn't let them give it up because he kept telling them I'd come back. Even after I'd walked away, he'd still believed in me.

I set my bags down and fell onto the bed I'd slept in for the last few weeks, and it felt as much like returning home as going back to my apartment. Except this room was much cleaner at the moment. I pulled out my acoustic guitar to play through "Behind the Mask" again so I wouldn't be rusty on Monday, but as soon as I picked off the first chord, someone knocked on my door. I knew who it was before I even opened it.

Jared was holding his guitar case, and today's villain shirt said, "Moriarty Was Real," from BBC's *Sherlock*. He had dark circles under his eyes and looked like he hadn't shaved in days, but he was still every bit as handsome as I remembered. You'd think after spending nearly every waking minute with him for weeks I'd be immune to the shock of his blue eyes, his perfect lips, his kissable neck, but no.

"Not okay?" he asked softly.

"Not okay." Very much not okay, especially now that he was here. "But I will be."

"Did you get my messages?"

"Yes, but…I couldn't listen to them."

He gave me a hesitant smile. "Probably for the best. They were pretty pathetic. There was a lot of groveling and begging. Some drunken singing. It wasn't pretty."

Now I wished I had listened to them. Maybe things would be different now. Or maybe I still wouldn't believe a thing he said. Jared was a master of words, of using his voice and looks to manipulate people, and I didn't need any more empty promises.

He looked past me into the room. "Can I come in?"

I nodded and stepped back, quickly putting distance between us. I didn't trust myself being so close to him. But he didn't move toward me; instead, he set his guitar case down on the bed, and I realized it wasn't his case—it was mine.

"What…" I held my breath and popped it open. My beautiful green guitar had been repaired, and you couldn't even tell it had been broken except for a small ring of lighter wood on the neck. I ran my hands over it, my eyes tearing up. My guitar was scarred, but it was whole again. Like me. "You got it fixed?"

"I wanted you to have your guitar, even if you didn't come back."

"Thank you." Jared knew how much this guitar meant, and my heart softened a tiny bit, knowing he'd done this for me. I closed my eyes and strummed a chord, enjoying the familiar weight in my arms. This must have cost a fortune, especially to have it done so quickly. "How much was it? I can repay you…"

Eventually. Somehow.

"No, definitely not."

"But—"

"Please, I want to do this for you. Let me try to be a hero for once."

I dropped my gaze. "All right."

He stood there a long moment, looking anywhere but at me, and our unspoken words hung between us. I felt like apologizing, but for what? For being honest about how I felt? I'd told him I loved him, and he'd let me walk away.

"I should go," he said, clearing his throat. "I just wanted to bring you that and to say I'm sorry for everything that happened and everything I said the other night."

"I'm sorry, too." Because I was, even if I wouldn't take back anything I'd said. I hated hurting him, but I couldn't let him keep hurting me either.

"I'm really happy you're back," he said. "And I know I might not be able to fix things between us, but I'm going to try."

I waited for him to say more, but he slipped out the door without another word. I wasn't sure how he planned to fix things. Nothing had changed between us since that night, even if he had gotten my guitar fixed. He obviously cared for me, at least a little, but that wasn't enough. He was still the guy who would do anything to win, who flirted with other girls, who flashed his stage smile for the audience and kept his real self hidden away. Maybe he wanted to fix things, but I refused to be his secret anymore.

CHAPTER TWENTY-FOUR

It was time. One last day of performances, with four bands competing for the prize: a contract with Mix It Up Records, plus all the opportunities that came with it. Spots on late night talk shows. Songs on the radio. Performances on future seasons of *The Sound*. Plus, the headlining spot on the tour next month.

Somehow, despite the odds, despite all the roadblocks thrown in our path, our band had made it to the finals. When I'd agreed to help the guys with their audition, I never in a million years dreamed we'd get this far. And yet, I knew we deserved to be here. I knew we had a chance at winning.

I'd only spent a day practicing "Radioactive" on my own, followed by one day with the rest of the band, but for once, I wasn't too worried. I could admit it now: I was a damn good guitarist. I had the song down, and what I might lack in practice, I'd make up for in energy. I wouldn't let anything hold me back tonight.

We did our soundcheck in the morning, and then had an hour break for lunch before we had to start getting ready for the live show. I headed for the food table with the other guys, but Jared stopped me.

"Come with me," he said, a slight smile on his lips.

I'd finally listened to all his messages the night before. He'd apologized a dozen times and pleaded for me to come back—if not for him, then for the other guys. He'd even sung me a drunken rendition of "Stay" that had morphed into "I'm Not Okay (I Promise)" halfway through. It had broken my heart all over again, but hearing how upset he'd been had mended it a tiny bit, too.

"Where are we going?" I remembered all too well the other times we'd sneaked off during a show. Not that I wasn't tempted, of course, but nothing like that was going to happen today.

"I want to show you something."

He led me out the side entrance of the theater and past the security guards to where the line for the audience wrapped around the block. People stood when they saw us approaching, and some cheered or shouted our names. I slowed, uncomfortable with all these people looking at me. This wasn't like on stage where I couldn't really make out faces in the crowd, where there was some distance between us and the fans. And it wasn't like when we'd met fans before, one at a time or in a small group. There were *hundreds* of people here. Maybe thousands. But Jared walked over without any hesitation, and I tailed behind him.

"Hey," he said, to the group of girls at the front of the line. They didn't look a day older than thirteen and had one very patient parent with them.

"Oh my god, you're Jared Cross! And Maddie Taylor! We love you!" The girls all shrieked and bounced and flailed, and I couldn't help but laugh. They were so enthusiastic, so excited to see us. *Both* of us.

"Thanks," Jared said, with a warm smile. "We love you, too."

"I'm freaking out. I can't believe you're really here," one of the girls said, fanning herself.

"Where are you from?" he asked.

"Portland. We've been camped out here all night."

"Wow, thank you for coming to see us. We're truly honored."

"You're, like, my all-time favorite guitarist," a girl in glasses told me. "I totally want to be you when I get older."

Her words hit me hard, right in the chest, and my throat closed up. "Thank you," I managed to get out. "That means so much to me."

"She *is* pretty amazing," Jared agreed.

"Please tell us you're together," the first girl said, looking back and forth between us. "Please!"

"You...want us to be together?" I asked. Is this what Jared wanted to show me? Even though I'd wondered if some fans might want us to be a couple, I didn't expect this reaction after all the nasty comments about us online and everything that had happened between us. But these girls looked like they might mash our faces together and force us to kiss in front of them.

"Yes! You *have* to be!" my fangirl said.

"You're just *so* perfect for each other!" the third girl added.

"I agree," Jared said and smiled at me. "We're trying to figure things out right now. But I'm hopeful."

The girls all clutched their chests and said, "Aww."

I stared at him, completely speechless. For the first time ever, Jared wasn't denying his feelings for me. He wasn't saying he was single. He wasn't saying we were just friends. Was he giving up the act finally? Or was he just joking around in front of these girls?

They all wanted photos with us and asked us to sign things, and the crowd around us grew. We carried on down the line, talking to all of the people who'd come to see our band, and encountered the same thing over and over. The fans loved our music, and they didn't care about Jared's player image. They wanted the fairy tale, the epic romance, the story of the reformed bad boy who fell in love with the good girl. Some people even had signs that read "Jared + Maddie" with hearts all over them, while others had drawn the Villain Complex logo on their arms and cheeks like tattoos. We even ran into some people wearing Villain Complex T-shirts.

"I didn't even know we *had* T-shirts," I said to Jared.

"News to me, too. How do I get one of those?"

"Here, you can each have one," the woman said. "I made them."

I held the shirt up to my chest. "Thank you, I love it."

Jared and I both pulled them on over the shirts we were already wearing, and I thought the fan might faint on the spot.

We spent our entire lunch break there, and I was sad when we had to go back inside but also more alive than I could ever remember being. Talking to the fans made every single thing we'd gone through worth it and gave me even more motivation to do my best tonight. That was the dream, right there—not winning the show or the recording contract or even the tour. It was knowing our music had touched other people's lives, that people had come to see our band, that they were rooting for us. And finally, Jared realized that, too.

Our special guests arrived just before the show started. Hector embraced his grandmother and his three little sisters, speaking to them in Spanish, while Kyle planted a huge kiss on Alexis. And behind them all stood Julie and Carla, along with my third guest: my mom.

"Mom, you made it!" I said, and ran to her arms. There was nothing like being hugged by your mother. Even if things between us had been weird for a while, it was still the most comforting feeling in the world.

"I can't wait to see you perform," she said into my hair. "I'm so proud of you, Madison."

I'd called her right after I'd rejoined the band, but I hadn't been sure she would actually come to the show. Getting out of the house was a challenge for her on most days, but she'd flown down to LA to see me, and that was huge for her. Even if she didn't approve of me playing guitar, she was trying and she was sober, and I was going to do my best to keep things good between us from now on. And maybe, someday, I'd even call my father, too.

Jared stood to the side, the only one who didn't have any family or friends waiting for him. We'd each been given two tickets for family members, but he'd given his to Hector, while Kyle had given me his spare. Jared's family—the only people he really cared about anyway—was already here.

Julie gave me a fierce hug and whispered, "I'm glad you decided to fight."

Carla hugged me next and wished me luck, and then I brought my mom over to meet Jared. "Mom, this is Jared Cross."

"Ah, yes. I've heard a lot about you."

Jared flashed her his most charming smile. "Only the good things are true, I promise."

"I'm not sure I believe that," she said but smiled back. When he went to say hello to Hector's family, she leaned close and whispered, "He's very handsome in person."

I laughed. Yes, yes, he was.

Our guests left to find their seats, and Dan called us over for one last pep talk.

"I know things haven't been easy these past few weeks, and some of that was my fault. I pressured you too hard to worry about what the producers wanted and about winning votes, and I apologize for that. Your brand and your image are important, but this industry can drag you down and turn you into someone you're not. Don't ever lose sight of who you are—both individually and as a band."

He nodded at each of us in turn, and I knew he was referring to what had happened this week. Dan had never questioned my departure or my return; he'd just accepted it, and I was so grateful to him for that. He'd given us space to work out our issues, and we were stronger because of it.

"You may not be what the producers want, but I know you can win this thing," he continued. "You're the most talented, most original band on the show, and the fans love you. And no matter what happens, I'm proud to have been your mentor."

He hugged each of us and wished us luck and then took his

place with the other mentors in front of the stage. Yes, Dan might have given us some bad advice, but he truly cared about us and wanted us to succeed. We'd learned so much from him in the past few weeks, and I was really glad I'd spilled coffee on Angel that day.

The lounge was mostly empty with only three other bands still on the show. While we waited for our turn to go on stage, Jared did his vocal exercises, Hector stretched his neck and shoulders, and Kyle paced back and forth. I flexed my wrists and fingers, trying to loosen myself up a bit. Tonight we'd gone for the full-out rock star look after Dan had pointed out that we were the only true rock band left. Black clothes and boots. Studded belts. Silver jewelry. Leather jackets. And Hector wore his normal Villain Complex hat, of course.

On the screens, we watched Brazen do a Katy Perry cover and Not Too Calm perform their song from the audition, which I barely remembered. Finally, it was our turn with "Behind the Mask."

When the stage rotated and we were hit with the lights and the roar of the crowd, I didn't know how I'd ever thought I could give this up. That familiar rush of adrenaline and endorphins swept through me, like a hit of my favorite drug, and I clutched my guitar, ready to begin.

We usually jumped right into our songs when the stage finished turning, since the producers were such crazy sticklers to the schedule, but Hector didn't start us off. Was there a problem? I turned to look at him and heard Jared speak into his mic.

"Before we start this song, there's something I need to say."

I spun around. What was he doing? The producers had a firm no-talking-to-the-audience rule. He was going to get us in trouble. I glanced at Kyle and Hector, but they were both grinning, so I knew they were in on this, too.

"It's amazing how a single moment can change everything." Jared smiled at me, a private smile hinting at all the things only the two of us knew. "This next song certainly changed my life."

The audience cheered, probably thinking of our audition. But from the way he looked at me, I knew he was referring to that moment when he'd caught me playing this song on his guitar, when he'd heard me belt out the lyrics like they were my own. The moment he'd said he'd first started to fall for me.

He pulled the mic from the stand and crossed the stage to face me. "Maddie, all my life, music's been the only thing that's ever made sense—until I met you. I know I messed up, but I'll do anything to get you back." He sank to his knees like he was begging, and the audience screamed, but they hushed when he spoke again. "You're the only woman in the world for me, and I don't care who knows it. I want to be with you and only you." He stopped and took a deep breath, staring up at me. "I love you, Maddie."

The crowd was silent, waiting for my response, but I was too stunned to speak. I couldn't believe he'd done this in front of everyone, on live TV. He loved me, and he'd just announced it to the entire world. No more lies. No more secrets. No more sneaking around or acting for the camera. No more watching him flirt with other girls and pretending I didn't care. Jared had made it possible for us to finally be together, for this thing between us to be real.

"Kiss him!" someone in front of the stage yelled, and I laughed.

I grabbed the collar of his jacket to pull him up to my lips. He wrapped his arms around me, and we kissed under the lights, in front of the crowd and the cameras, in front of the guys and my friends and even my mom.

"I love you, too," I said while the audience went wild.

Hector snapped his drumsticks, reminding me we were on stage for a reason. Jared moved back to his position, and I scrambled to control my racing heart so I could focus. Jared loved me, and he'd told everyone about us. I couldn't stop smiling.

We launched into "Behind the Mask," the same song we'd performed for our audition, but it sounded different now. Jared's bass playing had gotten much better, thanks to Dan's help, and I was no longer the terrified, awkward girl on stage. We'd all improved so much in the last few weeks—not just individually, but as a group. We'd learned how to work together as one cohesive unit.

I moved across the stage, letting the song pour out of me and into the guitar, feeling every note and every word deep inside me. And when Jared sang, his face twisting with the emotion behind the words he'd written, the audience sang along, too. I could even see some of the fans, the ones near the stage, swaying and shouting out the lyrics, holding their "Jared + Maddie" signs. The song took on new life, becoming a collaboration between us and the fans, an experience we all shared together. When we hit the bridge and the music went quiet to focus on Jared, the way the fans' voices echoed through the theater sent shivers down my spine. I joined in again with my guitar, and the rest of the guys rushed back in, and we finished the song even stronger, bolstered by the love from the crowd.

As soon as the stage turned around, Jared grabbed me and lifted me up, kissing me hard, sending flashes of heat throughout my entire body.

He set me back down, and I smiled up at him. "I can't believe you did that. I thought you would do anything to win, anything to make sure the band succeeds."

"I changed my mind." He ran his fingers through my hair, staring into my eyes like he hadn't seen me in years. "Don't get me wrong—I still want to win. But after you left, I realized winning the show wasn't worth losing you. Besides, you were right. I don't have to be the villain anymore for the band to succeed."

"You two are disgusting," Hector said, making gagging noises.

"Seriously, get a room," Kyle said.

"Oh, I plan on it." Jared kissed my neck in the spot he knew made me crazy.

Kyle opened his mouth to say something else, but his words died when we heard Fairy Lights start playing. Because they weren't doing the song they'd been scheduled to perform—they were doing a country version of "Radioactive."

Lacey had stolen our song.

CHAPTER TWENTY-FIVE

At first, we all stood there and listened, like we weren't sure what we were hearing. Maybe this was a joke. Maybe they were messing with us, and they would switch to their own song any second now. But when they got to the chorus, we knew this was really happening.

"What's going on?" I asked. "Is she…. Are they…." I couldn't even finish the sentence. It was too big, too horrible, too unbelievable.

Hector took off his baseball cap and tore at his hair. "Shit, what are we going to do? We can't do this song now!"

Kyle pulled the crumpled schedule from his pocket. "It says right here they're supposed to be covering 'Jesus Take the Wheel' by Carrie Underwood."

Jared grabbed the schedule and studied it. "This must be some kind of mistake."

"How can it be a mistake?" I asked. "They're doing *our* song! And they've clearly been practicing it. Lacey did this on purpose!"

Kyle shook his head. "She couldn't have done this alone."

"He's right," Jared said. "The producers must be involved with this, too."

"We need to talk to Dan," Hector said.

We moved to a spot where we could see the audience while Fairy Lights continued their country version of our cover song. Normally the mentors sat and watched the performances from their chairs, but Dan was standing next to Lissa and arguing with her. We couldn't hear what he was saying, but judging from his frantic gestures and wild eyes, he was pissed.

The guys left to find one of the producers to ask what was going on, but I waited backstage for Fairy Lights to finish their song. This was the kind of disaster that would have sent the old Maddie running, but no more. I was ready to fight.

When her band finished, I was all ready to go off on Lacey, but before I could, her mother stalked up to her and dragged her off the stage. The woman lightly smacked Lacey on the back of the head, making her wince.

"What was that? That was awful! I've trained you better than that!"

"Mama, stop, please," Lacey said, smoothing her hair. "I did the best I could."

"The best you could? You were way too pitchy in the chorus. We went over this yesterday. I thought you got it, but clearly we should have rehearsed it more!" When Lacey's head dropped, the woman grabbed her chin and tilted her head up. "Hey, do you hear me?"

Lacey nodded, and I actually felt bad for her. Dammit.

Her mother huffed. "You have one more song tonight, and you better not mess it up. You are *going* to win this thing. Don't embarrass me out there."

The woman walked off, glaring at me as she passed by. Lacey took a moment to compose herself, wiping at her eyes, and she looked so young. I'd forgotten she was only seventeen, since she seemed so much older when she was on stage. And now I couldn't yell at her because I related all too well to having a difficult relationship with your mother, even if mine seemed nowhere near as bad now. No, I had to remember why I was here. I cleared my throat, and she turned, eyes narrowing at me.

"You stole our song," I said.

"Have you come to gloat?" she asked, as if she hadn't heard me. "That was a nice publicity stunt back there. I knew all your 'we're just friends' crap was an act."

I clenched my fists. She was just trying to distract me. "You stole our *song*," I repeated, louder.

"I don't know what you're talking about."

I shoved the schedule in her face. "You were supposed to be doing a Carrie Underwood song."

"I covered Carrie Underwood last week. Why would I do one of her songs again? Besides, that's the song you're supposed to be doing."

She handed me her own schedule, and there it was. "Radioactive" was listed as Fairy Lights' song, and "Jesus Take the Wheel" was listed as ours. We'd been given completely different schedules. As had the rest of the show, I was sure. The world seemed to close in on me, tighter and tighter, pressing against my chest, and no matter how much I gasped for air I still couldn't breathe.

"Did *you* choose 'Radioactive'?" I finally got out.

"No, the producers suggested it. I thought it was a weird choice, but whatever."

Everything clicked. The leaked photo of me and Jared. Our last-minute song change in the semi-finals. My broken guitar. Steve encouraging me to leave the show. And now this. It had never been Lacey or any of the other contestants on the show; it had been the producers all along. They'd been sabotaging us for weeks, either for more drama and higher ratings or because they wanted America's sweetheart to win the show. Or both.

They would never let us win.

I rushed off to find the rest of the band. In the lounge, Dan argued with Steve, waving the schedule in his face, while the guys watched it all unfold. I joined them, too stunned to tell them what I'd learned. I needed to hear what Dan said first. Maybe I was wrong. Maybe there was some other explanation for all of this. Maybe there was a possibility we could still win.

Dan threw up his hands and stomped over to us. He dragged us out of the room and into a corner of the hallway, away from the cameras, where no one could hear us.

"This is bullshit. The producers fucked us over. I can't believe it."

I closed my eyes. It was all true. I explained what I'd learned from Lacey and what I'd just figured out—that the show had been sabotaging us for weeks; that we'd been doomed from the start and could never win the show. For a minute, the guys were silent, taking it all in, their faces frozen in horror. And then Hector erupted with a long stream of obscenities in both English and Spanish.

"I can't believe this," Kyle said. "This is so unfair."

"How could they do this?" Jared asked, his voice anguished. I'd known he would take this harder than anyone.

Dan paced back and forth, his movements stiff and jerky. "I'm so pissed I can't even tell you. They did this last season to Angel's team, but I was never sure if it was her incompetence or if the producers were actually manipulating things. I guess now I know."

Kyle rubbed his face. "What are we going to perform? We

don't know 'Jesus Takes the Wheel' but we can't do 'Radioactive' now either."

"They're probably hoping you'll still do 'Radioactive' and that you'll look like you were copying Fairy Lights," Dan said. "Or they think you'll choke and not even go on stage."

Neither of those was an option. Jared and I looked at each other and something unspoken passed between us, the same idea popping into both of our heads at once.

"'Bad Romance,'" we said together, but the guys just stared at us.

"We have to do 'Bad Romance,'" I repeated. "We already know how to play it, and we even recorded it the other week before they changed the song on us."

"Exactly," Jared said. "They didn't want us to do that song before, so we're going to do it now as one big middle finger to them."

Hector rubbed the back of his neck. "We haven't practiced that song in over a week. But I guess it's the only song we *can* do."

Kyle nodded. "We might be a bit rusty, but we can make it work."

"Do it," Dan said. "It's the last show anyway. What are they going to do—kick you off?"

We were scheduled for the last performance of the night, and we spent every minute until then brushing up on the song while Dan discussed the changes with the sound and lighting people.

We didn't tell the producers what we were planning in case they tried to stop us.

As we waited backstage for our cue, Jared pulled us all in for one final group hug. We laced our arms together, facing each other in a huddle, holding on to each other for support.

"The producers might not want us to win, but we're going to make it damn hard for them to stop us," Jared said. "And even if we don't win, look how far we've come in the past few weeks. A little over a month ago, we were lucky to get a gig, and now we're going to be touring the country and playing in giant concert halls. We have thousands of fans, who make signs and T-shirts and camp out all night to see us. As far as I'm concerned, we've already won."

I smiled at him, warmth spreading from my heart to the rest of my body. He really had changed since last week. But there was something I had to say to all the guys before this was over. "Whatever happens tonight, I'm really thankful you all took a chance on me. It was a huge risk letting me into the band, and I have loved every second of it."

"We couldn't have done this without you," Kyle said.

"I love you guys," Hector said to all of us, sniffing.

"Hey, don't get all weepy on us now," Jared said, shoving him a little. We all laughed, but we each choked up a little, too. Win or lose, our time on the show was over, and it was bittersweet.

We broke apart and took our places on the revolving stage, ready to face the audience one last time. Jared grasped the mic, his blue bass around his neck, looking dangerously sexy with his black leather jacket. I stood beside him, running a hand along my sea foam green guitar, the one the producers had tried to destroy. Behind us, Kyle hovered over his keyboard, and Hector twirled his drumsticks. My new family, all preparing to go to battle together.

When the stage turned, Jared spoke into the mic again, his voice soft. "This is for all of the fans who believed in us, who voted for us and downloaded our songs and came to see us tonight. Thank you."

The crowd cheered and waved around their signs, and he started the opening to "Bad Romance." We let his voice carry the song alone at first, hypnotizing every person who heard it. I joined him on the guitar when he started the first verse while Hector provided the steady beat that kept the rest of us in sync and Kyle added the perfect atmosphere. Our version was harder and darker than the original, promising a night of leather and lust, of pleasure and pain. Jared imbued the lyrics with all of his passion, giving them almost a desperate edge, filling each word with yearning and need. He sang to the audience, but in my bones I knew he was singing this for me, another reminder of what we'd shared and what was to come. And when the song ended, he grabbed me for another kiss, leaving the audience with that one final image of us.

Jared was right. Whatever happened with the show, we had already won.

CHAPTER TWENTY-SIX

At the results show, when Fairy Lights was announced as the winner of *The Sound*, we weren't surprised. Disappointed, yes. Angry. Sad. But not surprised.

In the morning, we would pack our bags and leave the hotel forever. The show was over and it was back to reality—except everything had changed since that first audition and our lives would never truly be the same. We had Comic-Con next week and the tour right after that, and then Kyle and I would start our senior year at UCLA in the fall. I still wanted to write movie scores, but I was going to hold off on graduate school for now and see what happened with the band first. One day I would find a way to do both, like my hero, Danny Elfman.

But before we left the theater for the final time, our mentor asked us to meet with him in an empty dressing room.

"I quit the show," Dan said.

"You *quit?*" I asked.

"I'm done. The producers put your cover of 'Bad Romance' on the website too late so the downloads couldn't be counted as votes. Or that's the excuse they gave me anyway. Such bullshit. Everyone knows you should have won." He gave a bitter laugh. "The Internet is going to go crazy with this one. You have some pretty devoted fans out there."

"But why?" Jared asked. "Why go to so much trouble to make sure we didn't win?"

"The record label wanted Fairy Lights from the beginning, so they pressured the show to make it happen. They plan to turn Lacey into some new Taylor Swift or something. And after the headache with Addicted to Chaos, the producers thought your band was too risky. With the network threatening to cancel the show, they wanted to make sure they had a winner who would keep out of trouble. And someone they could easily control, too, I'm sure." He shook his head, disgusted. "But forget about the show. That doesn't matter anymore."

Kyle exchanged a glance with his brother and asked, "What do you mean?"

"It's actually better that you didn't win because the show's contract is shit. Fairy Lights will be their slave for the next seven years, making no money and giving up all their rights to their music. But you're still free, and everyone wants you. My phone has been ringing off the hook since last night."

"Everyone?" Jared asked, raising an eyebrow.

"All the big record labels. Trust me, you're hot right now, and they want to sign you fast. Which is why I have a proposition for you: let me be your manager. My band is retired and I'm done with the show, but I know the industry, I know who you are as a band, and I've actually come to enjoy this crazy mentoring thing. Let me get you the best deal I can, and I'll make sure you become the next big thing. What do you say?"

We all looked at each other as we processed what he'd said, a hundred emotions flickering across our faces. Finally, I laughed. "Well, I vote yes."

"The lady has spoken," Jared said. "I vote yes, too."

"Yes!" Kyle said. "Hell yes!"

Hector slapped Dan on the back. "C'mon, was there any doubt we'd say yes?"

We went out and celebrated, just the four of us. After the live show, we'd gone out with Dan and his husband, plus our families and friends, but tonight's dinner was only for the band. We laughed about everything we'd been through, we ate off each other's plates, and the guys teased me and Jared about our relationship. Jared held my hand the entire time, not caring who saw us together, like he was afraid I might run away if he let go. But he was done pretending, and I was done running.

I don't know how we made it back to my hotel room without burning the entire building down. We were kissing and pulling at each other's clothes as soon as we got off the elevator, stumbling to my door and fumbling for the key to open it.

When the door shut, I tugged off his shirt and slid my hands along his chest, down his arms, kissing the VILLAIN tattoo and the dark and light triangles on his forearms. One day I'd ask him what all of his other tattoos meant, but later. We had time.

He let me explore him, like he sensed I needed to touch every inch of his body and mark him as my own. I removed his pants to worship his calves, his thighs, his hips, teasing my tongue along the dark hair trailing down his stomach, lower and lower. I tasted his entire body, kissing and licking and learning what drove him crazy, branding him with my mouth.

When he couldn't take it anymore, he spun me around and unzipped my dress, removing the last of my clothes. He trailed kisses across my shoulders and down my back, all the way to the curve of my butt and then up again. He wrapped his arms around me from behind so we stood naked together, skin to skin, him hard and ready against me. In the mirror, I watched as his mouth caressed my neck and his hands cupped my breasts, and for the first time, I agreed with the fans: Jared and I *were* perfect for each other.

He pulled me onto the bed and kissed me until I was begging him for more. We broke apart for him to put on a condom, and then he was on top of me again, between my legs. He held my face and stared into my eyes.

"I love you," he whispered.

"I love you, too," I gasped and clung to him as he stretched me, filled me, completed me.

For a minute, he rested his forehead against mine and held me, one body now instead of two. We moved together, slowly at first, savoring the feel of each other, but then picked up speed. I lifted my hips to meet his thrusts, digging my nails into his back. He ran his talented fingers down to that spot that drove me wild, playing my body like he played his guitar, and I swore I heard music.

I rolled us over so I was on top, and he grinned up at me. I grabbed his wrists to pull them above his head and ran my tongue along the lines of music tattooed around his arms. God, I loved his arms, whether they were holding a guitar or wrapped around me, and seeing them above his head like this, seeing him give himself over to me completely, made me even more excited.

I rolled my hips, sliding him in and out of me, the crescendo building as skin glided against skin. Our fingers entwined as we moved faster, the friction of our bodies lifting us higher, like an orchestra harmonizing and swelling just before the climax. He buried his face in my neck, his fingers tightening around mine.

"Maddie," he moaned, and I knew he was close, too, and that sent me over the edge. I gasped his name against his skin, rocking against him, tightening around him, dragging us both into bliss.

I released him, and he wrapped me in his arms and held me close. We lay together, breathing heavily and slicked with sweat, but complete. Whole.

"Not okay?" he asked with his real smile I'd come to know so well.

"Not okay," I agreed, tracing a finger along his lips. "I'm *much* better than okay."

Even though the show was over, this was only the beginning for us. I didn't know what would happen with the band, but I knew we'd get through it. Because what we had together was more than music. It was love.

ACKNOWLEDGEMENTS

Thanks to my husband, Gary, who encouraged me to follow my dreams and gave me the freedom to make them happen. I truly couldn't have done this without him.

Thanks to my mom, Gaylene, who bought me as many books as I wanted as a kid and always said I should write something romantic and fun. Thanks to my dad, Peter, for giving me his electric guitar long ago and for encouraging me to keep writing. And thanks to all of the Adams and Briggs families for supporting me and cheering for me.

A thousand thanks to the following authors who encouraged me to write this book and then helped make it much stronger: Rachel Searles, who taught me to a better writer and never let me give up (MELO!); Jessica Love, who graciously let me steal her concert stories ("Poor folk band! Where will they all sleep?"); Kathryn Rose, who knows all the guyliner references were for her; Stephanie Garber, whose never-ending enthusiasm always brightened my darkest days; Karen Akins, whose tireless cheering got me through the tough spots; and Dana Elmendorf, who came up with many of the band names in this book.

Many thanks to the following authors for their support, advice, and cheerleading: Cortney Pearson, Krista Van Dolzer, Susan Adrian, Amaris Glass, Jamie Grey, and Aileen Erin.

Thanks to my agent, Kate Schafer Testerman, who always believed in my books and said she was with me no matter which direction I went with my career.

Thanks to my cover designer, Najla Qamber, and my photographer, Lindee Robinson, for completely bringing Maddie and Jared to life.

Thanks to my copy editor, Rebecca Weston, for helping to make this book more professional.

To all the bands, musicians, and composers mentioned in this book (and many more I didn't mention), thank you for inspiring me and helping me through the difficult times, with special thanks to Thirty Seconds To Mars.

To the bloggers who reviewed and helped promote this book, I owe you all a virtual glass of wine.

And finally, to everyone reading this book, thank you!

ABOUT THE AUTHOR

Elizabeth Briggs is a full-time geek who writes books for teens and adults. She plays the guitar, mentors at-risk teens, and volunteers with a dog rescue group. She lives in Los Angeles with her husband and a pack of small, fluffy dogs.

Visit Elizabeth online for playlists & more!
www.elizabethbriggs.net
Facebook.com/ElizabethBriggsAuthor
Twitter: @lizwrites

26011388R00191

Made in the USA
San Bernardino, CA
16 November 2015